*THE HEIRESS'S CONVENIENT HUSBAND*

Cover Design and Interior Format
© KILLION
THE
GROUP INC.

GRACE
-BY-THE-
SEA

2

# The Heiress's Convenient Husband

## REGINA SCOTT

*To Kristin, who is rockin' her new adventure, and to the Lord, who walks beside us through all our adventures.*

# CHAPTER ONE

*Grace-by-the-Sea, Dorset, England, June 1804*

WHOEVER WAS USING HIS CASTLE was in for it. James Howland grimaced as he rode up onto the headland. He might serve as magistrate for the village of Grace-by-the-Sea and local steward for the mighty Earl of Howland, but the castle he approached now was hardly his. Everything he had, everything he'd accomplished, was a result of his distant illustrious connection to the Howland family. Well, almost everything.

He glanced down the slope beside him to the village. As the sun neared the horizon on the warm summer evening, lamps were beginning to glow. A few couples strolled arm in arm, heading home from some event at the spa that nourished the local economy with the hundreds of visitors it attracted each year. Among those thatched-roofed cottages lived the men he had recently organized into the local militia to save them from conscription. His smile tilted up. He'd almost forgotten how good it felt to defy his lordship.

That feeling wouldn't last, of course. Once the earl heard James had refused his direct order to stay out of the king's preparations to defend the coast from Napoleon's impending invasion, James would have to pay the cost. Perhaps it would come as a tithe on his income. Perhaps a refusal to summon him to London for some event. He could only hope it wouldn't take the form of a slight to his mother, who served as companion to the earl's wife. At least his lordship likely wouldn't remove him as magistrate. It came in too handy that the man enforcing the law was in the pay of the Howland family.

In the end, he would have to accept whatever punishment amused the earl. The cost was a small price to pay for ensuring the safety of his neighbors, his friends, and his village.

And there he went again claiming ownership he could never have.

He clucked to the roan, and his gelding, Majestic, obligingly broke into a canter up the graveled drive. Majestic was becoming accustomed to the trip. James usually checked the earl's hunting lodge of a castle quarterly, but a strange light had appeared in the window twice recently. Ghosts, Mrs. Tully in the village claimed. Rubbish. Someone was sneaking inside.

He'd thought it might be his old friend, Quillan St. Claire, who was using the caves beneath the castle proper, but the former naval captain had disclaimed all knowledge. Quill had his own battles to fight. James did what he could to help. It was the least that might be expected of any Englishman with Napoleon massing his troops just across the Channel.

Then there was the recent unpleasantness with a smuggling gang. Try as he might, he had found no connection between them and the mysterious light. So, to determine who might be lighting that beacon, he had been stopping by at various hours every day for the last week. He'd never spotted anything out of the ordinary.

Until tonight.

He reined in to stare at the turreted stone castle as it came fully into view among the trees that circled it. Light blazed from a dozen windows. Even the stables to the east were lit up. What affrontery! Blood roaring, he put heels to Majestic and galloped to the entry.

He leaped to the ground and looped the reins over the balustrade that edged the stone steps. Pulling out the pistol he'd brought with him as a precaution, he cocked it and took the steps two at a time to the terrace and the front door. His free hand was on the latch when it was yanked from under him.

The manservant in the doorway blinked as if just as surprised to find someone on the other side of the portal. He was tall and thin, with a thatch of black hair threaded with grey and a nose pointed enough to skewer apples. He didn't seem to notice James's weapon as he drew himself up.

"May I help you, sir?"

James pushed past him into the house, setting the fellow to sputtering like a wet teakettle on the hob. "Who are you, and why are you in my castle?"

The servant's bushy black brows came down. "*Your* castle? This moldering establishment belongs to the Earl of Howland. I have met his lordship, and you are not he."

"No, indeed." The warm voice came from above and danced with merriment. James glanced up the wide stairs that ran along one side of the great hall to the landing across the back. A lady was starting down the stairs. Her dark-brown hair was piled up at the top of her head in a loose pile of curls. Her ears dripped sapphires that caught the light as she moved. The simple blue gown showed off a slender figure.

She could not be called beautiful with that long nose and unruly hair. But as she reached the flagstone floor and started toward him, he felt the ridiculous urge to take a step back.

He held his ground. "Why are you here?"

Her eyes were the color of a perfect summer sky. They tilted up at the corners as she tsked. "I was banished here, sir. No need to introduce yourself. You must be James Howland, the earl's watchdog. I recognize that chin. I'm Eva Faraday, his prisoner."

He didn't respond. How very dissatisfying. But then, Eva could not say she had ever had a satisfying response from any of the Howlands.

He certainly seemed typical of the breed. He had the same golden-blond hair waving about a firm-jawed face, the same cold blue eyes that could spear her in place. His physique was as good as that of the earl's heir, Viscount Thorgood—tall, broad-shouldered. His many-caped great-coat swirled about long legs that looked ready to stomp on someone. Not that she cared. She'd refused to do the viscount's bidding, and the earl's, and she had no intention of doing this man's.

"I wasn't notified his lordship intended to house a prisoner in the castle," he said, watching her. Then he glanced at Yeager, her manservant. "Complete with jailer, it seems."

Yeager sniffed. "I've had the honor of serving Miss Eva and her late father since she was a girl."

"Thank you, Yeager," she said with a smile. "Would you see how Patsy is doing with the unpacking, then determine what's to be had for victuals?"

"Aye, miss." He cast Mr. Howland a narrow-eyed look before heading for the stairs.

Mr. Howland uncocked his pistol and put it away, jaw looking even harder. Did he eat rocks for breakfast? "Exactly how many people do you intend to house?"

"Five at the moment," she allowed. "I have a coachman

and groom in the stables. We'd hoped we could hire additional help once we settled in."

Was that noise his teeth grinding? "I have received nothing to indicate any of you are allowed here."

"So you said," she replied. "But it's only to be expected, really, when you go off in a fit of pique. The earl, that is. Not you personally. I don't imagine you have the luxury."

Oh, but those eyes snapped fire. "Tell your maid not to bother unpacking. You'll all be staying at the Swan until I can confirm matters with his lordship."

Eva shook her head. "I'm afraid that's impossible. I have no money to pay for an inn."

He nodded toward the upper story. "You're paying your staff."

"My father's will left funds for their wages," she informed him. "My portion is held in trust until I reach the age of five and twenty." Or she married, but she refused to dangle that worm. The earl liked to use it far more than necessary already.

He crossed his arms over his impressive chest. "Nevertheless, I must insist that you leave."

Was every Howland this pig-headed? If only she could wash her hands of the lot of them! But the earl was trustee over her funds, and he would give her nothing unless she bent to his will. This man might find it acceptable to live like that. She didn't.

"And I must insist that we stay," she said. "I promise to disturb as little as possible. I'll need a bedchamber, a withdrawing room, the dining room and kitchen, and quarters for the staff. From what I can tell, that's less than a quarter of the space in this pile."

She thought she caught a sigh. "The castle hasn't been used as a long-term habitation in years. You'll need coal, candles, food. How do you intend to pay for them?"

She smiled. "I intend to put them on the earl's credit. He

sent me here. He can pay for the privilege."

"No," he said, tone as solid as his chin. "The budget here doesn't allow for such expenses."

She waved a hand. "Then send the bill directly to the earl."

He caught her hand mid-air and held it, gaze fastened on hers. "Have a care, Miss Faraday. I'm only trying to protect you. This castle is more dangerous than you can know. It isn't safe for you here."

If he was trying to frighten her off, he was doing a good job. She could almost believe the concern in his voice.

But the earl could sound concerned too, even as he tried to steal her future.

She yanked her hand from his grip. "Then make it safe. Tell me what dangers to avoid. This is apparently to be my home until I earn my inheritance in ten months. Help me survive my imprisonment."

He eyed her a moment, and she steeled herself to keep fighting. Truly, what else was she to do? If her father had guessed the depths to which the Earl of Howland would sink to get his hands on her inheritance, he would never have made the man trustee and expected him to care for her. In the last six months since her father had died, she had learned to fight for what was best for her and her servants. James Howland would simply have to accustom himself to the fact.

"Very well, Miss Faraday," he said. "I'll help you. You may stay in the castle until I hear from the earl."

Best not to let him see her relief. "How very sensible of you."

He inclined his head. "But you must allow me to do my duty as well. I am responsible for safeguarding the earl's interests in Dorset."

And she would try not to despise him for it. "Of course. Shall I send you a report each week of what furniture I've moved? Which dishes we used?"

That smile could have frozen the waves on the Channel. "No need. I'll be able to verify all that on my own. I'll be moving into the castle with you, Miss Faraday."

# CHAPTER TWO

H ER EYES WENT WIDE, THEN narrowed at him. "No. I will not have my reputation called into question because you want to count the silver."

James met her gaze full on. "And I will not allow the earl's property to be disturbed." He stepped back. "However, I will give you a few moments alone to consider your position. I'll return shortly with my things."

He turned his back on her scowl and left.

Easy to put her and her so-called servants down as scheming opportunists, but he'd had too much experience with the earl's machinations. His lordship could readily consign those who defied him to some unsavory penance.

"Eva Faraday," he mused aloud as he retrieved Majestic's reins. He didn't recall hearing the name before. Of course, he hadn't been invited to London in nearly two years. That was plenty of time for the earl to have acquired himself a ward or two. Strange, though, that his mother had never mentioned her. They exchanged letters monthly. Or had the earl kept Eva away from the rest of the family? Why? Was she a threat of some kind? Or an advantage he didn't want to share?

The thoughts ran through his mind as he rode back into the village and down Church Street to the residence he had been given. It was an impressive house—the earl would have allowed nothing less to be associated with his name—though nothing on the order of the castle. Built of rough pale stone quarried from the area, Howland Cottage boasted two stories, with attics behind dormer windows in the pitched roof. As if determined to add a dash of formality, the earl had decreed that the front door and trim around the windows be painted black. There was a tiny yard between the house and the black, wrought-iron fence along the street. In his mother's time, it had been filled with flowers. Now it was mostly evergreen shrubs that tended to scratch against the windows when the wind blew. He had no time or inclination to change the arrangement.

He rode around back to the stables and remanded Majestic to the care of his groom, then went to tell Pym about the change in plans.

"Ooo, a mysterious lady," his manservant declared with a twinkle in his grey eyes. Short and fine-boned, with a way of looking out from under his heavy brows as if he was up to mischief, Pym had seemed ancient for as long as James could remember. But as his cooking was every bit as good as the inn's, he navigated the stairs with ease, and his eye for fashion had never failed, James had felt no need to retire him.

"I must pack your best waistcoat," he declared now, hurrying for the stairs.

"Clothes for five days should suffice," James called after him. "We should hear from the earl by then. And send for Priestly."

He turned for his study to the left of the entryway. He had a letter sanded, sealed with wax, and ready before his secretary arrived from his flat above Mr. Carroll's Curiosities in the village. Samuel Priestly had also followed in his father's footsteps. The senior Mr. Priestly had been secretary to James's father for years. Light brown hair carefully combed to hide the growing bald spot at the top of his head, Priestly bowed himself into the room, tugging his coat about him after being hastily summoned.

"Was there something you required, Magistrate?"

James held out the letter. "You'll be traveling to London first thing in the morning. Arrange for a horse from Mr. Josephs at the livery stable. Ride as fast as is practical. Deliver this note into the earl's hand, and don't leave until you have an answer."

Priestly swallowed, Adam's apple bobbing. "But what if the earl declines to answer?"

A strong possibility, given his lordship's capricious nature. If he had learned about the militia James had raised, he could well prefer to keep James waiting for an answer.

"Appeal to Viscount Thorgood," he told his secretary. "At least he can be counted upon to be reasonable."

"I'll pack now, sir." He bowed himself out.

One last task to accomplish. James glanced at the ornate ormolu clock on the mantel. Half past nine. Most of the village would be abed. A shame his task could not wait until morning, but Eva Faraday was right. They could not share a roof without a suitable chaperone. And he knew where his best hope lay of procuring one.

"Magistrate." Jesslyn Chance, the current hostess of the spa, blinked big blue eyes at him when she answered the door of her little stone cottage along the shore. Her nightgown was covered by a voluminous charcoal-colored cloak, but her blond curls clustered around her pretty face as if she was ready for her next dance partner.

"Miss Chance," he said, inclining his head. "Forgive me for coming so late, but I have urgent need of your services."

She opened the door wider and stepped aside to let him enter. He hadn't visited the cottage for years, not since the constable had given it up for better quarters, but he knew it contained only two rooms and a loft. She had added landscape paintings to the white-washed walls, a braided rug near the hearth. He caught the scent of warm stew and lavender, a combination both surprising and welcoming.

"Is it the trolls?"

Her aunt, Mrs. Tully, had come out of the bedchamber on the far side of the hearth. Her grey hair was wrapped in paper curls, and her red flannel nightgown billowed about her figure.

James inclined his head in her direction. "No trolls, alas."

She put her nose in the air. "You ought to be glad of that. They leave quite a mess. Don't expect us to clean up after them."

He managed a smile and leaned closer to her niece. "Is there somewhere we might have a private word?"

Miss Chance spread her hands. "My home is as you see it, Magistrate. I fear there is little opportunity for privacy, especially at this hour of the night."

She was also careful of her reputation, and he was trespassing.

"Of course." He straightened. "You recall the light that has been seen in the castle recently."

She paled. "Yes, but we caught the smugglers who put it there."

"So I'd hoped. But I have been checking every day, just in case. Tonight, I found someone." He went on to explain the claims Miss Faraday had made.

"So, I have no choice but to keep an eye on them until I hear from the earl," he concluded. "Therefore, I must have a chaperone."

She nodded, and he nearly sagged in relief. But then, he'd always admired her practical nature. And after the way she'd rallied the villagers to confront a gang of smugglers a week ago, he could only admire her ingenuity and courage as well.

"Of course," she agreed in her sweet voice. "I'll help my aunt gather her things."

"It will only take a moment," Mrs. Tully said, bustling back the way she had come.

James started after her, then glanced at her niece. "I had hoped you…"

She held up her hand as if to stop him. "I have only a week to finish setting the spa to rights for the new physician, and I must prepare to vacate this cottage. I cannot be spared from those duties. Maudie can."

He'd already had words with Mr. Greer, the president of the Spa Corporation, about the decision to release Miss Chance from her post. The first Chance in the area had decided to make use of the mineral waters for their healing properties, and there had been a Chance in charge of the spa ever since. The previous host had been Miss Chance's father, a physician, until he'd passed away last year. She had taken over then.

And she'd done a magnificent job of running not only the day-to-day operations but monthly events that the visitors so loved. Just yesterday had seen the annual midsummer masquerade at the assembly rooms at the top of the hill, an event enjoyed by all. But, no matter her skills, she wasn't a physician, and her brother was too young to take up the role, so the corporation had located a replacement. Apparently, Doctor Bennett had insisted he needed no hostess. Another time James might have appealed to the earl to fund her salary anyway, but he'd already used up any collateral he might have had.

"And may I say again how much I abhor the decision to discharge you," he said as something thumped from the other room. "But, because of that decision, you owe the corporation no loyalty now."

"I owe our guests only the most pleasant of times," she countered. "My aunt is an experienced chaperone, sir. She knows her duty as well."

"Where did you put my pixie trap?" Mrs. Tully called.

"Excuse me." Miss Chance went to help her aunt.

James paced from the stone hearth past the rocking chair toward the door. Could he trust Maudlyn Tully to do the job? Most of the people in Grace-by-the-Sea understood about her whimsical nature. The older widow claimed mermaids inhabited the cove, trolls the headland. She'd even whispered about French spies invading. Well, that story at least was more real than she could know, though James wasn't about to confirm it. Still, the last time she'd visited the castle with him, she'd horrified his other guests with tales of gruesome murders, chilling hauntings, and a hound with glowing red eyes. He could just imagine what Miss Faraday would think.

James stopped and smiled. Perhaps Mrs. Tully would make the perfect chaperone, at least until she scared his uninvited guest right out of the castle.

"Then are we to leave, miss?" Patsy asked, straightening in the act of removing Eva's gowns from one of the hastily packed trunks.

Eva had asked Yeager to join her and her maid, Patsy, in the bedchamber she'd chosen so she could explain the situation to them. Though the holland covers had been removed from the great box bed and walnut wardrobe, carved chest, and dressing table, the room still felt oddly empty, as if it were waiting for someone other than her to occupy it.

"No," she said, glancing between the maid and her man-of-all-work. "Here we were banished, and here we stay until the fortune is mine."

Yeager drew up his lanky frame. "Right you are, Miss Eva. His lordship sent us off. He'll have to deal with the consequences."

"Not him," Patsy said with a sniff, straight brown hair beginning to fall from her bun to frame her round face. "He'll find a way to wiggle out of any trouble. That's what snakes do."

"Now, now," Eva said, "I will not have you calling the earl such names."

Patsy hung her head, until Eva added, "After all, you malign the poor snake."

Patsy straightened with a chuckle.

"And what about his watchdog?" Yeager persisted. "Are we to fetch and carry for him as well?"

She had been trying so hard to find an ounce of sympathy for James Howland, until he'd declared his intent to move in with her. Why did he obey the earl's least command? Was he so fawning that the earl treated him better than most? Or was he so far away from the rest of his family that he did not know he served a corrupt master? She'd seen how his lordship worked to hide his plans from his heir, Viscount Thorgood. Perhaps James Howland really did think he was only doing his duty.

"If he requests your help, oblige him," she said, "unless you think it would harm us in some way. If you have any doubts, speak to me first."

They both nodded.

"There's no food in the house," Yeager reported. "We can eat what we brought in the hamper, but we'll have to see what can be had in the morning. How close is that village, do you think?"

Eva shrugged. "The earl made it sound like the closest habitation was leagues away. I have no idea where Mr. Howland normally lives. But he has to eat as well. He can point us in the right direction, at least."

"I'll call when I have the table set," Yeager said before bowing and leaving.

If only the Howlands were as easy to deal with. Eva couldn't help her sigh as she helped Patsy put away the rest of her things. Some she'd had to leave behind, but Patsy had thrown most of what she owned into the trunks they had brought with them. Fine lawn nightgowns reminded her of her bedchamber in London, done in pinks and blues, unlike this brown and white room that felt so cold. A riding habit in cerulean blue made her think of the times she'd ridden through Hyde Park in the early morning. But of course, the only horses she had here were the ones that had pulled her carriage. The earl had refused to release her riding horse, Blaze, from his stables.

The fancy gowns wrapped in tissue brought tears to her eyes. How many times had she worn them to events with her father? The theatre, the opera, balls and routs and soirees. And the dinner parties! Her father had found it endlessly amusing how he had seldom been welcomed at the tables of the *ton* until she'd reached marriageable age.

"Amazing what a daughter with an impressive dowry does for a fellow's standing," he'd joked more than once.

The positioning and maneuvering had amused her as well while he was alive. Papa had had no qualms about her choosing her own husband, and he had always been able to spot a charlatan. It was one of the traits that had allowed him to make the savviest of investments. Yet he had mistaken the earl's interest entirely.

"You needn't worry," he'd wheezed on his deathbed, robust frame shrunken, voice a whisper of its usual strength. "Lord Howland will see to your future. I know you will do me proud."

Would he be proud of her, refusing the one thing the earl demanded of her?

Far below, she thought she heard a bang, as if someone had slammed a door. Could Mr. Howland be back so soon? And why did that thought make her eager to rush downstairs?

Patsy must have heard the noise too, for she shivered. "I don't like this place, miss. It's too big and too dark. Who knows what's hiding in the shadows?"

"Dust," Eva told her. "Mr. Howland said the place hadn't been lived in for years."

"Mighty loud for dust," Patsy muttered, returning to the unpacking.

"Perhaps I'll just check," Eva said, straightening and heading for the door.

She had taken the bedchamber closest to the stairs, so it was only a moment before she reached the landing. She pitied anyone housed farther down the corridor in either direction. It was just like a Howland to make a castle out of what should have been a simple hunting lodge. Fine carpets graced every floor. Paintings hung on every wall. At least, she assumed they were paintings. Why else drape so much linen about?

She'd only explored a little so far, but if the other wings were anything like this one, the place could easily sleep two dozen, not counting the servants. Patsy was right. There were many ways to hide. She fought a shiver herself.

At least it wasn't easy to hide in the entry hall below. It had been designed to resemble the great hall of a real castle, with soaring ceilings veined in plaster and a stone fireplace big enough to roast an ox. The three people by the massive front door looked like dolls. She recognized James Howland. Who was the older couple with him?

As if he felt her scrutiny, he looked up, and something inside her fluttered like a startled dove. Eva raised her head. "Well, at least you know how to keep a promise."

He sketched her a bow. "Miss Faraday." Straightening, he turned to the woman at his elbow. "Mrs. Tully, may I present Miss Eva Faraday? You will be serving as her chaperone."

A chaperone? Oh, he really was doing it up right. Eva started down the stairs. "Mrs. Tully, how kind of you to come and at such a late hour."

"This is Mr. Pym, my manservant," Mr. Howland continued before the woman with the curly grey hair could answer. "He will assist with staffing."

The other fellow, who looked a little like the leprechauns her father had told her stories about, bowed to her.

As she reached the bottom of the stairs, she realized her perspective hadn't been so far off. Both Mrs. Tully and Mr. Pym were short; the top of their heads came only to Eva's chin. Mrs. Tully's black gown made her look even smaller, more fragile. Two bright blue eyes regarded her with interest from a round face that was beginning to show wrinkles.

"Have you seen the Lady yet?" she asked.

Eva glanced to Mr. Howland, but he merely offered her a smile. The set of his lips told her he was expecting a great deal from the exchange.

"The lady?" Eva asked her new chaperone politely.

She took a step closer and lowered her voice. "The Lady of the Tower. She wails for her love lost at sea. She was imprisoned here too, you know. Some say she haunts these halls to this day, seeking another to take her place."

Eva stared at her, chills running down her back.

"Mrs. Tully knows any number of tales about the castle," Mr. Howland put in.

She nodded, grey curls trembling. "Indeed I do. And you would be wise to heed them, before it's too late."

Eva grinned. "How delightful. I love a good ghost story." She linked arms with her new chaperone. "You must tell me more."

# CHAPTER THREE

JAMES HAD TO CLAMP HIS teeth together to keep his jaw from dropping as Miss Faraday led Mrs. Tully toward the withdrawing room to the left of the great hall.

"I imagine that's the first time Mrs. Tully has had such a receptive audience," Pym marveled.

James shook himself. "Find me a bedchamber in a different wing from hers, preferably one where I can keep a watch on the stairs."

Pym raised a rugged grey brow, but he started up the stairs for the chamber story. James followed the women into the withdrawing room.

Most of the furniture and statuary in the house was draped with holland covers to prevent dust from accumulating. Someone had removed the cream-colored cloth from the settee and chairs by the hearth, and a cheery fire was crackling. He was afraid to ask what they'd done for wood.

"The Hound of the Headland," Mrs. Tully was saying from her place beside Miss Faraday on the lime-striped satin settee as he approached across the thick emerald-patterned carpet. "Great white beast with glowing red eyes."

"Fascinating," Miss Faraday said, her own eyes gleeful. "And does it have a preferred prey? Children who don't obey their parents, perhaps?"

Mrs. Tully drew herself up, not an easy feat with the wide curving arms of the settee. "Nothing so common. It preys on young wastrels deep in their cups."

"Better and better." Miss Faraday glanced up at him. "Do join us, Mr. Howland. I had no idea your family history was so dreadful. I begin to see how the earl became such a despot."

And he'd never understood why the earl chose to wield his power like a sword to cut his family to its knees. "Mrs. Tully has a unique insight into the area," he said, but he sat on one of the matching chairs, hands on the chinoiserie-painted wood that edged the arms.

Their chaperone tapped the side of her short nose with one finger. "Comes from years of observing."

That he could believe. She was a fixture in the village.

"People tend not to notice chaperones and speak more freely, I suppose," Miss Faraday mused. "Have you been one long?"

"Since my Francis died," she replied. She cocked her head. "Thirty years? No, forty! My, how time flies."

Miss Faraday patted her hand. "Well, I am very glad Mr. Howland thought of you."

Mrs. Tully glanced at James, gaze knowing. "He didn't want me. He wanted my Jess."

"Mrs. Tully's niece, Jesslyn Chance, is hostess at the spa at Grace-by-the-Sea," he explained when Miss Faraday glanced his way as well. "She is closer to your age. I thought she might provide company."

Mrs. Tully waved a hand. "She's too busy."

"There's a spa here?" Miss Faraday asked eagerly.

"An excellent spa," Mrs. Tully assured her. "Mineral waters that will make your hair curl."

Not that Miss Faraday needed help in that area. That mass of curls at the back of her head looked as if it might have its own opinions and wouldn't be shy about sharing them. Why did his fingers itch to pull those curls free?

"Invigorating seaside bathing on appointment," their chaperone continued, warming to her theme. "And an assembly every Wednesday evening. I do hope you'll come."

"Assuredly," Miss Faraday said. "I have a carriage. We can travel that far, I would think. I had no idea there was society here. The earl made it sound as if he was sending me to the end of civilization."

"We are at the end of civilization," Mrs. Tully said solemnly. "The last, best hope of the kingdom, and the first line of defense against invasion."

Would that frighten the intrepid Miss Faraday at last? She certainly sobered.

"Is it true, then?" she asked. "Are the French coming?"

"Any day," Mrs. Tully said, like a bell tolling their doom. "And we have only the trolls to protect us, fickle fellows that they are."

Miss Faraday blinked, as if suddenly facing the sun. He ought to let live, but he felt compelled to explain. After all, the honor of his village was at stake.

"Grace-by-the-Sea has a number of sailors serving as Sea Fencibles, standing guard over our shores until the Navy can arrive," he said.

"And we have our own militia," Mrs. Tully agreed. "Led by our magistrate here." She smacked her lips. "There's something about a man in a red coat."

A week after it had been hastily formed, the Grace-by-the-Sea militia of thirty men had three red coats among them, but several more were in progress through Mr. Treacle, the tailor. A shame their military skills were as sparse as their uniforms, but they were going to muster every Monday morning for training. Quill would be helping when he could. The former naval captain knew something of discipline and order. At least, so he claimed.

James just had to make sure Quill wasn't too obvious in

recruiting men for his operations. It wouldn't do for word to get back to Larkin Denby, the new Riding Surveyor sent by the Excise Office to watch for smugglers. Fortunately, Lark was engaged to Miss Chance and busy making sure she and her family had a home and support before the new physician arrived to take their cottage.

Pym appeared in the doorway just then and coughed, and James rose to go see what he needed.

"It will take a bit of doing to settle everything to rights, sir," he said. "If you want to sleep soon, I might advise the settee in here."

James glanced over his shoulder at the ladies, who were regarding him as avidly as if he'd been a strolling player brought for their entertainment, then returned his gaze to his man. "Thank you, Pym. What about you?"

"I can find a spot, sir, never you fear. I'll just wait to help with your boots."

"No need," James said, laying a hand on a shoulder that had only grown more bowed in recent years. "I'll see you in the morning."

"Very good, sir." Pym inclined his head and left.

"Problem?" Miss Faraday asked as he rejoined them.

"Nothing I cannot handle," he assured her. "I am told I must make do with the settee this evening. Given all the excitement, I suggest we make an early night. Mrs. Tully, I regret that we won't have a room ready for you until tomorrow either. I'm sure Miss Faraday won't mind sharing."

He was imposing, but she merely offered him a tight smile before turning to Mrs. Tully. "The bed is plenty large, ma'am. If you wouldn't mind sharing."

"Not at all," she replied. "I share with Jess every night." She glanced around the room with a sigh. "Though we have no ghosts, worse luck."

"And apparently we have an excess," Miss Faraday said,

voice once more dancing with merriment. "I hope you have an opportunity to make their acquaintance, Mr. Howland."

No ghosts made an appearance that night. Not that Eva thought they would. Still, that didn't mean Castle Howland had never seen tragedy. She had to agree with Mrs. Tully: surely, she wasn't the only one who had been imprisoned in these walls.

"Have you met the Earl of Howland?" she asked her chaperone after Patsy had helped them change for bed and they had settled under the covers. With the lamps out, there was precious little light in the darkness.

"Once," Mrs. Tully answered, followed by a yawn. "I didn't care for him."

"Oh?" Eva asked. "Why not?"

"Too full of himself. And no imagination. The man wouldn't know a troll if it picked him up and heaved him."

Eva laughed imagining the look on the earl's lean face as he sailed through the air. "And Mr. Howland, the magistrate?"

"No troll would dare heave him."

Surprised, Eva rolled over to eye the dark shadow beside her. "Too proud?"

"Too scared. The trolls, that is. No one threatens our magistrate."

She sounded so pleased by the fact. "Then he's done good here," Eva said.

"He's nothing but a blessing," she insisted. "Twice when we had a bad harvest, he convinced the earl to forego his tithes. He raised a militia to keep our boys from being conscripted into the army and sent overseas. And I suspect the mermaids leave our fishermen alone because he's had a word with them."

She could almost see mermaids complying with James Howland's command. He had an air about him. And he was rather handsome.

If one cared for arrogant aristocrats.

He was already in high form when she and Mrs. Tully descended the stairs the next morning. A young man she didn't know was cleaning out the hearth in the great hall, and, through the open door to the withdrawing room, she spotted two women dusting.

"I thought you didn't want to go to an expense," she accused him.

"The castle is cleaned quarterly," he informed her, standing with arms crossed over his chest as he supervised the work. "I merely accelerated the time."

Today he wore a navy coat and chamois breeches that would have pleased any sporting mad Corinthian in London. There were no bags under his sharp blue eyes; no hint of a crick in that upright form. Sleeping on the settee apparently agreed with him.

He nodded toward the long table that had come into view when the holland covers had been removed. "You said you needed a dining room in addition to the withdrawing room. I thought this would do. It's close enough to the kitchen, down that corridor to the right, and keeps the disturbed area centralized."

"Why, Mr. Howland, you think of everything," she drawled.

Maudie, as she had insisted Eva call her, was eyeing the table. "Too small," she said. "Where will the smugglers sit?"

"Smugglers?" Eva teased. "Now, that's a story I'd love to hear."

Mr. Howland dropped his arms and turned to her. "Breakfast first. I took the liberty of sending to the bakery in the village. Do you prefer sweet rolls or toast in the morning?"

"Oh, jams!" Maudie was already heading for the table.

"Toast and tea would be fine," Eva assured him. He had a word with the young man, who trotted for the kitchen.

Eva settled herself next to Maudie on one of the high-backed wooden chairs that surrounded the table. Rather like old-fashioned thrones, hard, firm, with carved arms that ended in a leering dragon. The earl must adore them.

"I understand you've taken one of the guest suites above the withdrawing room," Mr. Howland said as he sat on the chair at the head of the table, of course. "Where would you like Mrs. Tully?"

*As close as possible.*

Odd. Where had that thought come from? Maudie had a delightful imagination, and she surely took Eva's mind off her predicament, but Eva was used to having her own room, making her own choices. Why did she suddenly want to clutch the lady close?

"So long as it's not the dungeon, I can manage," Maudie put in as Yeager returned with a tray bearing heavy porcelain cups that steamed. Pym followed with toast, butter, and jam.

"Does the earl have a dungeon?" Eva asked as they laid out the meal before them.

"No," Mr. Howland said with a look to Maudie. "This hunting lodge may have been built to resemble a medieval castle, but it's less than two hundred years old. The previous earls saw no need for a dungeon."

"Of course not," Maudie agreed, slathering raspberry jam on her toast. "They already had the caves."

"Caves?" Eva asked.

Mr. Howland was having none of it. "I will not house you there either, madam. I am not an ogre. Or a troll," he hurried to add when Maudie opened her mouth.

He reached for his cup and drank deep. Eva applied herself to the meal.

"So, where will you put me?" Maudie asked as they all finished and Yeager set about clearing.

"Since I am in a guest suite, there must be others nearby," Eva said. "Perhaps we should go look."

Of course, Mr. Howland joined them. He didn't seem to want to let them out of his sight for more than a moment. It was quick work to determine that the bedchamber directly opposite Eva's would suit Maudie just fine. She particularly liked the view down the drive.

"That way," she said, "I'll see them coming."

"I'll take the suite at the beginning of the wing on the other side of the landing," Mr. Howland said before Eva could ask who Maudie thought might arrive. "I can be near at hand if needs arise."

What needs did he think would arise? She had Yeager to protect her, and the magistrate didn't believe Maudie's stories.

Did he?

He certainly stuck to their sides the rest of the day as she explored a bit more of the main floor. She and Maudie had great fun pulling off various covers to find the hidden treasures. In the great hall alone, they exposed a high-backed carved bench and a chest with ivory inlay on the lid. The best part was the twin marble statues flanking the hearth, sculpted in classical lines to resemble a Grecian lady with a vase balanced on her head. Maudie studied her the longest, reaching around it as if to measure the circumference, smoothing her hands down the stone fabric of the gown, and peering up into the face.

"Odd," she said when Eva came to collect her. "I don't recall seeing a fairy this large before."

Mr. Howland looked away as if trying to hide his smile.

Beyond the great hall, they discovered a disappointing library with few books lying on mostly empty shelves. But on the other side of the withdrawing room sat a music room, gilt chairs lined up as if awaiting the next concert. Eva peeked under one of the draped cloths to find a harpsichord, lacquered in black with gilt appointments.

"Do you play, Miss Faraday?" Mr. Howland asked as she trailed a finger along the keys.

"I never learned," she confessed.

"I did," Maudie said. She pulled the cloth the rest of the way off and plunked herself down on the bench.

Eva wasn't sure what to expect, but a quite passible melody pranced from her fingers.

"I used to play at the assemblies too," she said as if she had noticed Eva's surprise, "but they have a fancy quartet now. I can't mind. More opportunity for me to dance."

Could Eva dance at the assembly? The earl had been adamant about her banishment.

"Perhaps a month or two in your own company will give you a different perspective," he'd said the last time they'd met.

"One month or ten," Eva had returned, "you will never convince me to accept an offer from your son. He doesn't love me, and I don't love him. He isn't finished mourning his first wife."

His hand had come down on his desk. The papers had no more than rustled, but in the quiet of his study the movement had been like the crack of thunder. "None of that matters. Thorgood will do as I tell him. I advise you to think carefully before contemplating otherwise."

She stood by her word. She would choose her own husband. The earl could keep her here at the worst ten months, when she would have access to her own funds and no longer have to rely on his good will. Of course, whoever she married would take control of her fortune. That was the law, and she had never heard of a way around it. But she would not allow the earl to mismanage her father's hard-won fortune the way he had mismanaged his own.

Besides, his lordship wasn't here now. He hadn't even sent word to his watchdog. There was no one to stop her from visiting the spa, dancing the night away at the assembly. Maybe she'd finally meet a man she could trust with her future, someone who would value her more than the money she could bring him.

For some reason, her gaze was drawn to James Howland. He had moved to one of the taller draped furnishings in the room. One hand rested on the peak, and his head was bowed, as if he was whispering to the thing. His golden hair reflected the sunlight coming through the narrow windows. He gripped the cloth and pulled it off.

Eva caught her breath. She was at his side in an instant. "It's beautiful."

The harp was crafted from maple, polished to a warm glow. The arch and head had been carved to curve like an ostrich plume. The glittering strings begged for her touch.

As if he felt the same, he ran a hand gently along the wood. "It was my mother's."

Her throat tightened. "I'm sorry for your loss."

He frowned at her, hand falling. "Mother isn't dead, Miss Faraday. She's as much a prisoner as you are. If you're as close to the earl as you claim, you must have met her. She resides in Howland House."

Eva blinked. "Does she? I never met a Mrs. Howland. The only other lady there besides the countess is Miss Marjorie."

"Miss?" He choked on the word. "My mother had the misfortune to marry a Howland, but marry she did. How dare he imply otherwise!"

"That is rude," Eva agreed. "I'm sorry I helped perpetuate the lie. I didn't see your mother often, mind you. Lady Howland required much attention, and she keeps her companion close. But Miss…Mrs. Howland was always kind to me."

He inclined his head. "She would be. My mother is one of the kindest people I know. Forgive me for my vehemence in defending her. It's difficult to see her slighted."

"I can imagine." She made herself focus on the harp. "And I can understand how sad she must have felt to leave this behind. My harp was the first thing the earl took away."

"You play?" Immediately, he bent to uncover the seat. "Please. Mother would be delighted that someone who loved it as much as she did was using it."

She had played for the earl once, and he'd taken her instrument from her. She could not make herself give away her feelings so easily now.

"Perhaps another time," she said, turning her back on the instrument.

Maudie began to play a dirge.

Somehow, they made it through the day. The servants finished setting the house to rights. The scent of lemon polish hung in the air. Men delivered coal, food, candles, and lamp oil from somewhere. She wasn't sure who had procured fresh fish for dinner, but she wasn't going to question the gift. She, Maudie, and Mr. Howland made quick work of the meal. Then he excused himself, claiming the need to work.

"He works?" Eva asked Maudie after they had returned to the withdrawing room.

Beside her on the settee, Maudie shrugged. "Doesn't anyone of any worth?"

Eva smiled. "My father would say yes. The earl would not."

"Then he should talk to the trolls," Maudie said. "They'd teach him a thing or two."

Eva leaned forward. "What would the smugglers you mentioned have to say to him?"

"Oh, they talk to the earl all the time. He funds their cargo."

"Does he?" Eva leaned back. "I wish I could prove that. Perhaps someone would bring him up on charges."

Maudie sucked her teeth a moment before answering. "Your best chance would be to watch the caves. Mr. How-land and the militia captured one band of smugglers, but those caves have been used for generations. Someone else must be using them now."

Eva nodded. "And how would I find these caves?"

Maudie pouted. "No easy way I know. But you might ask Jesslyn. She's sailed in twice."

Eva grinned. "I cannot wait to meet your niece."

They chatted about other things then, staying up per-haps later than was usual, until they decided it was time to retire. Yeager put out the lights behind them.

Eva gave Maudie a hug at the top of the landing.

"Thank you," she said. "I thought I would be abandoned here, but I feel as if I've made a friend instead."

Maudie beamed at her. "Me as well. You're even better than the mermaids."

Eva smiled as Maudie continued to her own room. Yea-ger had disappeared toward the kitchen, taking the last light with him. The corridor seemed empty suddenly, the house too silent. She couldn't even hear a clock ticking. She might well have been alone.

Below a movement caught her eye.

Someone was opening the door of the castle, for a shaft of moonlight widened across the floor. A shadow stepped into the light, cloak flowing, then darted into the great hall.

That couldn't be a servant.

It must be an intruder.

Eva opened her mouth and screamed.

# CHAPTER FOUR

J AMES HAD BEEN SITTING ON an armchair by the
fire, reviewing the reports from various properties
around the area, when a scream pierced the silence. He
was on his feet and moving before it finished echoing.
Pym darted out of the dressing room to meet him at the
door of the bedchamber he'd chosen.

"What could that be, sir?"

"Load my pistol," James said, and his valet's eyes went
round as saucers.

He did not wait for Pym to comply but strode out into
the corridor. Miss Faraday stood on the other side of the
landing, her maid peering from her room. Mrs. Tully's head
stuck out of her room as well.

Miss Faraday pointed down the stairs. "I saw someone
sneaking into the house."

James eased himself to where the corridor met the open
landing. Cautiously, he looked around the corner.

The stairwell to the main floor was empty. Below, her
man Yeager had come out of the corridor to the kitchen,
lamp in his grip. He stared up at James.

She must have understood the value of silence, for she
tiptoed to James's side and tilted her head to gaze down the
stairs as well. Her curls brushed his cheek, and he caught
a scent like ripe apples. Still, nothing else moved, and he

heard no noise of a sudden footfall.

He pulled back into the corridor just as Pym scurried up to him, offering the pistol with a shaking hand.

James steadied the gun. "Go with Miss Faraday and protect her and the other ladies."

Pym stared down at the mother-of-pearl handled pistol.

Miss Faraday opened her palm. "I know how to shoot. Do you expect an attack, Mr. Howland?"

"I don't know," James said as Pym surrendered the pistol to her with a shudder. "Lock yourself in your room just in case. I'll return as soon as I can."

She made a face. "Unsatisfactory. What if something happens to you? You may have a quarter hour, then I'm sending Pym to the village for help."

"Agreed," James said. He watched as she gathered everyone up, like a hen collecting her chicks, and vanished into her bedchamber. Then he started down the stairs.

"Did you see anything?" he asked Yeager.

The tall, gangly servant shook his head. "I was just making sure the fire was banked in the kitchen before retiring. Then I heard Miss Eva scream." He glanced up the stairs. "She doesn't scare easily."

"And she may have nothing to fear now," James said. "She said she saw someone coming into the castle. You're sure all the cleaning staff have left?"

Yeager nodded. "Saw them out myself." He lifted the lantern higher, sending shadows leaping up the walls of the great hall. "If she saw someone, we may have a thief."

An easy explanation, but James feared something more. "Grab the poker from the hearth, and follow me."

Together, they covered the great hall and library, but nothing seemed out of place. The two statues Eva and Mrs. Tully had unveiled stared balefully ahead. James ventured into the withdrawing room. The fire had been banked here as well, and all lights extinguished. The shadows from

Yeager's lamp made every piece of furniture seem bigger, darker.

"Look around," James said. "I'll check the windows."

But the narrow windows were all latched, their velvet draperies undisturbed.

Yeager completed his circuit of the room and returned to James's side. "Nothing, sir."

James faced the door to the music room. "Stand ready." He moved to take the latch and pushed the door open, dodging aside in case something came flying out.

No movement. Silence.

Yeager peered past him, lantern up. Besides the harp and the harpsichord, nothing else had been undraped. But then, nothing else was large enough to hide behind or under.

James pulled the door shut. "It appears Miss Faraday's scream scared him off. Perhaps you should stay with her tonight. It might ease her concerns."

Yeager snorted, then turned the sound into a cough. "I told you. She's not scared of anything. She sat her first horse at four, and it was a horse, not a pony. Her father had a saddle made just for her short legs. She was leaping fences by the time she was eight. He taught her to shoot and box as well. She can take care of herself."

Rather impressive. The earl had certainly mistaken his target this time. Then again, just because she could defend herself physically didn't mean she wasn't vulnerable to the earl's schemes. He knew how well his cousin played the game, to his sorrow.

"I promised to tell her what we learned in any event," James said. "She can decide whether she wants you close."

Yeager went ahead of him toward the great hall. James glanced around the withdrawing room again, but still he saw nothing out of place. He could not shake the feeling that Miss Faraday's stranger had been his mysterious lamp lighter. He risked much entering a building that was now occupied. Even if none of the remaining lamps showed outside, once he'd entered the great hall he would have seen the glow from above. He had to realize people were about. So why chance getting caught?

And why the great hall? Before, the lamp had been lit on the chamber story, where it could be seen by sea. The stairs to the caves were accessed through the kitchen. What would anyone want with the great hall, library, withdrawing room, or music room?

With a shake of his head, he followed Yeager. He paused at the top of the landing to listen again, but the castle kept its secrets well. He joined Yeager at Miss Faraday's door and rapped.

"What's the word to pass?" That was Mrs. Tully's voice.

Yeager frowned as if trying to remember it.

"I must speak to Miss Faraday," James called through the portal.

"Why can't any of you get it right?" she complained a moment before Miss Faraday opened the door.

She held the pistol in one grip. Seeing him, she uncocked and lowered it. "I heard no sign of a struggle. I take it you didn't find anyone."

"No," James admitted. "I suggest you may want to keep Mrs. Tully with you again. If you prefer, we can bring down a cot for Yeager as well."

Yeager's eyes narrowed over his sharp nose.

"No need to discomfort Yeager or Mrs. Tully," she said. "Patsy can stay with me if she's worried."

"Yes, miss." The maid's voice sounded relieved.

"Mr. Pym and I will be on guard across the landing," James promised her. "You should be perfectly safe."

She handed him back the pistol. "Very well, Mr. Howland. But you owe me an explanation in the morning."

He refused to share what he knew until he was sure of her. "I cannot explain what I cannot find, madam," he said.

He could not understand why what he said continued to amuse her, but her mouth quirked, and her eyes sparkled.

"Normally, I would agree," she said, "but you warned me of the dangers of this castle before I sighted our mysterious guest. You clearly expected something of this nature. I must know the truth if I'm to protect myself and my staff."

A shame he could not argue there. "In the morning, then, Miss Faraday."

He could only hope their prowler showed his hand before then, and James could end this before he had to tell Eva everything.

No one else disturbed Eva's sleep, even though she lay awake for some time, listening. At one point, Patsy, sleeping beside her, started snoring, making it impossible to hear anything else beyond the room. Still, the noise was rhythmic enough that she fell asleep anyway.

She woke to the sound of her maid stirring. Patsy's brown hair stuck out at odd angles as she sat up in the bed and glanced around.

"We're still alive," she said, as if she'd doubted that might be the case.

Eva swung her legs off the bed. "Let's hope we can say the same of Mrs. Tully and Mr. Howland."

Patsy shuddered. "I'll just stir up the coals before I go check."

But when Eva ventured downstairs a short while later, gowned in pink sprigged muslin, she found James Howland and Maudie at the table in the great hall, tucking into a hearty breakfast of liver and eggs. He rose as Eva approached.

"You look rested," she said, eyeing his tailored black coat and breeches. His cravat was intricately tied. She would not have taken him for a dandy.

"Pym and I spelled each other on watch," he said as she sat.

A likely story. He knew something more. Had he brought the stranger into the house just to frighten her? She'd seen the look on his face when Maudie had first started spinning tales. He'd thought Eva would run at the first hint of a supernatural presence. But what she'd seen had been no ghost.

"This would be an excellent opportunity for you to explain yourself, sir," she said as Pym brought her a loaded plate. Her companion continued eating with a happy sigh.

He glanced at Maudie. "Perhaps after breakfast."

So, he didn't want Maudie to know. There might be a good reason for that. She *was* good at telling stories. Perhaps others in the village believed them. But why did he need to hide the fact that they had found a stranger in the castle? Didn't he want help identifying the culprit?

"Very well," Eva allowed, picking up her fork. "But you can solve one mystery for me."

He hesitated. "Oh?"

"Who's cooking?" she asked.

He relaxed. "Pym has cooked for me for years. If you end up staying at the castle, we'll have to make other arrangements, but, for now, he can serve our needs."

It seemed she wouldn't even have to leave the castle to shop. He was proving a most efficient jailer, whether he meant to or not.

As if he'd noticed her glance toward the windows, he nodded in that direction. "The grounds are particularly fine this time of year. You might enjoy seeing them after breakfast. And Mrs. Tully could hunt for fairy circles."

Maudie's eyes lit. "Excellent suggestion."

Odd suggestion. She doubted he believed in fairies any more than she did. But she was willing to play along. It would get her out of the castle, and perhaps she could convince him to be more forthcoming.

When they had finished, Yeager fetched them their cloaks, and they ventured out at last.

It had been nearly dark when she'd arrived at the castle the other day. She'd only registered a lot of tall stone surrounded by emerald-colored lawns. Now she noticed the slender trees that encircled the hunting lodge, bark almost silver and spring green leaves swaying as if they kept a discreet distance from the castle's grandeur. Just beyond, wildflowers bobbed their heads, pinks, purples, blues, and reds vibrant.

"I believe you may find mushrooms in that direction," James told Maudie with a nod toward the trees. "We'll be right behind you."

Without a glance at Eva, she trotted off.

"That was badly done," Eva said as she followed at a slower pace. "What if she eats one?"

"And destroy the fairy circle? Never."

Eva kept her eye on Maudie's black-clad figure just in case. "What did you want to tell me that she cannot hear?"

She thought he might prevaricate anew, but he clasped his hands behind his back as if he had made up his mind.

"Someone has been placing a light in the castle window on occasion," he told her. "I have been checking the castle more often since it started. I was coming to look the night you arrived."

Eva frowned. "But there was no one in the castle when we reached it. The door was locked."

"The door is generally locked," he said darkly. "It was locked before you retired last night."

The air felt colder, and she wrapped her cloak closer. "So, we might have come upon this intruder at any time."

"Perhaps not," he hedged, as if he could tell he had rattled her. "We originally suspected smugglers, but the gang in the area was recently captured."

"And yet I saw someone last night," Eva insisted.

"Which begs the question—who is using the castle and why?"

Ahead, Maudie bent over the grass as if to study a spatter of white-capped mushrooms shaped like parasols. She straightened with a shake of her head and moved on.

"You said *we* suspected smugglers," Eva murmured as they followed. "Who else knows about the incidents?"

Again, he answered readily enough. "Captain St. Claire, a friend of mine. Mr. Denby, the Riding Surveyor for the area. Mr. Chance, the Riding Officer for Grace-by-the-Sea, and Miss Chance, the spa hostess."

"She's Mrs. Tully's niece," Eva remembered. "So surely Maudie knows too."

"I am never entirely certain what Mrs. Tully knows," he said, looking to where Maudie was now hopping through a patch of wildflowers, arms flapping.

Eva shook her head. "If you are this cautious about word getting out, you must suspect someone in the village."

"I dislike suspecting any of my neighbors," he said, gaze hardening. "But it's unlikely anyone would travel a great distance to sneak into the castle, and there has been no sign of a break in."

"So someone else has a key," Eva surmised.

"Indeed. I thought them all accounted for. I have one. Our employment agency owner has another, which he uses to open the door for those who come to clean."

"Obviously the earl sent me with one," Eva added. "I'm assuming he kept one as well."

"So you say."

Eva frowned at him. "Oh, come now. Surely you don't still think I made that all up. If I had been a thief determined to steal from you, I could have cleaned out the silver and run while you were fetching Maudie. And I would hardly have screamed at my own man last night."

"Agreed," he said, somewhat reluctantly. "But I wish I knew what drove our visitor to take a chance on entering an occupied building."

"Aha!" Maudie positively vibrated as she beckoned them closer. "Come see what I found."

She was standing in the center of a ten-foot circle of white-capped mushrooms. Easy to imagine rainbow-winged fairies sitting on each to have a chat.

Eva smiled. "How delightful. Don't you agree, Mr. Howland?"

When he didn't answer, she glanced up to find him staring out through the trees.

She could see why. Just beyond the circle, the wildflowers had been trampled, their stems broken, as if a large beast like a horse had been pastured among them.

And Eva doubted it had belonged to the fairies.

# CHAPTER FIVE

JAMES STARED AT THE BATTERED flowers. This had to have been where his quarry had tied his horse last night before making his escape. Had he come from a long distance after all? Why?

"Looks like our visitor left a trail," Miss Faraday said beside him. "Let's follow it."

She was so eager, but she couldn't understand the danger. If this fellow was part of a new smuggling gang moving into the area, he would fight to hide his identity, to the death if need be. Yet, surely they'd captured all the smugglers. Who had come to sneak into his castle now?

"Stay close," he advised, and she and Mrs. Tully gathered around him as he began walking through the trees.

"We must speak to my coachman," Miss Faraday said, scurrying to keep up. "Perhaps the horses reacted last night to a strange beast so near."

"Especially if it was ridden by fairies," Mrs. Tully put in helpfully.

"No fairies," James assured her. "But I doubt your coachman heard anything, Miss Faraday. You'd be surprised the number of ways thieves have found to move silently."

"You have extensive experience with such matters as magistrate, I imagine," she mused, pink-sprigged skirts swishing across the grass below the hem of her cloak.

"Less than other magistrates along the coast," he allowed, focusing on the tracks. The grove of trees was denser here, the wildflowers fewer. With the sunlight slanting through the leaves, he was hard-pressed to spot a sign of a horse's passing, much less determine the exact direction.

They moved back into the sunlight as they reached the edge of the headland nearest the sea, and he put out his arms to prevent them from stepping onto unstable ground. "Easy. The cliff erodes a little more after each storm."

Mrs. Tully shaded her eyes with her hand, gaze going out over the blue-green waves of the Channel. "No sign of mermaids."

"Or our thief," James agreed.

Miss Faraday frowned. "What's that noise?"

Funny. He'd heard the roar of the waves so often he no longer noticed. One of the reasons the area below the castle was called the Dragon's Maw was the sound the waves made when they pummeled the cliff at high tide, as they were now. The other was the boulders sticking up like teeth and guarding the entrance to the caves.

"The roar of the dragon," Mrs. Tully said, as if she remembered as well. "No one's getting into the caves right now."

"Getting in?" Miss Faraday looked around him at their chaperone. "You mean the cave entrance your niece sailed into is right below us?"

"No," James started even as Mrs. Tully nodded.

"That's how the smugglers reach the caves too," she said.

Of course she would know about the caves. He'd heard that some of the young men had taken to attempting to enter by sea as proof they had reached adulthood. As far as he knew, all had come back to boast of their achievements, and they'd left the caves relatively undisturbed.

"As Mrs. Tully has mentioned, there are caves under the headland," he admitted to Eva. "They were used for storage once, but they've been empty for years."

"Pft," Mrs. Tully spat. "They've been used by smugglers, you mean. And the French send their spies that way."

James speared her with a look. "That, madam, is a lie."

Both Mrs. Tully and Miss Faraday stiffened, but at his condemning statement or his vehemence, he wasn't sure.

Mrs. Tully narrowed her eyes. "I've seen them."

Along with fairies, trolls, and mermaids. "When?" James asked. "If you know the enemy is traveling through the area, it is your duty to inform me as your magistrate."

"Why?" she asked. "The mermaids don't."

"Mr. Howland is correct," Miss Faraday put in gently. "If you are aware of the enemy so close, we must alert the Home Office."

She scowled. "I've been speaking out for years, and no one pays me the least attention. Why, I've seen Napoleon on this very headland. For all we know, he's the one who snuck in last night."

James blew out a breath. "Mrs. Tully, forgive me for not paying sufficient attention in the past, but you must admit that finding the French emperor on English soil is unlikely."

She stood taller. "Unlikely, but not impossible."

"Not impossible," Miss Faraday said with a look to James. "But let's focus on more recent events. Someone was in the castle last night. Was that person a smuggler or a French agent?"

James turned from the view. "That, Miss Faraday, is what I want to know."

She turned as well, then froze, eyes widening. He jerked to a stop. What had she discovered now?

"The village is right there!" she declared.

James glanced over Grace-by-the-Sea, where Miss Chance was leading a group of Newcomers through the village. Mr. Carroll was already out in front of his curiosity shop in anticipation, sunlight sparkling on his spectacles.

"Did you expect it to have moved?" he asked Miss

Faraday.

Her reddening cheeks clashed with the pink of her cloak. "No. But it wasn't visible when we came in the other night, and my room faces the courtyard. The earl made it sound as if I would be completely isolated. The village is an easy walk."

"A quarter hour at a brisk pace," Mrs. Tully agreed. "Less if you're a troll."

Miss Faraday regarded him as if he'd somehow hidden the village from her. "I demand we visit."

He ought to refuse. He still had little knowledge as to why the earl had sent her here or if he even knew she existed. She could be a cunning thief or in league with those using the castle for their own ends.

But if his cousin had truly exiled her here, James would not add to her misery. And having her and Mrs. Tully out of the house would give him an opportunity to visit the caves, see if he could find any evidence of unauthorized entry. He might even find time for a word with Quill. At the least, his friend should be alerted to the visitor last night.

"Certainly you should go, Miss Faraday," he said. "Mrs. Tully knows the area well. She will make an exceptional guide. Take Yeager with you as escort. I look forward to hearing what you think of the place."

He'd given in entirely too easily. Maybe it was penance for the way he'd spoken to Mrs. Tully. He certainly didn't like the idea that the enemy might be near. Still, Eva wasn't ready to trust him.

She wasn't willing to refuse the chance to escape, either, if only for the afternoon. She led Maudie back to the castle to leave their cloaks and collect Yeager, their shawls, and their reticules, then set out for the village.

She wasn't sure how to get down from the headland, but Maudie showed them a switchback path that brought them out on a pleasant lane.

"Castle Walk," she explained as they passed white-washed cottages with thatched roofs. "Directly ahead is High Street. Left takes you down to the shops and the shore. Right takes you up to the spa and assembly rooms. Directly across is Church Street, which leads to the magistrate's house and St. Andrew's."

"So, Mr. Howland doesn't live on the castle grounds," Eva said as they reached the cross street.

Maudie snorted. "Not his family. The earl barely considers them relations, for all they share a common lineage." She leaned closer. "I suspect he was a changeling, switched at birth with a troll. That's why they obey him."

That would explain a great deal, if she believed in trolls.

"Which way, Miss Eva?" Yeager asked, glancing right and left.

She'd wanted to meet Miss Chance, see the spa, even do some shopping, but another idea held more interest at the moment. "Show me Mr. Howland's house."

If her choice surprised her chaperone, Maudie didn't show it. She obligingly led them across the wide High Street toward the steeple rising against the opposite hillside.

The houses were grander here—two or three stories, with brick or stone sides and window boxes or gardens bursting with blooms.

"That one's his," Maudie said with a nod toward one of the largest. "It was his father's before him. His grandfather built it. He was the second son of the earl's grandfather."

Eva calculated the connection in her head. "So, Mr. Howland is Viscount Thorgood's second cousin."

"And the earl's cousin once removed," Maudie agreed as they stopped in front of the wrought-iron fence.

Eva eyed the house. It was certainly worthy of the local magistrate, but it was a far cry from the earl's other properties in London and Somerset. How hard did James Howland have to work to keep it? How much had he had to compromise?

She turned from the sight. "I'd like to meet your niece next. Shall we visit the spa?"

Maudie led the way.

Eva had heard of Bath and Scarborough, but she'd never visited a spa before. She had thought to find bathing rooms, perhaps a tearoom, but the spa at Grace-by-the-Sea resembled nothing so much as a conservatory in one of the larger London homes. Pale blue walls encircled the pump room, as if a cloudless summer's day greeted her. A lacquered harpsichord sat in one corner, waiting to be played, and a stone fountain in the opposite corner bubbled with sparkling water. The scent of lavender floated around her.

An older, auburn-haired woman was holding court near a bank of wide windows overlooking the sea, her admirers seated around her in white wicker chairs. Maudie made for her side.

"What have you done with Jesslyn?" she asked.

The gentlemen looked her way, then rose. One, a rheumy-eyed fellow of narrow frame, frowned as if taking umbrage on the lady's behalf.

"Good morning to you as well, Mrs. Tully," the lady said in a warm, amused voice. "Your niece is leading a tour of the village. Now, do make us known to your friend."

"Why?" Maudie asked.

An older gentleman with silver hair and an impressive countenance stepped forward. "Allow me. Miss Chance mentioned you were chaperoning a Miss Faraday. May I present Mrs. Harding…"

The auburn-haired lady inclined her head.

"Mr. Crabapple…"

The rheumy-eyed man nodded with a sniff.

"Mr. Donner, a recent addition to our group, and his friend, Mr. George…"

The two brunettes, both young and dapper, bowed to her.

"Admiral Walsey…"

The portly older man attempted a bow and nearly over-set himself.

"And my own humble self, Featherstone." He effected a far more elegant bow.

Eva curtsied. "A pleasure to make your acquaintances."

"Will you be visiting long, Miss Faraday?" Mrs. Harding asked, gaze flickering over the two younger men in her train, who were regarding Eva with interest.

"Not now," Maudie said, tugging on her arm. "We must find Jess."

Well, that had been their mission, but Eva wouldn't have minded tarrying. Instead, she allowed Maudie to tow her toward the door. "I hope to see you again soon," she called to Mrs. Harding and her set. Lord Featherstone bowed again.

Yeager rejoined them as they exited and started down the hill into the village proper. So small a place would likely include no more than a grocer and blacksmith, so it shouldn't be so difficult to locate Miss Chance. Yet, any number of shops hugged the main street to the cove. Eva's smile turned up.

Maudie didn't appear to know which of the businesses her niece was visiting, so she took Eva into each of them, starting on the west side of the street.

"Mr. Carroll's Curiosities," Eva read on the gilded sign above the door before Maudie pulled her inside. Then she stopped and stared, turning to take in all the wonders around her. Books on brightly colored shelves, periodicals spread on tables, miniature automatons, and what was the huge charcoal-colored beast at the back? Yeager's mouth was agape.

"May I be of assistance?" A dapper fellow with a round face and a pleasant smile came forward.

"Have you seen them?" Maudie demanded.

He schooled his face to all seriousness. "Fairies or trolls?"

"Neither," Maudie said. "Jesslyn."

"She was here not a half hour ago," he assured her. "You might try Mr. Ellison's bakery."

"Oh, the bakery," Eva enthused. "The bread this morning was marvelous." She and Yeager followed Maudie from the shop.

"Excellent rolls," Maudie replied. "The cake's not bad either. But I understand the mermaids were most disappointed in the macaroons."

She wasn't sure how mermaids had managed to come by the little almond-flavored biscuits, but Mr. Ellison's bakery was slightly closer to the shore. Miss Chance wasn't there either.

"Try the linens and trimmings shop," the burly baker suggested as they left with a crusty loaf of bread, an iced cake, and a dozen cinnamon biscuits. Eva might not be able to pay for housing, but she had some pin money. Her father's will had stipulated that, at least.

The Misses Pierce, as the two older ladies introduced themselves, were happy to show off the bolts of fabric, ribbon, and braid that filled their shop, but it was easy to see that Eva was their only customer. The same was true of the milliner's they tried next.

"Perhaps we should have brought Patsy too, Miss Eva," Yeager said, balancing the baked goods with boxes holding the purple braid and pink leather gloves she'd purchased at the other two shops.

"Jesslyn has to be in here," Maudie said, leading them into a shop across the street from Mr. Carroll's Curiosities. Eva caught the name All the Colors of the Sea as she stepped inside to the ring of a bell.

This shop was more like an art gallery, with paintings crowding the walls and tables down the center with any number of unique goods from tatted collars to wrought-iron wall sconces and colorful pottery.

"You see," Maudie declared. "I knew we could find her."

Blond curls peeking out of her straw bonnet, a young woman turned at the sound of Maudie's voice. So did the others clustered around her.

"Aunt," she said with a pretty smile. "And you must be Miss Faraday."

Eva nodded as she and Maudie joined the group. "And you are Miss Chance, the spa hostess."

"Indeed I am. Allow me to make you known to our guests. Mrs. North and her son are visiting us from neighboring Wiltshire."

An attractive woman with honey-colored hair and a pink pelisse Eva could only envy, Mrs. North smiled a greeting. Her son, who appeared quite a few years younger than Eva, ogled her through his gilt-edged quizzing glass. Eva regarded him back, brows raised. He dropped the little square glass to the length of its black ribbon around the thoroughly complicated fold of his cravat.

"Miss Tapper and her companion Mrs. Baugh are touring the coast," Miss Chance continued.

"And I must say we've had the best welcome here at Grace-by-the-Sea," the younger brunette declared. Sturdy and rosy-cheeked, she looked as if she was ready to climb the highest hill in her tweed spencer and stout walking shoes. Her darker-haired older companion, dressed in black like Maudie, nodded her agreement.

"Finally, we have Mr. Harris," Miss Chance concluded. "He has been visiting us for the last fortnight. From London, I believe."

Mr. Harris had wavy brown hair and a trim mustache. He bowed to Eva and Maudie, bottle-green coat falling open to reveal a slender physique. "Ladies. Was any man so fortunate as to be surrounded by such beauty?"

All the women smiled at him. Mr. North yawned.

"Allow me to welcome you as well." Another woman approached, the shopkeeper by the canvas smock that covered her gown. Still, Eva wondered at the green dots sprinkled through her ginger-colored hair.

"All the Colors of the Sea carries any number of fine products crafted right here in our village," she told them all. "Please, look around, and let me know if you have any questions."

Miss Chance watched her charges wander off in various directions before moving closer to Eva. Those big blue eyes regarded her kindly. "Mr. Howland explained that you are visiting the castle as a guest of the earl."

That was one way to put it. Then again, Eva didn't know how the village, except for Maudie and Mr. Howland, viewed the earl. Best not to make enemies, or her ten-month sentence could be long indeed.

"Yes," Eva answered. "And thank you so much for allowing your aunt to chaperone me. She's been nothing but a delight."

Maudie beamed at her. "We're coming to the assembly on Wednesday."

"Excellent," her niece said. "I'll look forward to seeing you there. Excuse me." She hurried to where Miss Tapper appeared to be giving Mr. North the dressing down he deserved.

Maudie tugged on Eva's arm. "Come see the paintings."

There were several—wonderful landscapes that could well have inspired the shop's name. Eva stopped before a massive canvas showing a stormy sea with the sun just beaming through the clouds. Oh, to see so far, to feel so free. She peered closer at the signature.

"Archer," she said to Maudie, who was studying the piece so fixedly she might have been searching for mermaids in the waves. "Is this by a local painter too?"

"Indeed." The shopkeeper moved briskly to their sides, her poplin skirts rustling. "Do you like the piece?"

Eva nodded. "Mr. Archer is very talented."

"Mr. Archer, my father, wouldn't have recognized a work of art if I had smacked it over his head," she replied with a teasing smile. "That is one of mine."

Eva's face felt hot. "Please forgive my assumption, Miss Archer."

Miss Archer inclined her head. "It is rare to find a lady selling her paintings, I know. I am blessed to be able to pursue my calling."

"Jesslyn was pursuing her calling," Maudie said with a glance to her niece, who was examining a leather coin purse with Mr. Harris. "Now we're to be tossed out like yesterday's catch."

Miss Archer's face darkened. "I know. And I haven't given up, I promise you."

Eva glanced between them. "I don't understand."

"Jesslyn and Maudie are being forced from their positions," Miss Archer explained, voice as tart as a lemon. "It was a contested decision by the Spa Corporation Board. You would think people raised in this village would know better. Miss Chance's father was the previous spa physician. She assisted him in running the spa until he passed last year."

"They want a new physician," Maudie said. "Someone who can treat scrofulous coughs and other maladies." She sighed as if she'd have preferred to treat such things herself.

"The board looked hard for a replacement," Miss Archer agreed. "Now one's coming, but he thinks he can run the place all by himself. Just like a man."

"He might be persuaded to be reasonable," Eva said. "I've only met a few unreasonable men in my life." James Howland and the earl came to mind.

The shop bell rang as the door opened again, and Miss Archer turned toward the sound. So did Eva.

James Howland stood in the doorway. His head was up, his face set, his shoulders stiff.

In short, he did not look pleased to be here.

# CHAPTER SIX

ABIGAIL ARCHER WAS FROWNING AT him, and James did his best to remove the scowl from his face. The artist hardly deserved his frustration. Neither did Eva Faraday and Mrs. Tully. Only the earl would put him in such a position.

The day had not gone well. He'd waited until Eva, their chaperone, and her servant had left the castle, then made sure her maid and Pym were busy upstairs before heading for the door that led down to the caves. He'd wondered whether the thing would screech from disuse, but it had swung open on well-oiled hinges. He'd have to ask Quill about that.

Down the long, winding stairs he'd gone, lantern in hand. The stone walls grew damper, darker. At the bottom, he stepped out on the floor of the cave.

What once might have been sand was now covered with dark rocks fallen from the roof and sides of the low cave. Waves lapped at the edge, driven in through the Dragon's Maw on the high tide. In the distance, the glow of light and the dull boom of surf told of the exit to the sea.

Glancing around, he saw little sign of occupancy. If a boat had beached recently, he couldn't tell. At least Quill was doing a good job there. But someone had built a fire. The pile of ash looked silvery grey next to the black-tinged rocks that ringed it.

Yeager hadn't returned when he eased out into the kitchen, and there was no sign of Pym or the maid. As he shut the door carefully behind him, he caught the sound of voices echoing in the great hall. He strode in that direction.

Priestly and Pym were in consultation near the front door. They both looked up as James approached.

"You returned faster than I expected," he told his secretary. "Did you even reach London?"

"No, sir," Priestly said, pulling his dusty hat from his head and showing more of his bald spot in the process. "I met the earl's footman on my way north. He was carrying a note for you." He held it out to James with his free hand.

James withdrew to the table to open the missive, breaking the heavy red wax sealed with the earl's signet.

"I have sent you a challenge," his cousin had written. "Arden Faraday was a savvy fellow who provided some useful information on my investments. I agreed to take charge of his daughter when he passed. I have found her ungrateful, headstrong, and ill-disciplined. She will not heed my advice and counsel. For her own good and the good of the rest of the household, I have sent her to live in Castle How. She is to have no visitors. She is not to associate with anyone in the village. Expend as little time and money on her as you must to see to her basic needs. With seclusion may come wisdom. Send an update on her state of mind when you provide your monthly report. Howland."

The tone and direction were every bit what he'd come to expect from the earl. The only oddity was the signature. He was used to seeing the bold, black scrawl, feeling the supreme confidence with which it had been penned. This signature was thinner. Indeed, the pen hadn't even touched the paper in places, as if the hand that had written it had shaken.

He glanced up to find both his staff watching him. "You're certain the man you met was the earl's?" he asked Priestly.

His secretary nodded. "I'd seen him when you took me up to London last. He generally waits upon the earl in his study."

Dawson, then. No mistaking the strapping footman with his coal-black hair and bulbous nose. James folded the note and set it on the table. "Thank you, Priestly. Take the afternoon and your usual Sunday off, and get some rest."

Priestly bowed. "Thank you, sir. I'll see you on Monday. Here or…?"

"At the magistrate's house," James said. "The earl has confirmed that Miss Faraday is here as his guest. We will give her every courtesy."

They both inclined their heads. "Sir."

His secretary left, and Pym crossed to his side. It appeared Eva Faraday truly was the earl's prisoner. What had she done to earn his wrath?

And how could James protect her from the consequences?

"Then are we moving back to the house, sir?" Pym asked.

He would, except for the matter of the stranger in the castle last night. Would Eva be safe if he left? Bringing her home with him would only fuel speculation, even if Mrs. Tully stayed as well. Easy enough to avoid her in the castle. Impossible at the house.

"I'll give the matter thought," he told his man. "For now, assume we will be here at least another night. I'll go give Miss Faraday the good news."

James had walked the path down into the village. He might have ridden Majestic, but he would have had to take the drive to the cliff road, then follow it to the crossroads that led east to Lord Peverell's Lodge on the opposite headland, north to the village of Upper Grace on the Downs, and south into Grace-by-the-Sea.

He had thought Miss Faraday might have gone to the spa, so he'd checked there first. Miss Chance was missing from her usual spot near the welcome desk in the Grand Pump Room of the spa, but the auburn-haired beauty, Mrs. Harding, was lounging in her usual spot that looked down toward the cove. Lord Featherstone, another of those who attended regularly, detached himself from the group to meet James.

"Magistrate," the older man said as he joined James by the large bronze wall clock. "What brings you to our circle?"

"I was looking for a new addition to your set, a Miss Faraday," James answered. "I take it you haven't seen her or Mrs. Tully this afternoon?"

"Miss Faraday and Mrs. Tully were here not an hour ago, but they decamped for the village, where Miss Chance is leading a tour." He cocked his head. "An intriguing young lady to arrive here, no chaperone, no companion. What do you know of her?"

"Not enough at present," James assured him. "But I believe she will be with us for some time."

"Then I look forward to furthering the acquaintance," Lord Featherstone said.

With a bow, James left the silver-haired lord to his pleasures.

As he continued down the hill into the village proper, it was easy enough to spot Yeager lounging outside the gallery, packages piled at his feet. He scrambled straighter as James pushed past him into the shop.

"Miss Archer," he greeted the painter now, letting the door close behind him. "Forgive the interruption. I was looking for Miss Faraday."

"Oh?" Miss Archer glanced between them, reddish

brows up. "Am I to understand his lordship has returned at last and is hosting a house party?"

Who had started that rumor? It must be squelched immediately. While Grace-by-the-Sea was remarkably tolerant of visitors, a few residents would want to know why they hadn't been invited to any party in the castle.

"I regret the earl must remain in London for the time being," he told her. "Duty. He thought his good friend, Miss Faraday, might enjoy a holiday." He turned to Eva. "I see you've been enjoying the village."

"A great deal, Mr. Howland," she said brightly. "Everyone *here* has been very welcoming."

He glanced around to find a number of people gazing back, looks brimming with curiosity. "Ah, yes. Excuse me a moment while I pay my respects to Miss Chance."

Now Miss Faraday's look turned curious, but he moved to meet the spa hostess.

"Miss Chance," he said as the fellow beside her hurried off to study the pottery as if it held the meaning of life. "It appears Miss Faraday will be with us for some time. I will speak to your aunt about continuing her services as chaperone, but I'd like to pay their subscription to the spa."

Those blue eyes were wide and guileless, but he knew from experience they masked a sharp mind with the tactical skills of a general. "Speak to Mr. Lawrence," she advised. "As our spa treasurer, he records all subscriptions and lets me know who has paid and who is in arrears."

He knew the jeweler well. "I would prefer to deal with you directly. Questions would be raised about Miss Faraday's circumstances if it were known I was providing her funds as the earl's agent. Perhaps I could have Priestly provide the funds, and you could give the money to Mr. Lawrence. If Miss Faraday asks about the cost, assure her it has been met."

"I see," she said, and he feared she saw too much. "Very

well, Magistrate. However, you might want to pay for however long you expect Miss Faraday to be in the area rather than month by month. I am delighted to help, but I cannot promise the physician who is taking over will feel the same."

"And I can promise you that I will speak to this Doctor Bennett about your position," he told her. "The spa will not function without someone of your skills at the helm. Grace-by-the-Sea has no one finer."

"You are too kind," she said, lowering her gaze. He excused himself to return to Eva.

"Thank you for waiting for me," he said. "If you're ready to go?" He motioned toward the door.

She fluttered dark lashes at him. "I fear I hadn't quite finished my business in the village, Mr. Howland. If you insist on playing escort, you will have to amuse yourself for a while."

If that was how she'd addressed the earl, small wonder his cousin had found her headstrong. Still, James couldn't help admiring her bravado. He crossed his arms over his chest. "I would be delighted to wait for your least command, madam."

Once more Miss Archer glanced between them, then she grinned at Miss Faraday. "What can I show you, my dear?"

Eva kept one eye on James Howland as the energetic Miss Archer led her and Maudie about the gallery, pausing only to settle accounts with the other visitors and send them and Miss Chance on their way. Eva had a few coins left in her reticule, so she could buy something. Not that she needed to. The house her father had left her was still standing in London, filled to the rafters with fine furnishings, art, and statuary. She'd merely been trying to put James in his place. She hadn't expected him to agree so easily again.

What was he plotting?

He certainly looked as if he were contriving complex strategies as he stood to one side of the door. His blue eyes were narrowed just the slightest, as if he didn't want anyone to see the thoughts flying behind them. And he appeared to like that particular stance, arms crossed, booted legs braced. Did he know it made him look rather dashing, like a pirate king come to claim the village?

A giggle bubbled up at the image, and she turned her back on her distracting jailer.

"He is rather full of himself," Miss Archer murmured, handing Eva a lace collar to consider. "But you must know about the Howlands, being a particular friend of the earl."

She said it with all politeness, yet Eva knew that term could be used in far less kind ways. "I am, in a sense, the earl's ward," she explained, setting down the collar and picking up another with tiny glass beads that caught the light. "He thought I might learn obedience by sending me away."

Miss Archer's face stiffened. "Then you are in a difficult position."

Eva fingered the fine thread of the collar. "Nothing I cannot handle, Miss Archer."

"She has the trolls on her side," Maudie agreed.

"Not the mermaids?" Miss Archer asked with a fond look her way.

Maudie regarded her as if she'd gone mad. "Certainly not. Fickle and jealous, that's what they are."

"You can tell them they need not envy me," Eva assured her, laying the collar back down with the others on the display table. "And I thank you both for your concern, but I need no rescue. Should that change, I will be sure to let you know."

In the end, she'd purchased one of the purple-painted

lidded pottery jars, thanked Miss Archer for her time, and followed James Howland out the door.

Yeager hurriedly gathered up their belongings. Seeing his ungainly pile, Eva decided to carry the jar herself.

"Was there a reason you decided to come collect me?" she asked the magistrate as they started walking up High Street. "Or had I exceeded the limit of your patience? I imagine it's not excessive."

His mouth tightened a moment before he responded. "I heard from the earl. He confirms your statements."

She wasn't sure whether to be pleased to have been vindicated or annoyed he'd accepted the earl's word but not hers. "And so I am confined to the castle again."

"Those were his orders," he agreed.

"And you always follow orders," she guessed. She turned onto Castle Walk, Yeager and Maudie right behind.

"No," he clipped out. "I do not."

Eva eyed him, surprised. Once more that face was set, that jaw determined. Had she finally found a Howland with both backbone and integrity?

"What are you saying, Mr. Howland?" she asked.

He looked back at Maudie. "Mrs. Tully, forgive me. I would like to ask you to extend your time with us as chaperone. Miss Faraday will need your services for the next ten months. I will work out compensation with your niece."

Maudie frowned. "Why? Are you going to hire Jess too?"

"No," he assured her. "I thought perhaps she might have a better idea of the proper rate for chaperones."

Nicely done. Maudie might well have requested payment in fairy dust. This way, he made sure she was paid fairly without intimating she might not be her own best advocate.

"Given your prolonged stay," he continued, "you will want to collect a few more belongings to take back to the castle. Miss Faraday and I will wait for you on the bench at the first turning. Mr. Yeager can continue up to the castle with the packages. We'll be in full view of the village, so there should be no impropriety."

"Good," Maudie said. "Just remember, there's a fairy hole under the bench. I can always ask them if you've behaved." With a nod, she turned down the street.

"Miss Eva?" Yeager asked with a sidelong glance at the magistrate.

"Go ahead," Eva told him.

Her man squared his shoulders and started up the path.

"You're quite good about getting rid of witnesses when it suits you," Eva told James.

He turned toward the path, where Yeager was trudging upward. "A trait that comes in handy from time to time."

They climbed to where the path made its first turn, then sat on the little stone bench there. The sea glittered like a diamond over the tops of the roofs. James seemed content to gaze on it, long legs stretched in front of him.

"And?" Eva urged him.

He kept his eyes on the distance. "The earl seems to think that isolation will be your salvation."

Eva choked. "My salvation? From what exactly does he think I need to be saved? Besides him, of course."

His look came back to hers, as blue and bright as the waves. "Why has he taken that stance?"

So, the earl hadn't told him all. Should she? He was a Howland. Though he had sounded suitably defiant a moment ago, he must obey the earl's commands at least part of the time or the earl would not have allowed him to remain in this position. But if he was beginning to question those orders, shouldn't she encourage him?

"My father was Arden Faraday, the financier," she told him, fingers stroking the pottery jar in her lap. "He built a well-respected practice advising the rich and powerful on how to invest their funds. The earl was one of his clients."

"And, on his death, he remanded you to his lordship's care," he said.

"No," Eva said. "I'd already reached my majority when he became ill. I could have lived alone with a chaperone like Mrs. Tully. But my father thought I was too young to manage the wealth that would come to me as his only child. He made the earl trustee over my inheritance until I reached the age of five and twenty. And, because the amount of money I am allowed to access until then is ridiculously small given the total, I am beholden on the earl for a home and sustenance."

"I take it you found Howland House less than satisfactory, then," he said, voice neutral.

Her fingers were tightening. She took them away from the pretty jar. "It was as much a prison as the castle. The earl dictated when I might go out, where, and with whom. Within a few weeks, I was only allowed out with him or Viscount Thorgood. It soon became apparent he intended me to wed Viscount Thorgood."

The change was almost imperceptible, a slight shift of his shoulders, the twist of one knee. What had she said to discomfort him?

"Thorgood is a fine fellow," he said, but his voice had gone oddly flat.

"He was all kindness," she assured him. "But he is still in mourning for his first wife, and I am not ready to be a mother to his daughter. Besides, she despised me at first sight."

"Lady Miranda can take some getting used to," he acknowledged.

"The countess does her no favors by granting her every wish," Eva countered. "And her father will not stand up against his father. Regardless, I told the earl in no uncertain terms that I would not marry his heir. That's when he sent me here."

"It is unlike the earl to take such an interest in a lady," he observed. "He must have admired your father."

Eva rolled her eyes. "He admired what my father accomplished. He bears me no love whatsoever. In short, Mr. Howland, your cousin wants my fortune. My father has it tied up nicely, so the earl cannot lay a finger on it until I gain access. I will not let him have it, even if I must stay inside that castle for the next ten months without seeing a soul."

"Then you are determined to wait him out."

Eva swallowed. Up until now, he had been more understanding than she would have expected, rather helpful, really. It might all be an act to lull her into complacency. Yet the earl could have told him about the other stipulation of her father's will, and he hadn't. Did that mean he didn't trust his watchdog?

Did that mean she should?

Her father had been a man willing to take risks for the sake of reward. She should not be afraid to follow in his footsteps.

"Not necessarily," she told him. "There is another way to gain my fortune sooner." She met his gaze. "When I marry, whatever my age, my fortune goes in its entirety to the control of my husband. That's why the earl is determined that I marry a Howland, immediately."

# CHAPTER SEVEN

INGENIOUS, UNDERHANDED. EXACTLY LIKE THE earl, but for one thing.

"I didn't realize his lordship needed money," James said.

She made a face, sunlight picking out her thick lashes. "He borrowed from my father against a harvest he expected. It was lost to poor weather."

That would not have been enough to dim the fortunes of the Howlands. Yet he could not doubt Eva this time. The earl had been remarkably tight-fisted in recent months. Economizing, perhaps? Had the earl made other poor financial decisions? James's work only involved the properties in Dorset. Were the others less profitable? Would they lose the acres in Northumberland, the plantations in the Caribbean? How long would the estates in Dorset remain solvent if the earl began bleeding them dry?

"So," she said, fingers fiddling with the pretty lidded jar on her lap, "what will it be, Mr. Howland? Will you side with the earl, or me?"

There was no question about his answer. He'd been working to thwart the earl since before he'd reached his majority. He rose and offered her his hand. "The earl has no business separating you from your inheritance. You have my support, however much good it will do you."

She set the jar aside and popped to her feet to throw her

arms around him. "Oh, thank you! You cannot know what this means to me."

And she could not know the emotions careening through him.

Astonishment—it wasn't often anyone dared hug the magistrate.

Determination—once more he would stop his cousin's machinations.

Pride—he could still be of use to someone.

And pleasure.

He disengaged. "Do not thank me yet, Miss Faraday. We have a long way to go to defeat the earl."

"I know," she said, bending to retrieve her jar. "But between your understanding of him and my tenacity, we will triumph. If we are to be conspirators, you should call me Eva. I shall call you James, unless you prefer a nickname."

He eyed her.

She giggled. "No, of course not. I should have known. James it is."

He didn't argue the informality. It was surprisingly sweet to hear his first name on her lips and said with a tinge of awe, as if he'd done something praiseworthy.

"So, let us discuss this imprisonment of yours," he said, glancing down the hill but catching no sight of Mrs. Tully returning yet. "The earl orders strict isolation."

She sobered. "I understand. What do you advise?"

"Some hold that Grace-by-the-Sea is isolated enough," he told her. "But you'll find quite a society at the spa. We have Regulars who come for the summer or stay year-round. Irregulars visit occasionally. Newcomers generally come once and for a short time, though everyone generally starts as one."

"Are there pins denoting the categories?" she asked. "I wouldn't want to mistake anyone."

He could hear the humor in her voice. "Perhaps we should create some, especially with Miss Chance leaving soon."

She nodded. "Miss Archer explained the situation. This physician sounds high handed. Who recommended him, the earl?"

"The Spa Corporation chose him from candidates proposed by the Royal College of Surgeons in London, and I understand it took some convincing to get him to come. Not many want to relocate to the coast these days, not with Napoleon crowding the opposite shore."

She glanced out toward the sea. "Do you think the French will invade, then?"

James shrugged. "Napoleon would be mad to try it. The weather changes suddenly and capriciously on the Channel, and he must know we'll be ready for him."

She looked back at him again, smile turning up. "Spoken like a true Englishman. You may be right. Perhaps whatever he saw when Maudie spied him on the headland dissuaded him. Or it could have been his agent I saw last night."

He did not want to entertain that notion. "Whoever it was, I dislike the idea of anyone sneaking about my castle."

Her brows went up, and too late he realized that he had claimed ownership of the earl's property again. He was only glad to see Mrs. Tully approaching. Her arms were laden with boxes and fabric, and a carpetbag hung off one wrist.

As soon as she reached their sides, she juggled her pile to bend and look under the bench. "Everything all right, then?"

For a moment, he thought he heard a low-pitched squeak in response. Eva must have heard it too, for she started.

Mrs. Tully straightened. "Sounds as if you've behaved. Good. Shall we?" She began climbing the path before James could offer to help her carry her load. With one more look at the bench, Eva followed. James waited until they had made the next turning before bending to peer under the bench, but the shadows were too deep for him to make out anything.

Cheeks feeling hot, he straightened and lengthened his stride to catch up to the women.

The sun felt brighter, the breeze warmer. It seemed Eva had an ally, and it was the last person she might have expected. She took a deep breath, reveling in the scent of crisp brine and sweet wildflowers. Thanks to James Howland, she had every hope of defeating the earl and reclaiming her life.

She glanced at the man who had come to walk beside her as they started across the headland for the castle. Shadows from the leaves patterned his chiseled face, making it look more thoughtful, solemn. Did he never smile?

On a whim, she reached out and took his hand. He glanced at her, brows up in question, but he didn't protest or pull away. Her heart gave a little skip.

*Careful, Eva.* The voice in her head sounded suspiciously like her father's. *Look at the ledger. What's in the debit column? What's in the credit? Can this man do what he's claiming, or is he a bad risk?*

If only she could be sure.

He pulled away from her as they reached the terrace of the castle. Perhaps he was merely using that hand to open the door for her, but it almost felt as if he didn't want his staff to notice that he had been holding her hand.

He bowed to her and Maudie. "I have some arrangements to make. I'll see you both at dinner."

He was heading for the stairs before she could thank him once more.

"I'll just take this to my room," she told no one in particular.

Upstairs, she found that Yeager had brought her other packages, at least the ones that didn't contain edible items, and Patsy was standing by the bed as if trying to determine what to do with them.

"So, there must be some shopping here," she said.

"Quite a bit," Eva replied, going to put the jar on the dressing table. Funny how that made the room seem more like home. "I'll take you with me next time."

"Then it's true. We're staying."

She sounded so depressed by the fact that Eva turned to face her. Patsy's head was down, her shoulders slumped in her black bombazine gown and white apron.

"It won't be so bad, Patsy," Eva said. "Mr. Howland is on our side. And it's only ten months. Then we can return to the bustle of London."

Patsy heaved a sigh. "Will you bother changing for dinner, then?"

She hadn't the previous evening. Yet she'd had little hope then, and so much more now. "Yes. Lay out my purple gown and its sash. I feel like celebrating."

Patsy went to do as she'd bid. Eva had always favored brighter colors, but the countess had wrinkled her nose and declared that young ladies wore pastels. So, Eva had promptly used her allotment of monthly pin money to buy a length of purple satin, purple embroidered gauze, and a sash the color of the fuchsias in Kew Garden. The countess had averted her eyes whenever Eva wore the outfit.

Would James like it?

"I thought you might be moping after that letter the earl sent," Patsy said as she returned from the wardrobe.

Eva swiveled to let her at the fastenings on the back of her day dress. "Did you see it, then?"

"Not me, but that nice Mr. Pym was telling me about it. His lordship called you ungrateful, headstrong, and ill-disciplined."

Eva frowned as Patsy pulled the gown off over her head. "Well, that was the pot calling the kettle black."

"I thought so too," Patsy said. "But then, he's allowed to call anyone anything, isn't he? He's the earl."

"Well, there's only so much he can do now that James has agreed to help," Eva said.

In the act of closing the back of the gown, Patsy peered around her. "James, is it? Well."

Eva felt as if the carpet had grown hot under her feet. "It is only sensible, given that we will be working together to stop the earl's control."

"So you say," Patsy murmured, returning to her task.

Eva was quite glad to escape the room.

But as she descended the stairs, she saw that James had come down before her, and he had changed as well. He was wearing a deep blue velvet coat with silver buttons and breeches buckled at each knee, as fine a looking gentleman as any in London Society.

Maudie glanced from Eva to him as Eva came to stand beside them by the long table.

"Well, don't look at me," she declared, tugging her shawl up on her shoulders. "All I own is black."

"And you look very fine in it," Eva assured her. "Black is always appropriate."

She seemed to accept that, for she went to take her place at the table. James waited until Eva was seated beside him before sitting at the head. Pym brought a tureen of fish stew with plaice, mussels, and mushrooms. Eva could only hope they did not belong to Maudie's fairy circle. Yeager followed with baskets of the crusty bread they'd bought in town. James said the blessing before serving them.

"Tomorrow is the Sabbath," Maudie announced between bites. "Will you allow Eva to attend services at St. Andrew's?"

James met Eva's gaze. Now, there was a smile. The sight of it made her feel warm all over. "Eva and I are agreed that she is free to spend her time as she likes."

Maudie nodded. "Good. Church tomorrow, a review of the troops on Monday, the spa on Tuesday, and the assembly on Wednesday."

"No engagement with the mermaids?" Eva asked.

Maudie sniffed. "Certainly not. They're entirely too busy this time of year."

"And the trolls are unworthy of your company," James added.

Maudie nodded. "Exactly right. Though I understand they highly esteem you, Magistrate."

His mouth quirked, but he wisely applied himself to the meal.

Yeager brought out the iced cake for dessert. Eva took one bite of the orange-almond-flavored cake and sighed happily.

"Mr. Ellison's bakery is one place I could visit daily," she declared. "Alas, my pin money will only stretch so far. Have you worked out the funding yet, James?"

"His lordship neglected to provide details," he said. "As you suggested, I intend to send the amount due to his man of affairs monthly. I expect it another month before the earl notices and argues."

Eva's conscience pulled at her. "You're not concerned about spending the earl's money when he may be in financial difficulties?"

Something flickered behind his eyes. "If he is in such a difficult place, he should have considered the costs before exiling you to my care."

His care. A flutter started in her stomach. She ignored it.

"Join us in the music room after dinner," she suggested.

He hesitated. "I have work I should attend to."

"I'll come," Maudie said. "I can play for you."

Eva swallowed the last of her cake. "I was hoping to play for you both."

He set down his napkin. "In that case, I will make time."

That flutter sprang up into her chest, until all of her tingled. She'd rarely played in company other than her father's. She'd made it a point not to play for the earl again. He deserved nothing of her efforts. Before he'd confiscated her harp, she'd practiced when everyone was out except the servants. Playing for James felt big, important.

Vulnerable.

Yeager hurried ahead of them to light the lamps. She thought fleetingly about pleading a headache, but she raised her chin and marched for the music room. Someone had draped the harp once more in holland cloth. She pulled off the cover. Dust billowed, and she sneezed. Well, that certainly wasn't the elegant beginning she'd had in mind.

"If you'd take a seat," she said without looking their way. The whisper of cloth told her they had complied.

She gathered her skirts to sit on the little stool. The harp towered above her, the strings gleaming like strands of gold in the candlelight. She tucked the instrument closer, felt the weight of it on her shoulder. Positioning her fingers, she plucked a few strings. It was well tuned for being little used.

The sound of clapping surprised her, and she glanced over to the little gilt chairs to find Maudie beaming at her.

"An excellent rendition," she claimed. "Perhaps another."

She decided not to explain that she had merely been tuning. "Of course."

Her father had been fond of Edward Jones, the Prince of Wales's bard, so she launched into an old Welsh melody. In a moment, she was swept away, carried by the song of the harp like a leaf on the stream. The music swelled around her, inside her, brushing away worry, tension. The bright, pure notes filled the room and her heart, leaving her clean.

This time when she finished, both Maudie and James applauded. She met his gaze, basked in the awe, the wonder she saw there.

"I have never heard that instrument played better," he said. "You are clearly a master at the craft."

Eva smiled. "Thank you. I hope to be able to play often while I'm here."

"Whenever you like," he assured her. He rose and bowed to her and Maudie. "Now, I must see to my work."

She set the harp upright and rose. "Wait. I have one question before I release you, sir. Will you remain in the castle as well, knowing that I am truly here at the earl's demand?"

His face tightened. "You have no need for a jailer, but I cannot forget our visitor last night. I would prefer to stay until I know you are safe."

"Then stay," she said. "I am free to invite you when the entire castle belongs to your family."

She thought she heard a chuckle as he inclined his head. "I will do my best to resolve the issue quickly so as not to intrude."

"Thank you, James," she said. She watched him walk from the room.

Maudie stood and sidled up to her. "He's a fine man, the magistrate."

"And the trolls approve of him," Eva agreed with a smile.

Maudie nodded thoughtfully. "Still, there's something he's hiding."

The room felt colder. "Why do you say that?"

"They're always hiding something," Maudie said darkly, and she stalked from the room.

Eva hurried to follow, but she didn't have an opportunity to question Maudie further. James had only reached the middle of the stairs. He paused to allow them to proceed him, then accompanied them to their rooms.

"Good night, Mrs. Tully," he said with a bow.

"Keep your pistol loaded," she advised before slipping into her room and shutting the door.

He frowned after her, then turned to Eva. "If you see anyone tonight, or sense anything amiss, call for me. I'm a light sleeper."

Eva smiled up at him. "Why, Mr. Howland, something on your conscience?"

She thought he would deny it, but he merely bowed and headed for his own room on the other side of the landing.

*Can you really trust him?*

The worried voice seemed to echo in his footsteps, but she knew it was no specter whispering. She shivered and entered her room.

"What do you think of James Howland?" she asked Patsy as her maid helped change her for bed.

"He seems the upright sort," Patsy allowed. "Mr. Pym appears devoted, which is more than I could say for any of the earl's staff. They did their jobs from fear, not admiration and respect. But he's a Howland. None of them have ever done right by you."

"Viscount Thorgood was kind," Eva protested as she pulled on her lawn nightgown. "He seemed as reluctant as I was to marry at his father's command."

"And how long will he withstand the pressure?" Patsy asked as she took away the purple gown for pressing. "I wouldn't be surprised if he showed up here, ring in hand, pretending to be your hero."

Was James pretending? Eva shoved away the thought as she climbed into bed. "I can only hope the viscount finds another lady to love, one with a sizeable dowry."

Patsy shook her head. "No one has a dowry as big as yours."

She wasn't sure about that, but she decided not to argue the point. Men had been drooling over her since the day she'd come out, and she had no illusions that they had coveted her talents and charms more than the money.

She lay for a while after Patsy left, listening, but she heard only the usual sounds of a house settling around her. A coal shifted in the grate. The floorboards creaked. From outside came the faint sound of the waves against the cliff. She snuggled deeper under the covers.

Light was peeking under the velvet curtains when she woke to sounds of Patsy poking up the fire.

"Church today," she told her maid. "I'll wear the white muslin with the embroidery along the hem and my pink wool shawl with the gold fringe. You haven't had a day off in a while. Would you like the afternoon to yourself?"

Patsy straightened, broad face beaming. "That would be lovely, Miss Eva. Thank you. I've brought warm water. I'll leave you to it while I go check on Mrs. Tully."

Eva ventured to the fine porcelain washbasin and pitcher in the corner, but she hadn't even wet a cloth before Patsy dashed back into the room.

"Miss Eva, she's gone!"

Eva pulled her wrapper about her with a frown. "Gone? Did I oversleep? Has she already left for services?"

"It's only half past eight, miss," Patsy protested. "But her bedclothes haven't been mussed. I don't think she slept there. Where could she be?"

# CHAPTER EIGHT

JAMES WAS SHAVING WHEN HE became aware of a disturbance in the corridor. Even as he set down his razor in the porcelain basin, the door to his room burst open.

"Miss Faraday!" Pym protested, James's navy coat draped over one arm. "You cannot be in here!"

"But she's gone!" Eva cried, gaze going past him to James. "Maudie has disappeared."

He grabbed a towel and wiped the remaining lather from his face. "Out chasing fairies, perhaps?"

Eva shook her head. She was clothed in a pink quilted dressing gown, and her hair sprang in a wild nimbus around her face and shoulders. "I had Yeager check the grounds close to the castle. Patsy says her bed hasn't been slept in. What could have happened to her?"

James frowned. It was doubtful whoever had broken into the castle would seek to kidnap an elderly retainer, but Mrs. Tully might have wandered somewhere she would have a hard time escaping.

"Pym, fetch Miss Faraday's coachman and groom from the stables. We'll search the house. She may have fallen and is unconscious."

Eva pressed her hand to her mouth as if holding back the same fear.

Pym handed him his coat and scurried out.

"We'll find her," James promised. "Perhaps you could ask Yeager and Patsy to help as well."

She dropped her hand. "Of course. Thank you." She left too. James shrugged into his coat, then set about pulling on his boots before following.

She was already in the great hall with Pym and her staff when he descended a short time later. Her eyes blazing, she marched up to him.

"Dastard! Coward! Bounder! How dare you!"

James took a step back. "What are you talking about?"

Pym put himself between them as if afraid Eva was about to do James violence. "I spoke with Mr. Connors, the coachman, sir," his man said. "He noticed someone leaving the house last night. After everything that had happened earlier, he decided to give chase. It was Mrs. Tully. When he asked her why she was leaving, she said she'd been told to do so. He had Kip, the groom, escort her into the village."

"You sent her away," Eva accused.

"Why would I do that?" James asked.

"Because we just spent the night alone together," she said, voice echoing to the high ceiling. "You know what that means to my reputation."

Someone, likely her maid, gasped. James wasn't about to take his eyes off Eva. Her face was florid, her body trembling.

"Eva, I…" he started.

She held up one finger to silence him. "I won't let you get away with it. I wouldn't marry you if you were the last man on earth."

She could barely stand to look at him. Why, oh why, had she allowed herself to trust him, to begin to care for him? She wasn't stupid. She knew how the earl schemed. Why had she thought for one minute the man he relied upon would be any different?

He gazed down at her now, face impassive, as if he'd tucked any emotion safely away.

"I had nothing to do with Mrs. Tully's defection," he said.

"A likely story," Eva fumed. "She knew she was needed. Why leave without saying goodbye?"

"Perhaps the fairies suggested it," he said.

"That," she spat out, "isn't funny."

"I understand the ramifications of her actions," he said in that maddeningly calm voice. "But at the moment, the only people who know of the matter are the ones in this room and your staff in the coach house."

"And Mrs. Tully and her kin," Patsy put in.

"All of whom will be understanding," James assured her.

Eva glanced around. Yeager nodded in support. Patsy drew herself up as if with pride. Eva knew she could count on Mr. Connors and young Kip; they too had served her father and rebelled against bowing to the earl. Mr. Pym met her gaze and stepped closer to his master.

Eva narrowed her eyes at the pair of them. "And you'll tell no one?"

"You have my solemn promise," James said. "Would you like us to sign in blood?"

Mr. Pym looked at him askance, eyes widening.

Tempting, but Eva shook her head. "That won't be necessary. Besides, it would only put the matter in writing, and I'd just as soon pretend it never happened."

"Done," he said.

She couldn't believe him. "That easily?"

"That easily. Now, if you are determined to put your best face forward, I suggest you prepare to attend church services. I'll leave now and come in from the direction of the magistrate's house. That ought to keep any tongues from wagging. And perhaps we can locate Mrs. Tully and discover who exactly advised her to leave us so hastily."

All reasonable suggestions. "Very well," Eva said. "I'll see you at services, sir."

He bowed, then headed for the stairs, Mr. Pym right behind.

"That's a rare fellow," Yeager muttered.

"Yes," Eva said, watching the magistrate go. "At least, so he appears."

James remained on her mind as she finished dressing, breakfasted, and then rode in the carriage with Patsy down to St. Andrew's in the village. It was a small church compared to those she'd attended in London, long and narrow, with a white-washed face and a silver cross high on the steeple and shining against the grey of the cloudy sky. Inside, the box pews were stained a rich, warm color that had likely mellowed with age. She was standing in the shadowed narthex, contemplating where to sit, when Miss Archer, the painter, came up to her.

"Miss Faraday," she said with a nod that set the candle-light skipping along the ginger-colored hair which peeked out from her straw bonnet. "It's nice to see you again. Wondering where to sit?"

Eva nodded. "I know some churches have family pews. I wouldn't want to take anyone's place."

She tipped her chin toward the pews on the left. "First two rows belong to the Howlands. No one ever sits there."

"Not even the magistrate?" Eva asked with a frown.

"Not even the magistrate. But since you're a guest of the earl, I see no reason why you can't use them. I'll join you, if you like. My mother wasn't feeling well today, so I'm alone for once. And the Archers lost their family pew ages ago."

It was not the place to pursue that comment, but Eva

made a note to ask the lady why at another time.

"I'd be delighted for the company," she said, and she led Patsy and Miss Archer up to the first row, feeling curious gazes on her back.

They settled themselves just in time, for the service opened a few moments later. The vicar was an earnest fellow who bobbed his head while speaking as if to emphasize the point he was making. She couldn't quite agree with his sermon about being content with one's lot. If her father had been content, she'd have grown up in the rented room off the Strand with little chance to improve herself. As it was, she could barely remember what it was like to want for anything. She bowed her head and whispered a prayer of thanks—for her father's determination, for the opportunities that had come his way, for the blessing of a secure future he'd left her.

For James Howland coming into her life.

That last part slipped in before she'd thought better of it. She'd been so angry this morning when she'd thought he had betrayed her. She should have known better than to trust a Howland. Yet, he wasn't a Howland by choice. And he'd been very composed throughout the entire affair. Perhaps he truly was a man she could rely on.

She raised her head and glanced around. Easy to spot him on the other side of the aisle, his face in profile. The light coming through the stained-glass window made patterns on his hair, as if he'd been adorned with jewels. Easy too to spy Maudie just behind him in her widow's black, head bowed and lips moving as if she also recited a prayer.

And on either side, a dozen gazes were looking Eva's way, some curious, some with an emotion she could only call envy.

Eva faced front again, cheeks heating. She did her best to attend for the rest of the service.

As the words of the benediction faded, she rose with

the others to go. She turned toward the aisle, and her gaze collided with James's. He inclined his head. She responded in kind. She watched as he walked down the aisle, pausing to greet that person, exchange words with another.

She had just stepped into the aisle when another woman crossed her path.

"Congratulations, miss, and many blessings," she said, bobbing a curtsey.

"Thank you," Eva said, bemused, but she hurried off and an older couple took her place. She recognized Mr. Ellison, the baker.

"We were all delighted to hear the news," his wife said.

"If you celebrate in the village," Mr. Ellison added, "we'd be delighted to help."

Eva frowned as they moved past. "Do you have any idea what they're talking about?" she asked Miss Archer.

"Not in the slightest," her new friend assured her. "But stand your tallest. Here comes Mrs. Greer."

She said the name as if a storm was approaching. The woman looked a bit formidable. Tall and slender, she held herself as high as a duchess Eva had once met.

"Miss Archer," she said in a voice that trembled with emotion, "will you be so kind as to introduce me to your acquaintance?"

"Miss Faraday," Abigail said obligingly, "allow me to present Mrs. Greer."

The woman waited as if expecting more. When it wasn't forthcoming, she huffed. "My husband is the Spa Corporation president and the leader of the Grace-by-the-Sea militia."

"Under the magistrate," Abigail seemed compelled to point out.

Mrs. Greer's lips turned up, but she didn't argue the matter.

"I'm sure he's very needed," Eva said.

"Unlike our spa hostess," Abigail added. "We're about to lose her."

"And gain a noted physician," Mrs. Greer said before turning to Eva again. "Forgive me for presuming, Miss Faraday, but I wanted to add my congratulations. Such an esteemed family. You must be overjoyed."

The words were like fingers squeezing her shoulders. "I'm afraid you have me at a disadvantage," she said cautiously.

She smiled. "No need to be coy, dear. We are all friends here in Grace-by-the-Sea."

"At least, most of us," Abigail muttered.

Mrs. Greer ignored her. "It isn't every day we have the opportunity to entertain the woman who will one day be the Countess of Howland."

Abigail turned to stare at Eva. "You're to marry Viscount Thorgood?"

"No," Eva said, putting every ounce of will into the word. "I don't know where you heard that rumor, Mrs. Greer, but I am merely here on the order of the earl. I will not be marrying into his family."

Mrs. Greer's face fell, then flamed. "Oh! I knew I shouldn't heed anything that woman said. She believes in mermaids!" She flounced off down the aisle.

"From princess to pariah in a matter of moments," Abigail marveled. "That's a record even for her."

Eva glanced around. Many of the people had exited the church, but those that remained all seemed to be watching her. Several averted their gazes on meeting hers.

"Do they all think I'm betrothed to Lord Howland's heir?" she asked Abigail.

"Perhaps not all of them at the moment," the painter allowed. "But give Maudie time. Where did she get the notion, I wonder?"

"I have no idea," Eva said with a shake of her head. "I

certainly didn't give it to her."

She felt a movement behind her and turned her head to find Patsy cringing.

Her heart fell. "You didn't," Eva said.

Patsy bit her lower lip a moment. "I might have. I was just talking while I helped her dress. You know how I am. But I'm sure I said the earl *wanted* you to marry his heir. Not that you were going to."

Would that have been enough to establish the matter in Maudie's mind? Eva glanced around again, but her former chaperone was nowhere to be found now.

Instead, James was striding back up the aisle to their sides. He nodded to Abigail. "Ladies. If I might borrow Miss Faraday for a moment."

Abigail patted Eva's shoulder. "Let me know if there's anything I can do to help. I'll be sure to correct anyone who mentions the matter to me." She excused herself.

Patsy shifted closer as if to protect Eva.

"Let me guess," Eva told him. "You've heard the rumor that I'm to marry Viscount Thorgood."

"No," he said with a frown. "I've had at least a dozen people congratulate *me* on my upcoming marriage."

Now Eva frowned as well. "Who are you supposed to be marrying?"

"You."

She stared at him. "What is Maudie telling people?"

He seized on the name. "Mrs. Tully? Is she the one who started these rumors?"

"Mrs. Greer claimed she had told her," Eva allowed, "but Mrs. Greer was certain I was marrying the viscount."

He sighed. "All Mrs. Tully would have had to say is that you were marrying a Howland. With you staying in the castle, Mrs. Greer would assume you were marrying the earl's heir. Her less fawning neighbors assumed I was the groom. I've done what I could to convince them otherwise."

"That was good of you," Eva said. "But I think we must find Maudie and determine why she left and why she's telling tales."

The church was empty now. Patsy behind her, Eva walked with James down the aisle and through the narthex. The churchyard with its ancient gravestones and wrought-iron fence was nearly empty as well, except for Maudie standing with her niece and a handsome darker-haired fellow along the walk to the gate.

"Magistrate, Miss Faraday," Miss Chance said with a nod of respect as James, Eva, and Patsy approached. "If we might have a word?"

"Miss Chance," he said. "Mrs. Tully, Mr. Denby. Miss Faraday and I were hoping to speak to you as well."

"I can imagine," she said. "I was surprised when my aunt returned home last night, but she tells me you two are now betrothed."

"A misunderstanding, I'm sure," James said before turning to the older woman. Maudie looked up at him, eyes bright as a bird's. "Mrs. Tully, we were also surprised to find you gone this morning. May I ask why you left?"

"I was told," she said.

Eva glanced at James, but he merely nodded thoughtfully. "So I understand. By whom?"

Eva held her breath, but her former chaperone answered readily enough. "The cloaked fellow in the great hall."

Now James glanced at Eva. She shrugged.

"A castle ghost?" he asked politely.

She stared at him. "Of course not! The Lady of the Tower is a lady, sir, and I couldn't see through this fellow."

Eva couldn't see through the argument either. "Perhaps it was Mr. Yeager," she guessed. "Or Mr. Pym." Neither would have claimed her engaged, but they were the only other men in residence besides James.

Maudie made a face. "Certainly not either of them. They had already retired when I went downstairs to fetch my shawl. I'd forgotten it in the music room. Besides, what do they know about love and marriage?"

"Indeed," James said. "You've had opportunity to watch your niece in her role as matchmaker at the spa. Did you think, perhaps, to hurry things along between Miss Faraday and me?"

Eva blinked. Had Maudie seen something Eva had been afraid to name?

But Maudie shook her head, grey curls bouncing. "You two will sort things out soon enough. The fairies said as much. I wouldn't have thought it this soon, but he insisted Eva was going to marry a Howland. The earl told him."

The air turned frigid. "The earl?" Eva asked, leaning forward. "This man claimed to know the earl?"

"Oh, the earl knows most of the smugglers hereabouts," Maudie said. "I was sure I already told you that."

Mr. Denby had been hanging respectfully back. Now he stepped forward as if ready to take charge. "There was a smuggler in the castle last night?"

James watched Maudie just as avidly, but she waved a hand. "A smuggler, a French spy, one of the two. I couldn't make out his features in that hooded cloak. But he said you would be marrying, and it would be best if I left, so I did."

Her niece was staring at her. Slowly she turned her gaze to James and Eva. "I'm so sorry, Magistrate, Miss Faraday. I don't know who she saw or what he might have said."

"No reason to apologize," James assured her, voice kind. "Mrs. Tully, do you know why the fellow was in the castle last night?"

She glanced at him from the corners of her eyes, face sly. "He was looking for the note. Well, he won't find it. I took it."

"Aunt!" her niece scolded. "If you have something of

Mr. Howland's, you must return it."

She drew herself up. "Why? I found it. And he couldn't read it in any event. It's in the language of the fairies."

"Nevertheless," James said, "I would very much like to see it, if you would be so kind."

She pouted. "I don't have it with me. It's far too precious."

Her niece put her hand on her arm. "We'll locate it at home and bring it to the magistrate as soon as possible."

"After I've had a chance to look at it as well," Mr. Denby said. "I was always good at languages."

Maudie sighed.

James inclined his head. "I await your verdict, Mr. Denby. And thank you all."

Her niece apologized again and led Maudie off, Mr. Denby at their sides.

Eva shook her head. "Who do you think she saw?"

"You assume she saw anyone," James said.

"That was rather pointed advice for a fairy," Eva argued.

"But not for a troll."

She glanced his way, but she saw the gleam in those blue eyes. She shook her head with a smile. "Perhaps a troll might have ordered her to leave, but I doubt one was hanging about the great hall. Could it have been the fellow I saw the night before? Would he have been so bold as to return?"

"If he'd left something behind in the castle," James mused. "I'm as concerned about the mention of the earl. Could his lordship have ordered someone to spy on us?"

Eva laughed. "And he ended up sending off our chaperone so you and I would be compromised? That certainly didn't serve the earl well. Can you imagine the look on his face if he heard we were about to marry?"

James laughed as well. "Now, that would be a sight to see."

An idea popped into her head, far too tantalizing to ignore. Could they do it? It was a tremendous risk. The earl would seek revenge. There was still a chance James was not the man she hoped.

But oh, how she hoped he was.

She grabbed his arm. "Let's stun him, James. Let's get married."

# CHAPTER NINE

JAMES GAPED AT HER. "WHAT? You nearly took my head off at the very idea earlier."

"That's because I thought you were trying to trap me." She put a hand on his arm and gave it a squeeze. "I am willing to concede that you have my best interests at heart."

He'd certainly tried to take that perspective. "I'm still a Howland."

"The very best of the breed," she assured him. "Think, James. It is clear you long for independence. Admit it. If it wasn't for your mother, you'd have cut ties to the earl ages ago."

Was he that transparent? "His lordship is selfish and capricious, but he's still family."

She released him. "See how loyal you can be? I'd like to buy that loyalty."

James drew himself up. "My loyalty, Miss Faraday, is not for sale. I regret if I gave you that impression. If you'll excuse me, I must see about procuring you another chaperone."

She darted around him to put herself in his path. "Forgive me. I wasn't trying to impugn your honor. But a marriage between us makes perfect sense."

"It makes no sense," he argued. "You want your freedom as much as I do."

"Exactly!" Even on the grey summer day, her eyes sparkled. "Think of it: your ideals, my ingenuity, and my father's fortune. We would be able to do as we like, with no one to tell us how to behave, where to go. It would be the most convenient marriage of convenience ever!"

"Yet you lock us into a partnership with no hope of release," he protested. "What of love, madam?"

"Love might grow," she said, but she turned her gaze toward the gravestones in the yard. "Besides, I realized years ago that finding a man who could value me more than my father's fortune was unlikely."

There was more under her calm assessment. A sadness? A yearning?

James put his finger under her chin and tipped her gaze to meet his. "Not unlikely at all."

As if she saw more than he intended, her eyes widened. Such a warm brown, like polished walnut. And her lashes were as thick as her hair. So easy to lean closer, touch his lips to hers.

What was he thinking? He'd known her a scant three days. And she'd just asked for a marriage of convenience.

"Then you'll consider it?" she asked softly, as if she could see him weakening.

He dropped his hand. "I regret that I cannot."

"Why?" She sounded so wistful. "It benefits you. You will have all the money you need to break loose of the earl's control. You can free your mother as well. I imagine she would like her own home after serving the countess for so long."

She would. Before his father had died eight years ago, his mother had made their home a place of happiness, joy. She'd tended a garden in front of the house, bringing in flowers to fill the vases she put in every room. She'd used her plants in the stillroom as well, crafting lotions and elixirs that healed. And she'd played the harp in the evenings to warm his and his father's hearts. All of that had been denied her when the earl had demanded her presence in London. And James had seen firsthand that the countess could be as contrary as her husband.

Yet, could he do it? He'd once thought to marry for love as his father had. It had been the one time his father had refused the earl anything. But the earl had made it plain James was not to have that luxury. If he married, it would be to a lady the earl thought brought something to the family—land, connections. And it would be someone no one else in the family wanted.

The earl wanted Eva's fortune. Denying him that would be sweet indeed. Yet was a marriage of convenience right for him and Eva?

"Walk with me," he said, offering her his arm.

With a happy smile, she took hold.

"Go ahead and take your time off, Patsy," she called over her shoulder at the maid. "I'll just be walking with my betrothed. I'll expect you back at the castle in time to help me change for dinner."

"Yes, Miss Eva." With a sidelong look at James, the maid hurried around them and out of the churchyard.

"If I consent to your proposal," James said as he and Eva headed at a more leisurely pace for the wrought-iron gate, "we would have to reach an agreement on a number of factors first."

She nodded, curls trembling inside her bonnet. "Of course."

"The first thing," he continued, pausing to open the gate for her, "would be to have a lawyer draw up the marriage settlements. Generally the gentleman brings the greater assets, with the lady allowed pin money and funds set aside for any issue from their union."

"So I understand," she said, and there was that note of sadness in her voice again.

He shut the gate behind them. "You know that the law gives the husband complete control of all a woman's assets."

She shivered. "I know. That's one of the reasons I refused to wed Lord Thorgood. I couldn't be sure he wouldn't bow to his father's wishes."

"And you think I will stand firm."

She glanced his way as they started up Church Street, past the fine houses and flowered gardens his mother had so loved, to where her carriage was waiting. "Yes, James, I believe you would. But I guess I won't know for certain until I've married you."

He could not fathom the risk she was willing to take. Perhaps that was why he was so determined to mitigate it. "I propose a different sort of settlement. Give me pin money—an allowance, if you will. Make it sufficient only to pay for our sustenance and maintenance. Lock up the remaining funds for your use as dower and for the inheritance of any children."

She peered up at him. "I stipulated a marriage of convenience, sir."

"And you acknowledged that love might grow. I merely want to consider every contingency. Name a favorite charity to receive the remaining funds if we die without issue. The point is, Eva, this is your money. I am not entitled to it, no matter what the law may say."

Still she regarded him, as if trying to find the hole in his arguments. "You'd do this, build an agreement that would prevent you from accessing the bulk of my inheritance?"

"Madam, it is the only way I will agree to marry you."

She jerked to a stop, and he stopped with her. "James Howland, you are the very best of men. I knew I was right to choose you."

Her praise was like a warm wool blanket on a cold winter's night. "It isn't accomplished yet," he warned her. "Word is already circulating in Grace-by-the-Sea, but we cannot allow the earl to hear of it."

She nodded. "He'd try to stop us."

"He would make our lives miserable," he corrected her. "I'm used to it, but I will not have him harm you or my mother. I must start for London to extract her from his clutches and purchase a special license from the Archbishop, so we can marry as soon as possible. I will have to stay through the morning muster tomorrow, but I'll leave immediately afterward."

She clasped her hands together, eyes shining. "An excellent plan. Take Mr. Connors and the carriage. That way you can bring back your mother and her things."

He nodded. "Thank you. That would help. Perhaps while I'm gone you can broach the subject with the vicar."

"I'll make all the arrangements," she said.

"One last thing," he said. "I cannot like you staying at the castle unprotected, particularly after Mrs. Tully's story about a stranger there last night, one who claims to know the earl's mind. Tongues will wag, but we'll move you into the magistrate's house in the village. We'll have to find another place to live once we wed in any event. That house too belongs to the earl."

She sobered. "How badly can he harm us, if we pull this off?"

"It depends," James said. "He'll want revenge, but he'll also feel the need to make an example of us. Anyone who crosses him must know they will pay a price. Still, you're right—your fortune gives us an advantage. So does my background. My father and I worked for him for years. I know any number of facts his lordship might not want made public."

"Ooo," she said with a smile. "Ruthless. I like it."

James chuckled despite himself. "I hope you will not regret your proposal, Eva, but I will marry you. Now, let's see what can be done to put our plan in place."

What followed was a flurry of preparations. It was rather impressive, actually. Eva had been largely kept out of her father's business affairs, but she'd learned a few things since his death as a way to safeguard her fortune. She'd also listened to any number of gentlemen discuss their financial ambitions with him and heard how quickly and accurately he'd identified the problems and prescribed solutions.

Her father would have admired James Howland.

"List your wishes regarding your inheritance," he said as they rode back to Castle How together. "Your needs, your hopes. I'll take the list with me to London and find a solicitor willing to craft the agreement, but I'll bring it back for your review before signing. Did you leave anything in the earl's care?"

"My harp and my winter clothes," she told him. "But there are boxes of books and my father's things in the house he purchased in London, along with all its furnishings."

"Who cares for the house while you're away?" he asked.

"A small staff loyal to my father. Their pay is stipulated in his will along with that of Patsy, Yeager, Mr. Connors, and Kip, until I secure my inheritance. I will note their pay on my list of financial obligations I intend to continue."

"Good," he said. "We'll have to determine how to deal with the house itself at some point. I would prefer to stay in Grace-by-the-Sea. London puts us too easily in the earl's reach."

She knew he was right. She'd lived in so many houses in London that the last one didn't feel particularly like home, especially with her father gone. But she'd enjoyed the excitement of the city, the opera, the theatre. Was she willing to settle for a village on the seashore?

"We can stay here, for now," she agreed. "We could go anywhere we want, once Napoleon is done with his murderous threats."

He nodded, but he didn't make any promises. "Then we'll move you into the village today. I'll have Pym help you pack. Take nothing from the castle that isn't yours. I have no right to any of it, with the exception of my mother's harp, which I intend to remove today."

By the sound of it, he and his father had worked their entire lives to protect the earl's interests in Dorset. Whatever they had been given—houses, position, income—might be taken away at the earl's whim.

"Oh!" Eva pressed a hand to his arm. "I just realized. Will you lose your position as magistrate?"

"Quite possibly," he said, voice grim. "The magistrate is appointed by the landowners in the area. The earl, Lord Peverell, and a few yeoman farmers own most of the property, and the farmers may be persuaded to take the earl's side."

"Who would they appoint instead, then?" she worried.

"In truth, I don't know. Captain St. Claire or Mr. Denby would be the next logical choices, though neither is versed in the law and may not wish to serve given the position is voluntary. But, whatever happens, the results will be far less than what the earl does any time I question him. I will be my own man at last. That is priceless."

His voice was warm with conviction. She could not doubt him. She would not doubt their plan. It was the best, the only way, to save both them and the fortune her father had worked so hard to build.

When they reached the castle, he asked Mr. Connors to see to the horses, then join them in the great hall. The coachman returned with Kip a short time later. Yeager and Pym came in as well. James nodded to each.

"Gentlemen. You should know that Miss Faraday and I have agreed to wed."

Pym reared back, and Yeager looked as if he was about

to fall off his feet. Only Mr. Connors looked smug, and she wondered how much he'd overheard from his place on the bench.

Yeager recovered first. "May I wish you happy, sir, miss."

"Thank you, Yeager," she said as the others joined in to congratulate her. "Thank you all."

"You should also know that our marriage is in direct opposition to the wishes of the Earl of Howland," James continued. "He will not be pleased when he hears of it, so it is in our best interest that he hear nothing until it's accomplished."

They all nodded. Even Pym, it seemed, had had cause to learn about the earl's vindictiveness.

"Eva and I are united in our commitment to continue with your services," James added, "but if anyone fears what the earl might do, he is welcome to leave, and no questions asked."

Mr. Connors drew himself up. Kip's eyes widened.

"I'm not afraid of the earl," Yeager said.

"You should be," Pym put in. "But I see no reason to allow fear to rule me. We're all with you, Mr. Howland, Miss Faraday."

Eva's heart swelled.

James organized them in repacking so she could spend time making the list of her financial requirements. They also checked the ground-floor rooms again, but neither spotted anything out of place to show someone else had been there last night.

"Bit of fuss and bother," Patsy complained when she returned around the dinner hour, but she finished packing Eva's things in short order.

After dinner, Eva, Patsy, Yeager, and Pym rode in the carriage with most of the boxes and trunks down into the village. Kip drove a wagon that belonged to the castle with James to bring down the harp and the rest of their things.

"Only unpack what is necessary for the next week," Eva instructed her staff. "We intend to move to a different house shortly."

Patsy's sigh was audible.

Mr. Pym directed them once they reached the house. "The master's things in his suite, chamber story to the right. There are two guest rooms to the left. Save the front-facing one for Mrs. Howland. Use the rear-facing one for Miss Eva. Pile everything else in the storeroom off the kitchen for now."

James came in as Yeager went out to see about the harp. "If you are comfortable here, I will make a few other arrangements in the village."

"We'll be fine," Eva assured him. With another nod, he set out.

She was directing Yeager and Pym on where to put Mrs. Howland's harp when she heard a rap at the door. Turning, she saw a woman standing in the open doorway. She had that color of hair called Titian, after the painter who had favored it in his work. It sprang out in curls around the inside of her silk-lined bonnet.

"Have I come at a bad time?" she asked, gloved hands clasped over her pearly muslin gown.

Pym stepped forward helpfully. "Miss Faraday, allow me to present Mrs. Kirby, the village leasing agent."

"The magistrate asked me to contact you regarding a new house," the older lady said with a smile. "I gather it was rather urgent, so I thought I'd see about setting up an appointment for tomorrow. If you give me your require-ments, I can have appropriate properties ready for you to review."

Eva thought fast. "At least four bedchambers, a study for Mr. Howland to conduct business, a room to hold a harp or two, quarters for seven to ten staff—nice quarters, mind you, with plenty of light and heat—and a dining room and withdrawing room large enough to entertain."

Mrs. Kirby nodded. "Excellent. I'll see what I can do. Will half past ten be too early?"

Eva glanced at Pym.

He drew himself up. "Actually, Madam has an appointment in the morning. Half past one would be more appropriate."

"Then I'll stop by at that time," the leasing agent said. She turned to go. Pym shut the door behind her.

"What appointment do I have in the morning, Mr. Pym?" Eva asked as he returned to Yeager's side.

"I thought you would want to review the troops, miss," he said. "I expect the spectacle will be rather stirring."

She and her father had once gone to see a parade of the Life Guards, who protected the royal family. She struggled to think of the militia of Grace-by-the-Sea as so impressive, but perhaps she would be pleasantly surprised. "Very well."

"And that was very kind of you, Miss Eva, to ask for good rooms for us," Yeager put in.

"It will be your home too," Eva said. "Now, what else must we do to help everyone settle in here?"

They had unpacked what must be unpacked in the right rooms, and Pym was cooking dinner when James returned.

"Join me in my study, Eva," he said, moving toward a room at one side of the entry. His tone was so subdued she was almost afraid to follow, but she went inside, and he closed the door. It was a formal room, bookcases taking up much of the walls, the tomes lined up like little soldiers. A map between two of the cases showed properties around the area that must belong to the Howland family. A large desk, with papers neatly stacked, took up the back third of the room, with a chair behind and in front.

He nodded toward the closest chair. "Have a seat."

Eva sank onto the chair. "You changed your mind."

His brows rose as he sat behind the desk. "No. But you may change your mind about wanting to live in this village when you see this." He held out a folded piece of parchment.

Eva took it gingerly, unfolded it, and then peered closer. "What is this? There is nothing but random letters and numbers."

She glanced up to find him nodding. "That's Mrs. Tully's fairy language."

She frowned down at it. "Surely not."

"Neither Mr. Denby nor I can make sense of it, but he's concerned it may be a cipher of some sort, the kind used by agents passing secrets."

She dropped the parchment on his desk, feeling as if it had burned her fingers. "Surely you don't think Maudie is colluding with the French."

"Not in the slightest. Nor do I think that came from her friends the fairies or the mermaids. Someone had been in their cottage while they were at services today; they found things moved about, misplaced. Fortunately, the miscreant didn't locate the note. I can only wonder where Mrs. Tully had it stored. Regardless, I'm very much afraid a French agent has found his way into our midst and is using the castle to leave messages for his colleagues."

"Truly?" Eva asked. "Maudie said the man who told her to leave talked about knowing the earl. What connection does the Earl of Howland have with French agents?"

"That," he said, "is a very good question. I intend to do my best to see it answered."

# CHAPTER TEN

HOW COULD HIS COUSIN TAKE the side of the French? James kept asking himself the question as he and Eva ate dinner and talked more about the financial arrangements. He made sure everything in the house was to her satisfaction, then went up to the Swan to sleep. The innkeeper, Mr. Truant, looked at him askance, but James kept his face neutral. He knew how to keep a secret.

So did the earl. James could make no sense of the situation based on the information they had. Mrs. Tully seemed certain that his lordship hired smugglers. James doubted he'd go so far, but he wouldn't be the first aristocrat to purchase liquor, silk, and lace that hadn't come through legally. With the war on, it was hard to get those commodities, and the smugglers' goods were usually less expensive than those on which the tariff had been paid. How ironic that those who could most afford to pay the price refused.

But if Miss Chance's betrothed, Larkin Denby, was right, and that note was code from a French agent, the earl was dabbling in treason. Was the family in so dire a need of funds, as Eva had suggested? Surely the earl wouldn't sell his country's secrets to the enemy just to line his own pocket. As earl, he might be privy to some of the king's plans, but even *he* would stop short of jeopardizing England's security. Wouldn't he?

All the more reason for James to get to London quickly.

Of course, he must settle things here first. When he'd met with Lark to collect the note, they'd agreed that the Riding Surveyor and his officer, Miss Chance's younger brother, Alex, would keep an eye on the castle. The two of them would not be enough to watch all the entrances, but James didn't dare allow Lark beyond the front door to survey the interior. He had come to value the exciseman for his daring and insights. Lark had been part of the group that had ousted the smugglers from Grace-by-the-Sea two weeks ago. But even he didn't know about Quill's night-time activities.

So, someone else must watch the caves. That's why James had stopped to speak to Quill earlier that day before returning home to Eva.

He and Quill had known each other in school before Quill had enlisted in the navy. Now his old friend was supposedly recuperating from a war injury in Dove Cottage, a fine stone house on the way out of the village. Only Quill's manservant and James knew the injury had been healed for some time. Quill had a more important reason for remaining in Grace-by-the-Sea.

"So, you've finally been ordered to marry," Quill said after the two of them were nestled in leather armchairs near the stone hearth of his sitting room. The cottage had been sparsely furnished when Quill had leased it. He hadn't seen fit to change the fact, for the room boasted only a sea chest against one paneled wall and a triangular wooden table between the two chairs. James couldn't help noticing a new painting over the hearth, however: a view of a calm blue sea, the sun anointing the waves with gold, no doubt painted by Miss Archer.

"No one's ordered me," James said. "You'll be pleased to know Miss Faraday and I are marrying in direct defiance of his lordship's wishes."

Quill's brows rose into his thatch of coal-black hair. "You fell that hard."

James shifted on the chair. "I have the utmost respect and admiration for Miss Faraday."

"So much so that you continue to call her by her surname," Quill pointed out, relaxing.

"I call her by her first name in private," James explained.

Quill pressed a hand to his blue waistcoat. "Such daring! At this rate, you might kiss her by your fifth wedding anniversary."

"I didn't come here to discuss my relationship with my betrothed," James informed him. "There have been some developments at the castle. I thought you should know."

Quill stretched his legs toward the fire as if he hadn't a care in the world. "Don't get your back up, old man. You may deal with your bride as you like. Now, what's happening at the castle?"

James explained about the intruder Eva had spotted and Mrs. Tully's claim of talking with another stranger last night.

"This is what she intercepted," James said, pulling out the paper with the strange writing and handing it to Quill. "Someone had hidden it, though I've yet to determine where."

Quill frowned as he gazed down at the paper, then he stiffened. "It's code. I'm sure of it. Both the French and the English are using something like it, so I can't be sure whether it's one of ours or one of theirs."

"If my castle is being used by English intelligence agents, I am honored," James said. "Though I would have thought I might have been notified first."

"Trumpets at dawn?" Quill asked, setting down the cipher on his brown breeches. "Or a nice bowshot from a cannon?"

James shook his head. "I know they can't be so obvious.

But how'd they get into the castle to begin with?"

Quill gazed up at the ceiling as if consulting the dark beams that crossed it. "You've mentioned nothing of a break in, so they must have a key. And both Miss Faraday and Mrs. Tully saw the miscreant in the great hall, which isn't too far from the front door as I recall."

"A far enough walk if one was trying to sneak in and out of a house unseen," James allowed.

"An empty house," Quill reminded him. "At least, until recently."

James leaned back in the chair. "And you know nothing more about this."

Quill raised his hands. "Nothing. I swear." He dropped his hands. "But it does make me wonder where else they're visiting while in your castle."

James wondered as well. "You're thinking of the caves. I checked, but I didn't see anything but young Alex's fire circle."

Quill nodded thoughtfully. "We've left little mark. They'd do the same." He made a face. "I don't like it. We know too little. I've heard nothing of an English intelligence agent working in the area. And if the French have discovered us…"

The room grew darker. "I thought you might want to station a man in the caves. Lark and Alex will be watching the front of the castle."

"Which means I'm a man down again." Quill scowled at the fire, then looked up at James. "With Alex out, what about Lawrence? He must have a good head on his shoulders. He's spa treasurer."

"You promised not to recruit any more of my militia," James said. "We'll need them to defend the village should the French land."

Quill snorted. "If the French land, you'll never defend the village. The best you can do is use your militia to protect the villagers and our visitors while they flee inland."

James straightened in the chair. "We'll see about that. In the meantime, leave Lawrence out of it. I'll do what I can to help you once I return from London."

Quill frowned. "What do you hope to accomplish in London?"

"I intend to keep my cousin from harming Eva, me, and the rest of my family ever again."

"An honorable goal." Quill offered him the cipher. "Take this with you. I'll give you the name of someone in the War Office. They may know what this means."

"First, I'll make a copy," James said, accepting the note. "We might as well try to decipher it ourselves. Carroll is clever about such things. At the least, he'll enjoy the challenge."

Quill saluted him. "I wish him the best of luck. And you as well. How long do you intend to be gone?"

"I hope to be back by Friday evening, and I'll be bringing my mother with me. Will you keep an eye not only on the caves but Miss Faraday?"

Quill chuckled. "Expect her to bolt, do you?"

"No," James said. "But she is not well acquainted with Grace-by-the-Sea yet, and I don't know what else the earl might be planning to bring her to her knees."

"That hard on her, was he?" Quill asked.

"He sent her here as punishment for failing to comply with his wishes. I was to be her jailer."

He grinned. "Nicely thwarted, even for you. Very well, I'll watch over your bride. But I cannot promise I won't have stolen her heart before you return."

Something poked at him. Jealousy? Ridiculous. He and Eva had a civil arrangement. Besides, she'd see through Quill's disarming charm in a moment.

"If you make Eva Faraday change her mind, I'll dance at your wedding," James replied.

"And if I don't, I'll dance at yours," Quill countered.

And James wasn't entirely sure what they'd just agreed to.

Given everything that had happened—her impending marriage to James, the possibility of French spies in the area—it felt rather frivolous to review the troops on Monday. Eva almost didn't go, but the sight of James coming down the stairs in his red coat and sash, saber hanging at his side, changed her mind. He had slept at the Swan but returned after breakfast to change into his uniform.

"Don't you look impressive," she said.

Was that pink climbing in his cheeks? "Looking like a soldier is only part of the battle, madam," he said. She schooled her face until he had left for the stables. But she smiled as she followed in the carriage, top folded back on either end to allow her to take in the view.

She was one of many, as it turned out, making the pilgrimage to the Downs above the village. Other carriages backed the wide stretch of grasslands, their occupants peering out the windows, and women and men from the village sat on blankets, chatting. Children darted in and out among them, playing catch-me-who-can. A few enterprising souls had even brought chairs so they could better enjoy the spectacle. The sea breeze tugged at the ladies' bonnets, set the grass to rippling like the waves.

Glad she had worn her serpentine-colored redingote, Eva climbed down from the carriage to join Maudie, her niece, and a number of people who had come from the spa.

"Regulars, mostly," Maudie murmured to Eva as they took up positions to one side of the group of men clustered in the center of the field. "You met Lord Featherstone, the tall fellow with that magnificent mane."

Always regal, Lord Featherstone looked particularly

striking in his navy coat and buff-colored breeches. He bent his head to listen to something to Mrs. Harding was saying.

"Some call her the Winsome Widow," Maudie confided in Eva. "I don't see it myself. Mr. Crabapple has set his sights on her. The mermaids don't give him much of a chance."

Eva could understand why. Mr. Crabapple seemed as willowy as the widow was curvaceous, as quiet as she was vivacious. Her husky laughter floated on the breeze. He nodded so hard in response his long nose trembled. His gaze positively glowed when she aimed her smile his way. For his sake, Eva hoped the mermaids were mistaken.

"Give them what for, lads!" the Admiral ordered, shaking a cane over his head and tipping to the right in the process.

"I think he might have been a pirate once," Maudie told her.

She couldn't quite imagine that. "And what do you think of Mr. Harris?" Eva asked with a nod to the last fellow.

Maudie shook her head. "He's not worth the powder to fire upon."

Eva raised her brows at the statement, but, at that moment, James rode to the front of the men, who hastily formed an uneven line. She recognized Mr. Ellison, the baker, white smock replaced by a red coat; and Mr. Carroll, spectacles gleaming as brightly as his brass buttons.

Another man, taller than most with a way of holding his head thrust forward as if he was peering at the world, joined James at the front. Remembering what Abigail had said, Eva guessed this was Mrs. Greer's husband, the president of the Spa Corporation.

"All present and accounted for, sir," he reported in a voice designed to carry.

"Very good, Mr. Greer," James said. "Marching drill first."

Mr. Greer nodded. He started to turn away, silver braid

on his facings flashing in the sun, but James cleared his throat.

Greer hastily righted himself. "That is, marching drill it is, sir."

He turned on his heel and addressed his colleagues. "Young Mr. Lawrence, strike the pace."

A lad of about fifteen, drum slung about his slender frame, lifted his sticks and beat the tattoo. The men of Grace-by-the-Sea marched forward, the grass bowing before them as if in homage.

"Huzzah!" Mrs. Harding cheered, waving her lace-edged handkerchief.

Some of the troop lifted their chins.

"Right face!" Mr. Greer barked.

Most pivoted to their right. A few turned left and collided with the others, and they all came to a stop in a tangled mess. James said nothing, but Eva thought his jaw tightened, as if he was clamping his teeth against a harsh word.

"What's this!" Greer demanded, wading into the center of them. "I said right. Right!"

"Yes," someone complained, "but is that your right or ours? I've never been clear on that."

"And is it a sharp turn or more of an angle?" someone else asked.

"What if there's a tree in the way?" a third demanded, even though there were no trees any closer than the castle in the distance.

"Gentlemen, if we may proceed," James called, and they hastily aligned themselves again.

"We are all learning our paces," he told them, riding his horse back and forth along the line. "None of us has been a soldier before. But if Napoleon's troops land on our shores, we must be able to defend our families, our friends. We must have the discipline and knowledge to succeed.

Now, follow me."

He turned his horse to point toward the sea and shouted. "Forward, march."

Drum beating, they marched out across the waving grass.

"Right face!" he shouted, wheeling his mount, and they turned as well. This time Eva joined Mrs. Harding in cheering.

"Left face!" he shouted. Once again, some turned left, others turned entirely around, and the company ground to a halt.

"You're stepping on my toe!" a burly fellow proclaimed, shoving his colleague.

"You're facing the wrong way!" he countered, surging up and shoving him back.

Once more James rode closer. "Enough! Do you want to die on the first volley?"

That sobered them.

He had them line up again. "We will continue this drill until you can do it right," he told them.

"Left as well?" someone asked.

She could almost see the smoke pouring from his ears as he fought to contain his frustration. "Right, left, forward and back. And then we will start on musket drills. I will be gone the next few days, but I expect you to practice marching in the meantime. Choose an acquaintance, and drill together. We will try again as a troop at this time next Monday. Dismissed."

With sagging shoulders, they broke formation and began trickling back to the village. James stopped to talk to a balding fellow, who nodded almost as much as the vicar. The rest of the audience packed up to leave as well.

"Not an auspicious beginning," Eva commiserated when James rode up to them at last. "But they seem to want to get it right, and perhaps left."

That won a smile from him. "They are good men. They

will learn. They care too much about their country to do otherwise. Now, allow me to accompany you back to the house. I'd like to get on the road as soon as possible."

Of course. He was leaving today for London. She'd nearly forgotten. She bid Maudie farewell and returned to her seat in the carriage.

James rode beside them as Mr. Connors drove her down into the village. Miss Chance, her Regulars, Maudie, and Mr. Harris were heading for the spa. Maudie waved at Eva. Mr. Harris appeared to be watching James.

"It seems I'm not the only one impressed by your efforts," Eva teased as they passed the group. "Mr. Harris looks positively adoring."

James shook his head. "Another petitioner, no doubt. I receive at least a half dozen every summer, all seeking to ingratiate themselves with the earl through me."

"Well, you won't have to worry about that shortly," Eva said with a laugh.

"True," he allowed. "Everything is about to change."

She felt it too. Her world had upended on her father's death, and it had never really settled, thanks to the earl. Once she married James, she could finally claim her fortune, and her future.

While Mr. Connors made sure the carriage was ready for the journey, including closing the hood against the dust of travel, James changed his clothes and gathered the things Mr. Pym had already packed for him. Eva accompanied him out to the coach.

"I've asked a friend, Captain St. Claire, to look in on you," he told her after handing his bag up to her coachman for storing. "You know Miss Chance and Miss Archer now as well. They can be of great assistance should you need it."

Eva nodded. "I am well situated. Thank you." She swallowed. "Be careful, James. You know how wily the earl can be. I would not want anything to happen to you."

Were those tears gathering behind her eyes? She blinked away the hot pressure.

As if he saw her effort, he bent and brushed his lips against her cheek. "I'll return for you, Eva. I promise."

He straightened and climbed into the coach. Hand on the cheek he had kissed, feeling as if warmth and hope radiated from it, she watched them pull away from the house. She held his pledge, his promise.

Would the earl convince him to break them both?

# CHAPTER ELEVEN

JAMES REACHED LONDON WEDNESDAY morning. He left a weary Mr. Connors at the coaching inn on Hay's Mews and walked through the busy Mayfair streets to the London residence of the Earl of Howland. The three-story block was set off from the square with a garden behind and its own coaching house and mews. With the four Corinthian columns across the front and the golden stone imported from Bath, the placed looked more like a Grecian temple than a home.

If he went through the front door, the earl would be told immediately of his presence, so James slipped in through the terrace doors on the south side. He had at most a half hour before one of the staff noticed him and alerted the earl, so he had to move quickly. His first task was to speak to the viscount. He took the rear stairs up to the top story of the house where the schoolroom lay.

Miranda spotted him first. "Uncle James!" She dropped the book she had been holding, sprang up off the Aubusson carpet, and ran toward him, muslin skirts flapping.

James held up his hand and put on a stern face. "Now, then, who is this young lady? What have you done with Lady Miranda? She is a moppet no more than this high." He lowered his hand to brush the bridge of her nose.

She giggled, blond ringlets shining. "It's me, Uncle James.

I'm all grown up now."

"Perhaps not yet," her father said, rising from his place on the carpet. He and James had always looked enough alike to be brothers, though Thorgood was slightly thinner, his face longer, as if life had pulled at him. It couldn't be easy being the heir. He came to shake James's hand. "Good to see you. What brings you to town?"

"Questions," James said. "Do you have a moment?"

Miranda glanced at her father. "No. We were about to discuss the differences between hippopotami and water buffalo."

"An important taxonomic distinction," James acknowledged. "I'll only keep him a moment. I hope to see you at Grace-by-the-Sea this summer."

Miranda brightened, but her father shook his head at her. She stomped back to the rug, threw herself down, and crossed her arms over her chest, lower lip out in a pout.

Ignoring the irrepressible nine-year-old, Thorgood led James out into the corridor. "What has the earl done now?"

"What do you know about Miss Faraday?" James countered.

His cousin grimaced. "Bad business, there. I was never clear on what she said to Father, but he lashed out as only he can."

"Then you have no intention of marrying her?"

James tensed to hear the answer. Did Thorgood remember a similar conversation, when he'd been the one asking James that question?

His cousin raised his head and looked down his nose, and all at once James saw the resemblance to the earl. "Certainly not. I have no interest in marrying."

He could not stop the relief that surged through him. He wasn't sure he had it in him to step away this time. He was a different man. And he'd given his promise to Eva. Still, he had to be sure.

"You must know you can't hold out forever," James cautioned. "He's expecting the line to continue unbroken."

"I know." Thorgood sighed, shoulders slumping. "And I will do what I must to ensure that. Just not now, not yet."

James put a hand on his shoulder. "There are few like Felicity. You have my everlasting condolences."

"Thank you," he said. "That means a great deal considering how Felicity came to be my bride." He rallied. "Now, what of Miss Faraday? Is she fighting her exile? Giving you trouble?"

James smiled. "I find her company invigorating."

His cousin laughed. "That's one way to put it. Like you, she was quick to take up a cause and fight to the death for it. Are you here to plead her case, then?"

James cocked his head. "Is he willing to listen to reason?"

"Doubtful." He glanced down the corridor as if he expected to see the old man striding toward them even now. "He hasn't been well recently, James, and it's got his back up."

"It must be hard being reminded he's mortal," James drawled. "And you've heard nothing of financial difficulties?"

Thorgood frowned. "No. You manage the southern properties, Walsingham the north, and Rodrigo the east. All three of you know what you're about."

Normally he would agree, but he couldn't forget Eva's story. "There appear to be some questions. Watch yourself."

"You as well," Thorgood said. "He can do little to me—I'm his only hope for a legacy. But he can think of too many ways to inconvenience you."

And more. "I'll be careful," James said. "And I meant what I said to Miranda. Bring her to Grace-by-the-Sea this summer. The sea air will do you both good."

"I'll consider it," Thorgood said. "It depends on how the earl is faring. Will I see you at dinner?"

"Not if I can help it. I hope to have my business concluded and be back on the road."

Thorgood shook his head. "Do you never stop working?"

"Never," James said. "That's the way the earl prefers it."

As he took his leave of his cousin, a clock chimed the hour nearby. His mother next.

He located her in the countess' sunny sitting room at the back of the house.

"How can Society survive when two of its loveliest ladies hide themselves away?" he asked from the doorway.

His mother, who had been working at an embroidery loop on her lap, glanced up. Then her eyes lit. "James!"

"What an unexpected pleasure," the countess said from her place near the hearth.

He bowed to them both. "Countess, Mother. May I join you?"

The countess looked him up and down. She persisted in the fashion of yesteryear, gathering her hair up in a high peak over her head. At least it was silvery enough now on its own that it didn't require powder. His mother had taken to wearing lace-edged caps, a fancier version of what the maids wore, so that in no way would she eclipse the countess.

"In all your travel dirt?" the countess said with a wrinkle of her nose. "Surely you can do better, sir."

His mother's smile faded, but she didn't question her employer.

"I regret that I will only be in town a few hours," he said, closing the distance to his mother's side. "I had business with a solicitor and thought to look in on you as well. I have a request of you."

The countess raised a finely etched brow. "Oh?"

He must go carefully if he was to convince her. "You will be repairing to the country house shortly," he said. "I was hoping Mother could visit me for a time."

Once more his mother brightened, but one look at the countess' face had her fiddling with her embroidery.

"I'm afraid I cannot do without her," the countess said with a sniff. "You know my sensitivities to any disruption in my routine."

James inclined his head. "Of course. I wouldn't have suggested it except I heard you were looking for a new wife for Thorgood."

She frowned at him. "What has that to do with the matter?"

James kept his face neutral. "Naturally, I assumed you would prefer to invite one of the ladies to travel with you so you could interview her more thoroughly. Unless you want Mother's assistance?"

His mother looked up with a helpful smile.

"No," the countess said with a curl of her lip. "That will not be necessary. Very well. When we leave for Somerset, you may visit your son, Marjorie."

His mother beamed. "Wonderful news. Thank you."

"Actually," James put in with his most ingratiating smile, "to save you the trouble of going out of your way, I thought I could take her with me now."

The countess blinked. "What?"

"He'd like me to leave today," his mother said, as if the countess could have mistaken him.

"I understand that," Lady Howland snapped. "Really, the pair of you are entirely vexatious. Perhaps you deserve each other."

"Oh, I…" his mother started, but James lay a hand on her shoulder.

"I only thought to spare you the travel time, my lady," he told the countess. "Detouring through Grace-by-the-Sea would add several hours to your trip. But if you are willing to stomach the discomfort, the dust…"

She held up a hand. "Even this discussion fatigues me. Go. But I expect you back by the end of June, Marjorie."

James bowed but made no promise. "I'll leave you to pack, Mother. The weather has been uncertain. Bring both your summer and winter clothes, and feel free to take every bit of your wardrobe. I have a coach."

"How did you acquire a coach?" the countess demanded. "The earl has been remarkably difficult with our town coach. Last time I called for it, I was told it was no longer in the coaching house, as if it would be anywhere else." She humphed.

Jonas, the Howland butler, appeared in the doorway just then. Black head high, silvery gaze out in the middle distance, he spoke with the solemnity of an archbishop crowning the new king of England. "Pardon the intrusion, your ladyship, but the earl requests Mr. Howland's company."

Neither his mother nor the countess moved to protest as James followed the butler out.

"How angry is he?" James asked as he walked the familiar carpeted corridor toward the earl's study on the opposite side of the house.

"About as angry as the year you advised him to raise the salary of the staff or risk losing them," Jonas said.

That had been a memorable quarrel. But he'd been fresh from university, his father still alive and groveling, and James had thought he knew better how to handle the earl.

He'd learned otherwise since then.

"Any particular issues I should avoid mentioning?" James asked as they neared the paneled door.

"Viscount Thorgood's future and the price of coffee," Jonas advised. "And may I wish you the best of luck, sir." He opened the door. "Mr. James Howland, my lord."

James moved past him into the room and heard the door close behind him.

He couldn't help glancing up at the ceiling, painted brown and gold to etch out a map of the world, as if the earl owned all of it. Glass-fronted bookcases across the back of the room held tomes of law, history, and philosophy, though James doubted the earl consulted any to guide him. Another man might have sat behind the teak desk, spread papers about to look as if he had been studying them. The earl's desk was clean. Other men did his studying and merely brought him their conclusions to be accepted or rejected on his whim.

His lordship was seated on one of two black leather armchairs near the white marble hearth, book open in his lap, gaze on the door.

"James," he said. "Explain yourself."

And that should be his cue to shuffle forward, head bowed, like a schoolboy summoned before the headmaster. James held his ground and met the earl's gaze.

"The situation in Grace-by-the-Sea has changed. I thought I should apprise you personally."

The earl's heavy-lidded eyes were half closed, as if the conversation already bored him. "What could possibly be so urgent?"

"I chartered a militia."

His face didn't change, though he leaned back ever so slightly in the chair. "I gave you direct orders to do no such thing."

"You did," James acknowledged, moving closer. "But since receiving your orders we discovered smugglers in the cove."

He dropped his gaze to the book, as if it was far more important than James would ever be. "You are the magistrate. Surely you are capable of dealing with such matters."

"It took the entire village to route them," he said. "And they are in Weymouth, awaiting trial. But in the process of removing them, I discovered that someone had placed a beacon in the castle. I thought it was the smugglers, but we've stumbled upon strangers in the night. Do you know anything about the matter?"

The earl's nostrils flared. "If I did, I would either have instructed you to be alert or told you to look the other way."

That was what James had feared. "I thought perhaps that was what you had done—told me to look the other way and forget about chartering a militia."

He sighed as if he was tired of dealing with recalcitrant underlings. "I had other reasons."

"So, you are not in the habit of funding smugglers or French agents," James said, knowing the statement was dangerously close to a challenge.

The earl shifted on the chair. "If you must ask the question, you are not the man I thought you were."

Slippery. But he always had been. "In any regard, to protect your holdings, I thought it best to have armed men keep an eye on the castle from here on out."

He looked up at last. "And have they uncovered the miscreant using the castle?"

"Not yet, which is one of the reasons I am concerned about Miss Faraday living there."

His smile was grim. "On the contrary. If her life is in danger, she may be more amenable to changing her attitude."

James took a step closer, and the earl's eyes lit. He was spoiling for a fight, and James knew who would win.

"She certainly has some interesting opinions," he said, keeping his voice level. "She seems to think we're nearing Dun Territory."

The earl's gaze flickered. "I will not have rumors threatening this family."

"Nor will I," James told him. "I assured her she was mistaken. If there was something wrong, I would have been asked to transfer funds."

"You have wasted your time," he said. "All of this could have been put in a letter."

"Perhaps," James allowed. "But I wanted to add my voice to hers. Miss Faraday has a right to her own future. She is of age. She can marry who she likes."

The earl set his book aside and slowly rose to his feet. The banyan enclosed a figure that was thinner than James remembered, but perhaps he was seeing the earl as merely a man for the first time.

"You dare to presume to lecture me about what is best for this family?" the earl asked, gaze drilling into his. "Perhaps you need a reminder where you live, your purpose for existing."

James bowed. "Like my father and grandfather, I have ever served the House of Howland."

"And, like them, you do not deserve the name." The earl raised his chin. "Get out of my sight. And tell Miss Faraday since she sees fit to darken my name with claims of insolvency, I have no further interest in storing her belongings. I will put her harp on the market this very afternoon."

James bowed again. "My lord." He backed from the room.

But he would never back down.

# CHAPTER TWELVE

I F SHE SPENT THE ENTIRE four days thinking about James, Eva knew she would go mad. So, she was very glad she had an appointment Monday afternoon with the leasing agent.

"I have several properties that might suit your needs," Mrs. Kirby said as she, Eva, and Pym set out from the magistrate's house. Eva had decided to take the man-of-all-work with her so he could consider the houses from James's point of view. It wasn't as if she knew her betrothed well enough to select a house for him.

*Her betrothed*. Soon her husband. Something zinged through her, as fast as one of Maudie's fairies. It was the excitement of choosing a home. It had to be.

The first house Mrs. Kirby suggested was a tall stone cottage on High Street, and Eva objected to the busy thoroughfare.

"Though I like the look of that one," she confessed as they started up the hill past an elegant house with a fanlight shaped like a cockleshell.

"That's Shell Cottage," Mrs. Kirby said with a smile. "It was leased for the summer, but the lady has graciously agreed to relocate so that Miss Chance and her betrothed can make it their home when they wed. Miss Chance was raised in the cottage, you see. It was her family home until her father died last year."

"How nice that she can return to it now," Eva said. Her father had moved five times since they'd left the rented room where she had been born, always to larger, more impressive surroundings.

"If you want to deal with those having money," he'd said, "you must look as if you have money yourself."

She would have far preferred a home with warm memories attached to it.

The second house was along a quieter street but at the very back of the village closer to the top of the hill.

"It seems too far for everyone to go to find their magistrate," Eva said. "And I don't think James would approve appearing above them."

"But he is above us, merely by the fact that he is a Howland," Mrs. Kirby pointed out.

Did they all subscribe to the myth that the earl was omnipotent? What a wretched way to live.

As if Pym saw the set to her face, he stepped in politely. "It's a long way to the market as well. Perhaps something more centrally located."

Mrs. Kirby led them back down the hill and turned onto Church Street. "The summer leases have all been set, so there are only a few houses available at the moment. There is one more that might suit your needs, but I hesitate to point it out. I'm not at all sure Mr. Howland will approve."

Eva glanced at Pym, who shrugged. But as the leasing agent stopped before a thatched-roof house just down the street from the magistrate's home, the servant drew himself up and scowled at her.

"That house isn't for let," he declared.

Mrs. Kirby raised a brow. "It most certainly is. The Turpin lease lapsed this past March."

"No one alerted Mr. Howland," he protested. "He would have had something to say in the matter."

"Very likely," she said, voice coming out clipped. She turned to Eva. "Butterfly Manor may look smaller than the others around it, but there's an addition at the back. I think it will suit you perfectly. You'll just need to convince the magistrate."

Eva looked to Pym. "Why would James protest, Mr. Pym?"

He nodded toward the pretty stone cottage, where gold, blue, and yellow butterflies hovered among the flowers that crowded the front garden. "This was his grandfather's house, where his mother was raised, miss. The earl had insisted that Mr. Howland could not marry her. The magistrate's father disobeyed him. It was the bravest thing he ever did, but the earl insisted we couldn't associate with them from then on or he would bring trouble on everyone. I doubt Master James has set foot in it since he was a lad."

Anger pushed up inside her. Eva squared her shoulders and turned to the leasing agent. "I would very much like to see this house, Mrs. Kirby."

With a nod, the leasing agent opened the latch on the wrought-iron gate and let them in among the flowers. Such fragrance had never smelled sweeter.

Inside, the rooms featured creamy plastered walls and warm wood molding. The main floor boasted a sitting room overlooking the harbor, a dining room with a table opened to seat twenty, and a study lined with bookcases, with a kitchen and a servants hall in the addition. On the chamber story, there were four large bedchambers, each with its own dressing room, and ample room for the staff above.

"With a connecting door between the master's and mistress's suites," Mrs. Kirby noted.

Eva's cheeks heated. She looked to James's manservant. "What do you think, Mr. Pym?"

His eyes were bright, as if with unshed tears. "I think Master James would be pleased, miss. If you're certain it's what you want."

Eva nodded. "It's perfect. We'll take it."

"We will, of course, have to wait to have Mr. Howland sign the lease," the agent explained as they descended the stairs. "And his lordship must agree to the lease, but that's only a formality, especially given Mr. Howland's standing."

The house felt suddenly confining, and Eva was glad to step out into the sunlight. "Then this land belongs to the Earl of Howland."

"Actually, it belongs to Lord Peverell," she said as they crossed through the garden. "His holdings and that of Lord Howland bisect the village. It's an odd arrangement, but one that has stood us in good stead over the years."

And stood her in good stead now. Very likely the Earl of Howland would refuse to allow James and her to set foot on any of his properties, but he was less likely to be able to sway another aristocrat.

"So, when may we move in?" Eva asked as a butterfly danced past her face.

"A week after Mr. Howland signs the papers, most likely," Mrs. Kirby said, letting them out the gate. "That will give us sufficient time to have them signed by Lord Peverell's agent as well. When do you expect the magistrate back?"

"He should be available to sign the papers on Saturday," Eva said. "I'll send him to visit you at his earliest convenience."

"I'll have the lease prepared and waiting for him," she promised. "And congratulations on your upcoming wedding, Miss Faraday. You marry into a prestigious family."

Perhaps not as prestigious as the leasing agent thought. "Thank you," Eva said. Mrs. Kirby bobbed a curtsey and headed back down the street. Pym and Eva crossed the street for the magistrate's house.

"Mrs. Howland will be overjoyed by your choice, miss," Mr. Pym said. "She missed her family home so much."

Eva couldn't imagine being able to look just down the street and know she wasn't allowed to visit. "The earl really is a horrid fellow. Why did he take the Turpins in such dislike?"

"Oh, it wasn't the Turpins," Pym said as he held open the door for her. "It was the fact that Mr. Howland had disobeyed him. His lordship tends to punish those who fail to fall in line."

"Then James and I will just have to find a way around him," Eva said.

"We're all hoping that to be the case," Pym assured her. "There are a few things in the house that Mrs. Howland brought with her on her marriage. Those should not be left to the earl. If I may show you?"

She spent the rest of the afternoon conducting an inventory and making more lists. Mrs. Howland had brought most of the linens with her, but the silver and plate belonged to the Howlands and would have to be left behind. Her father's staff had always made such decisions before. All Eva had had to do was climb into the carriage and step out at her new home. There was something rather pleasing about making the decisions herself.

She spoke to the vicar Tuesday morning, but, as she could not set a date until James returned, the best she could do was talk about options and possibilities.

"Will you want to be married quietly like Mr. Howland's parents?" Mr. Wingate, the vicar, asked. "Or will you want something grander? I know many in the village would appreciate the opportunity to wish their magistrate well."

She certainly didn't intend to hide her marriage. But it was rather daunting to think of it as a village event. She let the vicar know she would send James to see him as soon as he returned.

"I'm making a great number of promises for your master," she told Pym when she reached the house again. "I hope he'll be amenable."

Pym smiled. "Master James is as determined as you are to make this arrangement work. Have you given any thought as to who you'd like as your attendant?"

There was only one choice. And that meant she must visit the spa.

She didn't mind in the least. It was an elegant space, with fluted columns and potted palms. Ladies—Mrs. Harding and Mrs. North among them—lounged in white wicker chairs along the light blue walls or by the windows looking down to the sea. Gentlemen strolled the parquet floor. So did Miss Tapper, her companion watching from the safety of the far wall. Eva spotted Lord Featherstone and Mr. Crabapple playing chess near a stone fountain where mineral water bubbled. Mr. Harris stood with arms crossed as if studying their every move.

"Miss Faraday," Miss Chance greeted her from her place behind a tall desk holding a large book. "Maudie is at the harpsichord at the moment, but I know she'll want to greet you too."

As if to prove as much, the song ended in a crescendo its composer had never intended, and Maudie hopped up from the lacquered instrument in the corner and scurried to their sides.

"Eva! You look tired. You need a drink."

Eva blinked, but Miss Chance put a hand on her arm. "I believe my aunt means a dose of the mineral waters would do you good."

Maudie frowned. "Well, of course that was what I meant. I don't understand why I must keep repeating myself."

Miss Chance released Eva with a smile. "Why don't you go pour her a glass, Aunt? I'll just acquaint her with some of our offerings."

Maudie toddled off. Miss Chance leaned closer.

"I'm sure the magistrate told you about our assembly on Wednesday evenings. I merely wanted you to know that Lark and my brother, Alex, were on duty at the castle Sunday night and last night, and they spotted nothing unusual."

"So, our mysterious stranger remains at large," Eva said.

She nodded, straightening. "I'll be sure to send word if there's any news."

Eva thanked her and headed to the corner, where Maudie stood holding a crystal glass. Eva took a cautious sip—warm, tart, with a hint of effervescence. She drank some more.

"When's the wedding?" Maudie asked.

Eva regarded her, lowering the glass. "Who told you there'd be a wedding? Last time we talked, James and I hadn't agreed on it."

Her smile was knowing. "I saw how the magistrate looked at you when you were playing the harp. A man doesn't look at a lady that way unless he has marriage on his mind."

Perhaps she'd taken too many sips of the mineral water, for the effervescence seemed to be rising inside her. Could James have feelings for her? He hadn't known they might marry when she'd been playing the harp. Her father had always claimed she transported him when she played. Could she have carved a place for herself in James's heart?

Suddenly, Maudie brightened. "Oh, look, the pirate!"

Eva turned, even as she heard the rush of air, as if every lady in the room had exhaled at once. A gentleman had just come into the spa and was surveying the room as if trying to decide upon his prey. His brown coat was common, his breeches worn. But that shock of coal-black hair, that air of command, made him seem taller, bigger, than he likely was. For once, she had to agree with Maudie's assessment.

He moved to Miss Chance's side, listened to her response to his question, then turned toward Eva. She took a step back and bumped into the fountain.

He strode to their sides. "Mrs. Tully, be a dear and make me known to your charming companion."

Maudie frowned at him. "The fairy or the mermaid?"

"Is she one?" He pressed a hand to his heart. "That must explain her ethereal beauty."

Eva started laughing. "Does any lady take you seriously, sir?"

Now he effected a wounded look. "Miss Faraday, did you steal my heart merely to crush it by your disregard?"

"I have it on good authority the only person who steals things around here is you," Eva told him.

He dropped his hand, but his look veered to Maudie. "Indeed. What have you been saying about me, Mrs. Tully?"

Was that concern she heard in his flippant tone? Surely not. This fellow was enough of a coxcomb to believe himself the best in all situations.

"You're a pirate," Maudie stated. "You know it's true. I've seen you sailing at night."

Something flickered behind his eyes. "Alas, I haven't been able to sail for some time. Bum knee, you know." He tapped his right knee with one knuckle as if to prove it.

Maudie grabbed another glass and filled it. "You need a drink."

"You are too kind." He accepted it from her, but he didn't take a sip. Instead, he looked at Eva. "I'm Captain St. Claire. Your beloved asked me to be at your disposal while he was away."

So, this was James's friend. She could not imagine what he and James had in common. "That's very thoughtful of you, Captain, but I have friends and staff. I'll be fine."

"Ah." He made a show of slugging back the water, then lowered the glass. Maudie watched him as if she thought he might spring up and twirl. "Then you have an escort for the assembly tomorrow night."

"No," Eva allowed, "but I wasn't planning on attending this week."

He set the glass on the lip of the fountain and took one of her hands in his, cradling it close. "And deprive the men of the area of such a treasure? Tell her, Mrs. Tully. She must dance."

"There are some very fine toadstools on the road out of town," Maudie offered. "I'll go and dance with you if you'd like."

Eva bit back a laugh. "I think I might enjoy that more than the assembly."

He dropped her hand and bowed. "Very well, madam. You can tell your betrothed that I tried and failed and that he is the most fortunate of mortals." He turned and strode for the door.

"I take it you're not interested in the toadstools," Maudie said with a sigh.

Eva shook her head, then turned to her companion. "I have a great deal to do to be ready for this wedding. But I must ask you a favor. When the time comes, will you stand up with me as my attendant?"

Maudie blinked. "In a church?"

"Yes."

She narrowed her eyes. "Will you make me wear pink?"

"You may wear whatever you like, and if you'd like a new dress, I will gladly pay for its creation."

She grinned. "Done. And afterward, we can dance. The mermaids will be so jealous."

Eva wasn't so sure about the mermaids. But some of the other ladies at the spa looked a bit green when she asked Miss Chance if she might borrow Maudie to visit the dressmakers.

The shop near the bottom of the hill smelled of wool and

linen as Eva and Maudie entered, and the shelves behind the counter were overflowing with bolts of patterned cotton and pale muslin.

"I'm to be married within the week," Eva explained when the two sisters asked what they might do for her, gazes darting from her to Maudie and back. "Mrs. Tully has graciously agreed to stand up with me."

"In a church?" one asked, brows going up.

Where else did they think she might wed? Or did they think Maudie only attended the weddings of the fairies?

"In St. Andrew's," Eva clarified. "I've already spoken to the vicar. I don't want to put you to any trouble, but I would love to have a new gown for me and one for Mrs. Tully."

The shorter of the two sisters hurried to pull down some bolts of pastel satin.

"We have some lovely lace as well," the taller sister said to Eva. "Must the other be black?" Her long nose wrinkled, as if she found the thought distasteful.

Eva looked to Maudie. Her former chaperone was gazing about the shop as if considering it from all angles or listening to other voices. She nodded and faced Miss Pierce.

"Purple," she announced. "And none of that lavender, mind you. That should be saved for the pixies."

Eva grinned. "I've always been fond of purple. Make that two gowns."

Miss Pierce looked as if the room was suddenly devoid of air. "Purple? Deep purple? For a wedding?"

"Why not?" Maudie asked with a frown. "It's good enough for the trolls."

Miss Pierce swayed back to the shelves to deposit her bolts and select new ones. By the time they were done choosing styles, having their measurements taken, and determining finishes, the other shops were closing.

"I'll walk you back to the magistrate's," Maudie said.

"That way you won't have to talk to that fellow."

"Mr. Howland is on his way to London," Eva reminded her as they set off up the street. "I don't expect to talk to him until Thursday evening at the earliest."

"Not him," Maudie said. She nodded toward Miss Archer's gallery on the other side of the street. "That one."

Eva just caught the back of a man going into the painter's. "Was that Mr. Harris?"

"Maybe," Maudie said. "He's been following me. I told him my heart was already taken."

"Very wise of you," Eva said, leading her onward. "We wouldn't want to give him expectations. Though I do wonder about Lord Featherstone. He's rather handsome, don't you think, and of an age with you."

"He's far too old," Maudie said. "And he looks nothing like my Francis."

"Your husband," Eva reasoned. "Was he a shopkeeper here?"

"No, he was a sailor, a very fine one. Don't let anyone tell you otherwise. He'd have come home to me if the mermaids hadn't wanted him more. They wrecked his ship. I'm certain of it. It took a long time for me to forgive them for that."

"I can imagine," Eva said softly. "The earl merely tried to steal my fortune, and I've yet to forgive him."

"He's a pirate too," Maudie said with a nod. "He'll get what's coming to him. You wait and see."

Eva certainly hoped she was right.

As it was, she was bone-tired by the time dinner was over. She stood for a moment, looking out the window as the lights of the village went out, one by one. Above, stars came into view in the depths of the sky.

"It's a lovely village," Mr. Pym said from behind her. "I hope you'll be very happy here."

"I believe I will, Mr. Pym." She began to turn, but

another light caught her eye. She started. "What is that?"

Mr. Pym squeezed in beside her, then stiffened. "That's a fire, that is. Someone's burning the fields near the castle!"

# CHAPTER THIRTEEN

EVA SENT PYM TO ALERT Mr. Greer and the militia. She sent Yeager to make sure Mr. Denby and Mr. Chance at the castle could see the fire from their vantage point. She hated waiting for news, but there was little else she could do. She and Patsy remained near the window, watching the flames climb higher until she could see the castle in their glow.

"How could this have happened?" she worried aloud.

"Someone's playing a prank," Patsy said. "Young folk thinking it's all fine and good to hold a summer bonfire on the headland now that you and the magistrate have moved out of the castle."

If only the reason was so innocent, but Eva couldn't shake the fear that this was the work of their mysterious stranger.

Mr. Pym returned first.

"The militia are on their way," he assured her and Patsy as he came back into the withdrawing room. "They didn't even wait to don their red coats."

"Did they at least take buckets, a water wagon?" Eva pressed.

"The village hasn't needed one before now, miss," Pym replied. "The last fire we had was at least twenty years ago. It was from a lightning strike on the hill above the spa, and it burned itself out before reaching any building. But never you fear, they have spades and wet cloth. That will have to do."

Yeager took longer to return. "Stayed to help the militia," he reported. "Took a bit for them to figure out how to work together, but they have it under control now. The fire was nearly spent when I left."

She wanted to feel relieved. "What was the cause?"

His face darkened. "It was hard to see into the center of the burn, but it looked to me like someone had set the grass on fire."

"Someone out to harm the castle?" Eva guessed.

As if she was just as concerned, Patsy cringed, but she stayed up with the rest of them until the glow from the hillside had subsided, and the smoke had melded with the night.

The next morning, Eva took her key to the castle to Jesslyn Chance for Mr. Denby to check the interior. The spa was nearly as ablaze as the hillside when Eva entered. Guests stood in groups, heads close together, and words like *fire* and *danger* hung in the air even above the sound of Maudie's playing at the harpsichord.

"They sound worried," Eva murmured to Jesslyn as she handed over the key.

Jesslyn nodded. "It's not often we have such a disturbance here. But it will fade."

As Eva turned to go, Miss Tapper intercepted her.

"Were you at the castle last night, Miss Faraday?" she asked, brown brows up. "I could see the flames from the Swan."

"Terribly concerning," her companion, Mrs. Baugh, agreed, large hands worrying before her spring-green gown.

"I've been staying in the village," Eva assured them. "But I saw the flames too."

Lord Featherstone strolled up to them. "Ladies, I would not be unduly concerned. Lightning strikes and the dry grass of summer conspire to start trouble. Wouldn't you agree, Harris?"

The younger man had been following in his orbit like a moon a planet. He offered Eva and the others a smile as he joined them. "Of course, my lord. I see no reason for concern, particularly with the local militia to protect us."

Eva realized the music had stopped a moment before Maudie squeezed into their group. "It wasn't a lightning strike or dry grass. Are you afraid to name the true culprit?"

Miss Tapper smiled at her. "Trolls?"

"Pirates?" Mrs. Baugh suggested gamely.

Maudie frowned at them all. "No. French spies."

Mr. Harris snorted, then turned the sound into a cough. "Forgive me. I must partake of the waters." He hurried off. Miss Tapper and Mrs. Baugh excused themselves as well.

"What do you know, dear lady?" Lord Featherstone asked Maudie.

Eva held her breath, waiting for the answer.

"French spies started that fire," Maudie insisted. "They can't get into the castle, not with my Alex and Lark watching. So, they must alert their ships another way."

Eva exhaled. It certainly made sense. Lord Featherstone must have thought the same, for he turned to Eva and asked, "When do you expect the magistrate back?"

"Not until Friday," Eva told him.

"Then you must assist me," he said solemnly. "I would not see the spa in such an uproar. It is not conducive to the civility Miss Chance works so hard to maintain."

Maudie rubbed an ear. "It's loud too."

"What would you have me do?" Eva asked.

"Calmer heads may prevail," he said, glancing around. "Speak to Mrs. Harding. If she is assured of her safety, it will go a long way to assure others. And do me the honor of escorting you to the assembly tonight. Seeing our magistrate's lady enjoying herself will also shore up flagging spirits."

Another offer of escort? No one in Grace-by-the-Sea except James and their staff knew the extent of her fortune or that she was even an heiress. How nice to be valued for what she might contribute instead of her father's money.

"I would be honored, my lord," she said.

She did not regret the decision. The assembly rooms at the top of the hill were shining with light as she arrived in her carriage. Lord Featherstone was waiting, resplendent in a black tailcoat with satin lapels and a silver-shot waistcoat. He was graciousness personified as he led her around the room, introducing her to spa guests she had not met and the mother and sisters of Jesslyn Chance's betrothed.

Eva took an instant liking to Miss Rosemary Denby, the younger sister. She kept twirling a lorgnette before her saffron-colored gown, and when young Mr. North dared to ogle her through his quizzing glass, she ogled him right back through her glasses. He hurried off, cheeks pinking above his high shirt points.

"I must get one of those," Eva said.

"It does come in handy," Rosemary agreed, fingering the little square glasses. "And it's useful for reading as well."

Eva laughed.

She also danced nearly every set—with Lord Featherston, the Newcomers Mr. Donner and Mr. George, and Mr. Harris. She only wished James had been there to dance with her. She could imagine taking his hands, feeling his strength as he turned her. Standing out at the bottom of the set while he flashed her admiring looks. And perhaps, as they passed shoulder to shoulder, he might whisper something sweet that would bring a blush to her cheek.

"Go fetch Miss Faraday refreshment," Rosemary told Mr. Harris when he led Eva back to her side. "Can't you see she's overset?"

That only made Eva blush all the more.

James reached Grace-by-the-Sea as the sun was setting on Thursday. He'd accomplished most of what he'd intended in London, including leaving a copy of the cipher at the War Office. The clerk Quill had told him to approach would not allow him to speak to more senior staff and had been noncommittal about who would review the cipher. One thing he was clear on, however: James need not expect an answer or involve himself further in any way. So, James did not tell him Mr. Carroll was working on the piece as well. The War Office had the responsibility to safeguard England. It was still James's job to safeguard Grace-by-the-Sea.

As they reached the crossroads above the village, he directed Mr. Connors down the hill to the magistrate's house. The coachman would have to unload his mother's things before returning the carriage and horses up to the livery stable for keeping.

James had tried to explain the situation to his mother on the way, but she had persisted in taking the earl's side.

"You mustn't provoke him," she'd said, hands worrying in her lap. "Your father always said so. You can be sure his father never provoked the previous earl. We owe the House of Howland everything."

"And that loyalty *cost* you everything," James argued. "Your family, friends, even your position in the village when the earl forced you to move to London."

Her face puckered. "You never understood. I remember how you and your father fought over the matter. It grieves me to this day."

It grieved him too, but for an entirely different reason. He'd grown up seeing his maternal grandparents sitting across the aisle in services, watching his mother give them no more than a nod in greeting. He had been eight when he'd first run across the street after dark to see them. They'd welcomed him, encouraged him, but always sent him carefully home with a promise not to tell anyone where he'd been. Howlands were not to associate with Turpins. He'd been fifteen before he'd truly understood why.

The earl was exerting his prowess, his position. His petty, cruel vengeance. From then on, it had been war.

"I never wanted to hurt you, Mother," James had said as the city had fallen away and they'd driven toward the shore. "But we cannot allow him to dictate our lives. Were you happy in London? Did you enjoy trying to meet her ladyship's least whim?"

"She isn't so bad, most days," his mother demurred, though she didn't look at him as she said it. "And I have my own room."

"You'll have your own room with Eva and me as well," James told her. "And a great deal more freedom. We all will."

"But at what cost?" she protested. "It's safer to acquiesce."

"I'm simply no longer willing to acquiesce," James said.

She'd turned her face to the view.

Now she gazed out at the house she had once called home as the carriage drew up before the door. "We'll lose this too, you know."

"I know," James said. "But Eva has been looking for houses while I was away."

She sniffed. "Eva this and Eva that. It seems you've just exchanged one master for another."

He certainly hoped not.

Eva must have heard the carriage pull up, for she was

waiting just inside the door of the house. She dropped a deep curtsey as his mother came inside. "Mother Howland, welcome home."

His mother glanced around, lower lip beginning to tremble. "It looks just the same," she murmured. "I could almost believe if I called, John would come out of his study to greet me. Oh, James, how can you give this all up?"

His gut tightened. "Because it is only a house, Mother. Being my own master is worth far more to me."

Eva nodded. "And we hope to give you something better, something that will bring you equally warm memories. Do you recall Butterfly Manor?"

His mother regarded her with a frown. "Certainly I recall Butterfly Manor. I always thought it was the prettiest house on Church Street. My parents had the lease. You remember, James."

"I remember, Mother," he said.

Eva's eyes gleamed. "Then perhaps you will be pleased to know that I've leased it for us all to live in."

His mother waxed white, swayed on her feet, and James stepped forward, prepared to catch her and defend Eva's choice.

But his mother didn't faint. She rushed forward and enfolded Eva in a hug.

"Oh, my dear, dear girl! What a treasure you are! Welcome to the family."

Eva felt warm all over as Mrs. Howland released her. She couldn't remember her mother, her father had never had close female acquaintances, and the countess had discouraged familiarity. How surprisingly lovely to feel that a lady of maternal age approved of her.

"I'm so glad she liked the idea," Eva told James after they had settled his mother in her room and returned downstairs. "Mrs. Kirby seemed to think you might object."

"My family's connection to Butterfly Manor is long and contentious," he said as they sat in the withdrawing room by the fire. Pym came in to draw the drapes against the darkening sky. "But I'm hoping for happier memories now."

Eva leaned forward. "And what of your trip to London? Did you achieve your goals?"

"Not exactly." He turned his gaze to the fire, the red glowing on his cheeks. "I managed to extract Mother, but the earl and the countess think she's on holiday. And the earl refused to listen to any idea that he might be mistreating you."

"Only to be expected," Eva commiserated. "And the settlement, the special license?"

"I located a young solicitor named Julian Mayes who was willing to draw up the necessary papers. But I decided against the special license. I realized if I go to the Archbishop, word would get back to the earl immediately. I secured a license from the local bishop instead on the way home. We can be married Wednesday or later next week."

"That long?" Eva bit her lip.

"Already reconsidering?" he asked, turning to look at her as if he could see the thoughts swirling through her mind.

"No," she said. "At least, not very often. And I suppose there's still much to do."

He nodded. "Not only for the wedding but to set matters to rights should the earl sever all ties."

"I hope it won't come to that, at least for your position. I understand Mr. Greer had some trouble leading the militia while you were gone."

He frowned. "The militia was not to drill while I was away."

"It wasn't a drill. There was a fire on the hillside near the castle. Mr. Greer mustered the militia to fight it. No one was hurt. I had Jesslyn give my key to Mr. Denby so he and her brother could check inside. They found everything as it should be."

"Good," he said.

Eva regarded him. "Good? I thought you wanted the miscreant plaguing the castle to be captured."

"I do," he assured her, "but I would prefer to be involved in the process."

A bit territorial, but she supposed he had that right after caring for the place all these years.

He pushed up from the chair. "I'll go see to the castle myself before retiring. At least I can confirm that the earl hasn't sent anyone else into exile."

"Yet," Eva predicted, rising as well. "Take Yeager or Pym with you."

His brows went up. "I appreciate your concern, but I'll be fine. Lark and Alex should be back on duty. Do not feel you must wait up." With a bow, he left.

Eva walked slowly to her room. She could almost see the wall he'd put up at her questions. He had to be tired—four days to and from London meant he'd traveled from dawn until dusk. Why insist on visiting the castle?

Their mysterious stranger had been cordial to Maudie, and they had no evidence he'd disturbed anything inside the house, but, if he'd been the one to start the fire, he was far from harmless. Was it only his duty that forced James out of the house now, or did he suspect something more than he'd confided?

Despite his admonition, she did wait up until she heard the stairs creak. Then she slipped from the bed and tiptoed to the door to crack it open enough to peer out. He was entering his bedchamber down the way. He didn't appear to be limping or nursing an arm, so he must be fine. She shut the door and allowed herself to go to sleep at last.

The next few days passed in such a rush she did not even have time to visit the spa. She reviewed the agreement Mr. Mayes had drafted and signed two copies. Yeager and Mrs. Howland served as witnesses. James mailed one copy to London to be filed with the solicitor and gave the other to Eva for her safekeeping.

"So you never need be concerned about your future again," he told her.

They also signed the lease agreement for Butterfly Manor.

"Lord Peverell's agent was quite pleased with it," Mrs. Kirby said. "I expect a signed counter-copy returned shortly. You should be able to move in immediately following your wedding."

Then there were the little details that went into planning a ceremony. Theirs was not a love match, but that didn't mean it shouldn't be memorable. Eva hardly intended to be married more than once.

"The vicar wanted to know how private we wished the wedding to be," she explained to James as they were helping the servants by packing books in his study.

He cocked his head as if considering the matter. "If I was marrying at the behest of the earl, it would either be an ostentatious thing in London or my own sitting room with only the necessary witnesses in attendance."

Eva made a face as she placed a book in the crate. "Well, I like neither of those. You are the village magistrate. They admire you—I can see it. We'll wed in St. Andrew's and allow anyone to attend."

His mouth quirked. "Even Mrs. Tully's trolls?"

"Well, perhaps not them," Eva said with a smile. "And I imagine it might be terribly inconvenient for the mermaids, but they'll simply have to make do."

James laughed.

Now, that was a fine sound. She felt rather clever to have

given him a moment of joy. Let's see what could be done to make their wedding just as pleasant.

She and Maudie met for fittings of their gowns from the Misses Pierce, who allowed that the purple was rather fetching, particularly with the cream lace that edged the neck and short sleeves. Mr. Inchley, the grocer, agreed to cater the wedding breakfast, which was to be held in the assembly rooms. Mrs. Kirby offered to arrange for flowers to decorate the space. And James took Eva down to Mr. Lawrence, the jeweler, to select a ring.

"Choose whatever you fancy," he murmured beside her ear as they entered. "I've money until the earl decides to discharge me."

She could certainly have put it on her credit, as she should have more than enough to pay for any ring in the shop, but it had been a long time since anyone had assumed they would pay for her expenses. She came to stand by the counter, where the jeweler stood beaming over the tray of rings. He was a dapper fellow, with a trim figure and a curling mustache. His brown eyes brightened as if he couldn't wait to see what she would select.

Eva picked up a simple gold band etched in the center with a heart. "This one."

James nodded to the heavier, plainer version. "And that for me."

Eva glanced back at him in surprise. "Do gentlemen generally wear rings? My father didn't, but my mother had been gone for some years."

He met her gaze. "We have a partnership, Eva. If you wear a ring, so do I."

Warmth pushed up inside her.

"An excellent choice, Magistrate, Miss Faraday," Mr. Lawrence said as she looked his way again. "Let me just take your measurements, and I'll have these sized appropriately. They will be ready by Tuesday."

"One more thing checked off the list," Eva said as they left the jeweler's. "Have you decided on your attendant?"

"I asked Captain St. Claire," he said.

"The pirate?" Eva asked.

He stumbled then righted himself. "Pirate? Where did you...let me guess. Mrs. Tully supplied his occupation."

"Yes," Eva admitted as they started up the hill. "But I cannot argue with her. All that swagger and bravado seems too large for anything less."

"He was a captain in the Royal Navy," James explained. "A war injury forced him into seclusion, but it's nearly healed now."

"That's not what he claims," Eva told him. "He says his knee prevents him from ever sailing again."

"A shame," James said, and she wasn't sure if it was Captain St. Claire's supposed injury or his claim of such that inspired the comment.

She stopped as they reached the corner of Church and High Street. "I'll leave you to your work. I must go up to the spa and speak to Maudie. I realized I don't know whether she needs new gloves. I'll see you at the house shortly."

He inclined his head. "As you wish." He started up Church Street.

And there was swagger enough for any lady to see. Such an impressive build, such a confident step. The black top hat contrasted nicely with the gold of his hair.

He was going to be her husband.

Once more she heard her father's voice. *You've purchased yourself a good one, Eva. Quite the bargain.*

She shuddered as she started for the spa. She'd loved her father, but one of the reasons he'd done so well for himself was because he'd viewed every person, each activity, as a transaction. She could not see James that way.

Yet, how else was she to view this marriage? A partnership, he'd called it. And she'd held out hope that more would come. Now that he would be dependent on her for his income, would he ever learn to love her for herself?

No! She would not think of that, or she'd be tempted to call the entire thing off. At least by marrying James, she saved him and his mother from the earl. That had to count for something.

She stepped inside the spa, inhaled the clean air. The hint of lavender she remembered seemed fainter than usual, but perhaps that was because she'd walked more in the sea air. She should have a chat with Miss Chance, compare notes on how they were planning their weddings. Miss Chance was supposed to be something of a matchmaker, James had mentioned. She probably had all kinds of insights to share. And Mrs. Harding was always in the first stare of fashion.

Eva moved beyond the entrance into the columned space. The utter silence pressed in on her. Every wicker chair stood empty. The chessboard sat abandoned. The fountain was dry and lacked a single crystal glass waiting to be filled.

"Is anyone here?" she called. Her voice echoed.

A door in the far wall opened, and a gentleman stepped out. He was tall and well built, with a noble brow from which waved back warm-brown hair. As he came closer, she could see wise grey eyes and solemn lips. He was dressed in a tailored navy coat and buff breeches like a London gentleman.

"May I be of assistance?" he asked politely in polished upper-class tones.

"Where is everyone?" Eva asked. "Miss Chance, Mrs. Tully, Lord Featherstone and Mr. Crabapple, Mrs. Harding, Mrs. North and her son, Miss Tapper? And you can't have hidden the Admiral."

His smile remained pleasant, but it did not reach his eyes.

"Gone," he said. "Apparently, they found my presence offensive. Allow me to introduce myself. I'm Doctor Linus Bennett, the new director of the spa."

# CHAPTER FOURTEEN

JAMES CAUGHT HIMSELF SMILING AS he remembered Eva's awe in looking over the rings. Lawrence had a gift with metals and gems and an eye for beauty. But James thought it was more than the gleam of gold that had fascinated her.

He'd felt the weight of those rings as well. These weren't rings designed to match a gown that would be out of style next Season. They weren't produced to proclaim a person's position or pedigree. Wedding bands spoke of commitment, promised forever.

He'd always wondered if the earl would allow him even the choice of a bride or if he would order him to marry a particular lady for the good of the family. Never had he considered that, if the choice were his, he would not be marrying for love.

Yet there was something about Eva. That sparkle in her eyes, that conspiratorial grin. His father had feared James would go too far in his determination to protect his friends and family from the earl's predations. His mother had abandoned him for London. His role as magistrate often kept the rest of the village at a distance. Quill followed his own star. It had been a long time since James had felt he had a friend, someone who would stand beside him, no matter the cost.

What, was he succumbing to the sentimental? Loving anyone had never been safe. If the earl knew of it, he would use the person against him. Or remove her from his life forever as he'd done with Felicity.

He opened the door of the magistrate's house to find Pym hopping from foot to foot in the entryway, as if the marble tiles had suddenly grown hot.

"Oh, good, you're back," he said, rushing forward. "I didn't know how much longer I could keep him from going in search of you."

His gut clenched. "The earl is here?"

Pym washed white. "Certainly not. I *would* have gone in search of you in that case. No, it's Captain St. Claire. He's in your study. Mr. Priestly promptly claimed business elsewhere."

"And my mother?" James asked, turning toward his study.

"Went down to the market to inspect the goods on offer herself," Pym said, scurrying along beside him. "I will not be surprised if she returns with a cook as well. She feels cooking isn't my place."

"Discuss the matter with her if she returns," James instructed him, hand on the latch of the study door. "Keep her busy until I'm done with the captain."

"Of course." Pym quickly withdrew.

James went into his study and shut the door behind him. Seated in James's chair, booted feet on the desk, Quill saluted him with a glass of lemonade. "Hail the conquering hero. I understand your trip to London was successful and congratulations are in order."

"A change of accommodation is in order," James countered, coming around the desk. "Move."

Quill tsked as he lowered his feet and rose. "If this is how you react to your impending nuptials, I shudder to think how well you'll respond to wedded bliss."

"What do you need, Quill?" James asked.

His friend ambled around the desk and studied the chair on the opposite side a moment before deigning to sit. "There was a fire at the castle while you were gone."

"Eva told me," James said, taking the seat Quill had vacated.

"Did she also tell you she roused the militia to deal with it? And let Denby into the castle proper? Gave me and my men a good few moments of concern, I can tell you."

"I imagine it might have. I went up last night hoping to find you."

"We won't go over again until next week at the earliest," he said. "But I thought you should know that we may have a bit more insight into your mysterious visitor."

Pulse quickening, James leaned forward. "Oh?"

"We weren't the only ones at sea the night of the fire. We nearly ran afoul of another vessel coming in toward the cliffs. I can't be certain because it veered off, but it looked to be making for the Dragon's Maw."

James frowned. "Other smugglers?"

"Too small to be very profitable, and I never caught sight of a larger vessel that night before spotting them. No, I fear it was the enemy."

He swallowed. "French spies?"

"It's a distinct possibility. It would explain why someone would be so bold as to enter an occupied castle, not once but twice. Leaving evidence behind jeopardizes the lives of hundreds of French soldiers when military intelligence is involved."

"The code we found," James agreed. "I left a copy with the War Office, as you instructed. They did not give me the impression they intended to be forthcoming."

"Well," Quill said, leaning back, "there is a war on."

James shook his head. "A war you and I are willing to help fight, if we are given the information we need to do so. As it is, perhaps you'd better relocate your efforts.

The earl was determined to make Eva pay, so I didn't bother asking him to bless our union. Once the marriage becomes known beyond Grace-by-the-Sea, I could well lose all access to the castle and the maps and ledgers in this office. That would make me of little use to you."

"Never, my friend," Quill assured him. "In fact, with you being out from under the earl's thumb, you could be of even greater use. Come with us next run. Take the news to Whitehall. You and Majestic can move faster than most of my men and with fewer questions as to why you might feel a sudden desire to visit the metropolis."

His shoulders felt lighter, as if a burden had lifted. "I may take you up on that offer, particularly if I'm replaced as magistrate."

"You think the earl would go so far?" Quill asked with a frown.

"I think he'll go farther," James told him. "I merely suggested he might ease up on Eva, and he ordered her most precious possession sold. I was able to get word to Thorgood to purchase it anonymously, so I hope Eva won't lose it in the end. But I have no doubt the earl's punishment for our marriage will be swift and harsh."

Quill nodded in understanding. "So that's why you brought your mother home with you. You're trying to spare her the lash too." He raised his glass again. "When this is over, I hope you can finally stop having to play the martyr."

"So do I," James said, but he had a feeling that day was a long way off.

Linus Bennett wished Miss Faraday good afternoon and watched as she traipsed from the spa, dark curls bouncing. Their conversation had been the first one approaching normalcy since he'd arrived in Grace-by-the-Sea last evening.

He and Ethan had barely settled their things at an inn called the Swan when the Spa Corporation had descended upon them *en masse*. He wasn't sure how they'd known of his arrival. Then again, word might travel faster in a small village than it did in London.

"Welcome to Grace-by-the-Sea," Mr. Greer, the president, had declared. Linus had only corresponded with the fellow, yet he wasn't surprised to find him tall and lean, with sandy hair that was receding and a way of thrusting his head forward. The beginning signs of a degeneration of the spine, perhaps?

"I regret that you may have to stay at the inn for a day or so," Greer continued. "Your cottage should be ready shortly."

Linus glanced at his son. The nine-year-old was sitting on the bed, brown eyes weary but watchful. Ethan tended to keep his thoughts to himself. Linus was never sure what was going through his mind. And it was of no little concern to him.

"I've already informed Miss Chance and her aunt that they must be out by tomorrow evening," Mrs. Greer assured Linus with a glance at Ethan. He would have called the look more curious than motherly. "They don't have much, so it shouldn't be any bother."

"On the contrary," one of the board members said, standing taller, "it is a great deal of bother, with nothing to gain from it."

"Yes, yes, Miss Archer," Mr. Greer said with a sigh.

Greer might have been president, but this lady had far more presence. Hair the color of bruised ginger protruded from her straw bonnet, and there appeared to be a speck of blue on one cheek. Curious. He found himself studying it a moment, trying to determine its source. Not a natural mark of her complexion. Not for effect—he was heartily glad the fashion for false spots had faded. Paint?

She must have caught him looking, for she frowned at him. "I must protest again that we are depriving Miss Chance and Mrs. Tully of positions in which they have served faithfully and well. I, for one, doubt a physician can take their place." She narrowed her eyes at him, as if she could see every last flaw in his character.

"We have discussed this and voted," Greer reminded her testily. "You are overruled." He looked apologetically to Linus. "I mentioned the matter of additional spa staff to you in my letters, sir. You had indicated you needed no assistance."

Greer had asked him about other staff, but Linus had taken the question to mean they were considering part-nering him with another physician. If he was to share patients, he needed to choose his colleague. Not everyone had the same philosophy of care, the ideas of how to treat an illness.

"I'm sure we'll muddle through," he had told the board members.

Miss Archer had scowled at him.

So had the only person to join him in the spa that morn-ing before Miss Faraday had arrived. Greer had given him the key, and he and his wife had come to the Swan to walk Linus to the spa. For now, Linus had left Ethan in the care of the innkeeper's wife, a temporary solution he would have to remedy as soon as possible. Other lads might be on their way to Eton or Harrow at that age. Linus had no intention of separating himself from his son. Bad enough that Ethan no longer had a mother.

He hadn't been sure what to expect of the spa. He'd vis-ited Harrogate and Scarborough. Both had become more social center than medical facility, and Bath was even more famous now. Would he find crowds of aristocrats here, who came to drink only to appear fashionable or people who truly needed a physician? Assembly rooms or examining rooms?

The spa at Grace-by-the-Sea was all he could have wanted. The pale blue walls and view to the sea welcomed patients into tranquility. The fountain stood ready to dispense the waters on his prescription. Examining rooms across the back offered reclining couches, the latest instruments and medicines. His head had risen, his breath come easier. This was going to be his place, his home.

The gentleman who'd arrived shortly after the Greers had left seemed to think otherwise. He'd been a long-limbed fellow with rheumy eyes and a pasty complexion, and Linus had immediately begun considering what he might do to effect a remedy.

"I am Warfield Crabapple," he'd announced, as if the name should mean something to Linus. "I'm a Regular at this spa, but I will only continue my subscription if you reinstate Miss Chance and her aunt immediately." He blinked and stepped back, as if astonished by his own temerity.

"Thank you for letting me know," Linus said. "I hope to make the acquaintance of Miss Chance so I can resolve what is evidently a misunderstanding."

He drew himself up. "A misunderstanding? You sacked her, sirrah. None of us take that kindly. Good day."

It was clear Miss Archer and Mr. Crabapple expected him to give the spa up, hand it back to those who had managed it before him. None of them could know how important this position was to him, how badly he and Ethan needed a new start. And so he would fight—for the spa, for the village he hoped to call home, and for the son he had nearly lost.

Eva had to tour through part of the village before she

located Jesslyn and Maudie in Abigail's gallery, All the Colors of the Sea. The former spa hostess was admiring the painter's latest creation, a canvas showing the castle with a turbulent sea below and a single light gleaming.

"I call it Hope in the Storm," Abigail was saying as Eva came up to them.

"I call it excellent," Eva assured her.

Jesslyn and Maudie turned. Though both smiled in welcome, Eva could see dark shadows under the younger woman's eyes, as if she hadn't been sleeping well.

"Thank you," Abigail said. "I'm holding a sale, Eva. Everything in the shop is half off, and I will use the funds to mount a crusade to remove Doctor Bennett from his position."

Jesslyn shook her head. "Please, Abigail, I wish you wouldn't. It's hardly his fault."

"No, indeed," Eva put in. "I was just up at the spa. It's empty, and he seems sincerely distressed by the fact. Yet I doubt he has any idea why or what to do about it."

Abigail snapped a nod. "Good. Perhaps he'll rethink his decision to oust others."

"We should consult the trolls," Maudie said. "They know how to deal with such matters." Her eyes narrowed as if she was considering a dark fate for the poor physician.

"He didn't oust anyone," her niece reminded them all. "Mrs. Greer hasn't appreciated me taking over for Father. I'm sure her attitude influenced her husband in making this decision. Besides, the spa is the lifeblood of this village. We wouldn't want to poison it. Too many other livelihoods are at stake."

Maudie brightened. "Poison?"

"No," her niece said emphatically.

"Is the spa the chief employer, then?" Eva asked.

"In a way," Jesslyn said. "A few families are directly involved. The Inchleys cater, Mr. Ellison provides baked goods. But many more derive income from those who come to visit."

"Mrs. Kirby, the leasing agent," Eva realized.

Jesslyn nodded. "And the inns and shops like Mr. Carroll's and Abigail's. And any excess income not required for maintenance or improvements goes into the corporation's profits to be divided among every family in the village on a quarterly basis."

Her father would have been impressed. "An excellent arrangement," Eva said. "I can see why you wouldn't want to ruin it. Perhaps someone should explain the matter to Doctor Bennett."

Abigail shuddered. "Better you than me. I can barely stand to look at him."

"All pock and warts?" Maudie asked. "With a hooked nose and a humped back?"

Eva laughed. "No, indeed. I found him rather charming."

"He is tall and well favored," Abigail allowed. "But his goodness may well be only skin deep."

"Time will tell," Jesslyn predicted. "And now we've monopolized your time quite enough, Abigail. Eva must have business."

"Actually," Eva told her, "I was looking for Maudie. I had a couple of questions about the wedding."

Maudie nodded. "Whatever you need."

"It was very sweet of you to ask Maudie to be your attendant," her niece put in.

Maudie frowned. "Who else was she going to get? The fairies are busy."

So was Eva. She managed to determine what else Maudie might need to stand up beside her and went on to attend to a myriad of other details. But before she knew it, the day of the wedding had arrived.

Mrs. Howland shooed James out of the house that morning at dawn so Eva could prepare.

"We have until half past ten before we must be at the church," Eva protested when Mrs. Howland came for her as the clock struck five. "It won't take me that long to dress."

"Nonsense," her soon-to-be mother-in-law insisted, waving at Patsy to open the curtains. "You must be bathed in lavender water, have your hair washed in essence of roses, and apply the Wash of the Ladies of Denmark."

"Never heard of that one," Patsy whispered to Eva.

Mrs. Howland must have heard her, for she nodded eagerly. "It's a wonderful concoction made of bean flour; seeds of the cucumber, gourd, and melon; and fresh cream."

"I'll smell like the grocer's," Eva whispered to Patsy, who giggled.

Still, soaking in the warm, fragrant water wasn't unpleasant, though she decided against the vaunted Wash of the Ladies of Denmark. And while Patsy rinsed her hair in the essence of roses Mrs. Howland supplied, instead of the apple vinegar Eva usually used, the black tresses still stuck out around her face.

"It certainly has a mind of its own," Mrs. Howland said when she bustled back in to check on them. "Have you tried wax?"

"No," Eva said with a stern look to Patsy. "I like the curls."

"Perhaps more organized curls," Mrs. Howland said, meeting her gaze in the mirror with a hopeful smile.

"I'll do what I can, ma'am," Patsy promised.

Somehow, Eva survived the pulling and crimping, the lacing and the dressing, until the three of them stood before the Pier glass mirror in Mrs. Howland's room.

The Misses Pierce had outdone themselves with the gown. The simple, square-necked bodice was edged with lace and made her skin look creamy. The rich color brought out the depth of her eyes. Her hair had been tamed into a closer nest of curls that framed her face. She looked soft, sweet...

"Beautiful," Mrs. Howland said.

Patsy nodded, eyes bright.

"He won't know who he's marrying," Eva predicted.

And she wasn't sure who she was marrying.

She stood with Maudie in the narthex of St. Andrew's. Every pew was filled, and she'd had to walk through other villagers as she'd come from the carriage to the church. It wasn't every day the local magistrate married.

And my, but the magistrate looked fine.

His golden hair was waved back from his face. His shoulders in the black coat were straight and true. Those white stockings outlined powerful calves. He glanced back at her.

Their gazes brushed, locked, and she knew. He was as certain as she was. This was meant to be. Every butterfly in the manor garden fluttered into flight inside her.

Maudie nudged her. "Don't we have to walk?"

Eva shook herself. Mr. Wingate, the vicar, was nodding to them.

"You go first," Eva whispered to Maudie.

Maudie frowned. "Why? I'm not marrying him."

"You're the attendant," Eva explained. "You are the most important person after the bride. And you have such a pretty dress to show off."

Maudie preened. "It does look rather fine. Perhaps I'll dress in purple from here on."

With a satisfied nod, she set off down the aisle.

Eva followed her, past the Greers, Abigail, Mr. Carroll and the Ellisons. Past Lord Featherstone, Mr. Crabapple, Mrs. Harding, Mrs. North and her son, Miss Tapper and Mrs. Baugh. Past Jesslyn and Larkin Denby. They were all smiling, all encouraging. Like horses harnessed to a chariot, the butterflies inside her pulled her heart up into her throat.

Maudie moved in beside Captain St. Claire, who was wearing his naval uniform. "You should have worn purple," Maudie informed him.

Eva's gaze was on James. That smile said he had been waiting for this moment, for her. She barely heard the minister perform the ceremony, nodded and responded as required. A few more moments, and they would be forever united.

And free.

"And such are the duties of a husband and his wife," the vicar finished with a pleased smile. "All ye of the parish of St. Andrew's, I give you Mr. and Mrs. Howland."

Eva and James turned. Everyone was beaming at them. Mrs. Harding had her head on Mr. Crabapple's shoulder, and the fellow was doing his best to stand up under the pleasant burden. Abigail was grinning from ear to ear. Farther back, Pym, Yeager, and Patsy were nodding with pride.

The church door banged open, and the Earl of Howland stormed into the space to plant his feet, greatcoat swirling and eyes blazing.

"Stop this marriage," he ordered. "I forbid it."

# CHAPTER FIFTEEN

HAD THE CHURCH WALLS COLLAPSED on him, James couldn't have felt more trapped. He gripped Eva's hand, held it tightly even as the vicar spoke into the stunned silence.

"I'm afraid you are too late, sir. Who are you to contest what God has joined together?"

The earl looked down his nose. "I am Charles, Earl of Howland. And you owe your living to me."

Gasps rang out, and James could only guess the vicar had turned white.

The earl pointed a finger at James. "Arrest this man at once for seducing my ward."

More gasps. James straightened to his full height, but Eva spoke first.

"There was no seduction. I married of my own free will. I am of legal age. And I am not your ward."

It was as if she hadn't spoken. "Will no one step forward to uphold the king's law?" the earl demanded, gaze spearing the others.

"I will," Mrs. Tully said helpfully. "But he's bigger than me, and he *is* the law."

Mr. Wingate's breath brushed James's ear. "Magistrate? What do you advise?"

James glanced at Quill. His friend squared his shoulders

and started forward. He could only hope Quill meant to confront the earl and not him, but Lark rose and moved out into the aisle at the same time. As Quill hesitated, Lark nodded to James and Eva, then turned and bowed to the earl. "My lord, I am the Riding Surveyor for the area, and I have the utmost respect for your relation, our magistrate. I can assure you that everything about this marriage was done legally."

"Were the banns read?" the earl snapped.

"No." Lark glanced back at James.

"We married by license from the bishop," James supplied.

"And in church before noon," Mr. Wingate seemed compelled to add.

"In front of witnesses," Quill put in.

"And not a mermaid or troll in sight," Mrs. Tully agreed.

Everyone else in the church seemed to be holding their breaths. Eva's fingers trembled in his.

"You two," the earl said, meeting James's gaze over Lark's head, "will attend me. Now."

Clothes rustled as everyone looked to James. Eva squeezed his hand, face resolute.

"Now is inconvenient," James said. "But you are welcome to join us at our wedding breakfast."

The earl's eyes narrowed. "A wedding breakfast I paid for."

Eva's head came up. "No. *I* paid for it, with the fortune you tried to steal from me."

Surprisingly, their guests had enough breath to gasp yet again.

James had had enough. He turned to the minister. "Thank you, Mr. Wingate, for officiating at our wedding. Please join us as we celebrate."

The vicar glanced around him in the earl's direction and swallowed. "Perhaps another time."

Right. James wasn't the only one serving at the earl's

behest. Just the reminder from the earl had been enough to let the minister know how tenuous his position might be.

"Of course," James said. He threaded Eva's arm through his. "Shall we, wife?"

Her smile curved up. "Delighted, husband."

They moved down the aisle. James kept his smile pleasant. Beside him, Eva was doing the same. Lark stepped aside with a respectful nod to let them pass. The earl remained blocking their way.

James bent his head and lowered his voice. "If you contest me here, you will only lose the respect you crave. Many come to the spa. Word will get out that you were so desperate for funds you disrupted a church service."

The earl's face tightened, but he moved out of their way. James led Eva past. In the back row, Yeager raised his clasped hands in victory. Patsy and Pym looked more concerned.

"What do we do now?" Eva whispered as she and James stepped out into the sunshine and began moving toward the waiting carriage. The remaining villagers were clustered along the walk to the gate. Children tossed flower petals into the air. The soft pinks and purples drifted down on him and Eva. Some lodged in the dark of her hair. Someone had managed to confine it for the wedding, but his fingers itched to let it loose, see it return to its usual bounce.

"Now," James said as he smiled his thanks all around, "we brazen it out. We wanted our freedom. It seems we'll have to fight for it a while longer."

A Roman general returning from conquest had never looked more sure of himself, Eva thought. James smiled and nodded to his friends and acquaintances, all of whom were beaming. People she'd never met threw flowers, called best wishes for her health and happiness. Of course, they hadn't been privy to the scene inside the church. Eva had thought her heart would stop in her chest when the earl had appeared and started issuing orders.

"May you be blessed with many children!" someone called.

Children!

Eva glanced at James, but he kept nodding graciously, as if he were the king dispensing benevolences. As they reached the coach, which was bedecked with garlands of flowers and ribbons, he helped her up onto the seat. Mr. Connors had laid back the top, so she had an excellent view of the church, the happy masses, and Maudie and James's mother coming to join them. Maudie was chatting away to Mrs. Howland, who was white. Kip helped them up into the carriage as well.

"Lovely wedding," Maudie said as she arranged her purple skirts. "I haven't been more entertained in years."

"James," Mrs. Howland moaned, shoulders as tight as her face. "What have you done?"

"It will be fine, Mother," James told her. As if he wasn't as sure as he sounded, he glanced toward the church. Their wedding guests had followed them as well, and many still looked stunned. There was no sign of the earl.

"Will he join us, do you think?" Eva asked James.

"It depends," James said, tapping the coachman's box to signal Mr. Connors to head out. "He will have to decide which is more important at the moment—behaving in a manner that draws no attention to his circumstances or punishing me."

"Punishing *us*," Eva reminded him as the coach began to move through the crowds toward High Street. "We are in this together, sir."

"For better, for worse," he said, bringing her hand to his lips.

At his kiss, warmth went through her. She could not

claim it was from the sun.

"Funny," she said as he lowered her hand. "When I recited those words, I thought the *for worse* part might be longer in coming."

"So did I," his mother murmured, gaze haunted.

Maudie glanced among them, clearly perplexed. "You never know when the *for worse* part is coming. That's why you have to make the best of the *for better* part."

James cradled Eva's hand closer. For a moment, she let herself dream of a future without the earl. Her and James, together, growing closer. Perhaps finding love...

They reached the assembly rooms a short time later. Purple bunting had been draped about the tall columns at the front, as if she and James were royalty. The elegant hall with its sea-blue walls held a long table down the center with a white cloth, a porcelain service edged in silver, and silver place settings. James led her to the two seats at the head of the table, and their guests came to fill up the sides. She was just thinking she might enjoy the meal after all when the earl arrived. He took the seat near the end of the table, and none of the people around him looked pleased by the fact. Mr. Crabapple went so far as to hold Mrs. Harding's chair so she could rise and find another place.

Mrs. Greer, who was closer to the top, leaned around the others between her and James. "Your cousin, the earl, should not be so low. Mrs. Tully must exchange places with him."

Maudie glared at her.

"Mrs. Tully has more than earned her place," James said. "So has the earl."

Mrs. Greer's eyes widened, but she sat back.

"You *are* starting a fight," Eva said, unable to keep the admiration from her voice.

"Give him an inch, and he'll take a mile," James returned. He smiled as the servers began bringing in the food.

And suddenly it wasn't so very difficult to make herself eat. She had gone over the arrangements with the caterers, Mr. and Mrs. Inchley, but she hadn't appreciated how well the Italian-dressed asparagus would go with the buttered prawns. Still, she far preferred the chicken and mushrooms, even though Maudie kept frowning at the dish as if she suspected the mushrooms had been stolen from a fairy circle.

"Allow me to congratulate you," Captain St. Claire said to Eva partway through the meal from his place on her left. "It isn't every day a villain like the earl is made to strike his colors."

"Has he troubled you as well, Captain?" Eva asked, digging into the apple pie that made up part of the second course.

"Not directly, but I've seen his influence around the village. And I know how much he's hurt James and his family."

She glanced at her husband, who was having a spirited debate with Maudie on his right. They appeared to be discussing the educational prospects of trolls.

"When I first came here," she said to the captain, "I thought he was one of the earl's puppets."

"James Howland is no one's puppet." He popped a stewed plum into his mouth and chewed a moment. "Neither are you, I think. Tell me, once the old boy comes to his senses, will you stay in Grace-by-the-Sea? You have a fortune, I hear. You could live anywhere."

She could. All at once the future looked vast, endless. Eva drew a breath. "I don't know. I hadn't thought much farther than this moment."

"Then think carefully," he advised. "The earl may lean on his prestige and force James out of his position, but James has been advocating for this village all his life. It will not be easy for him to let it go."

She could imagine that. She had never felt such affinity for a place before coming here, but already she looked forward to meeting with Jesslyn and Abigail over tea, discussing books with Rosemary, helping decorate the church and assembly rooms for the next wedding, studying mushrooms with Maudie, and dancing and promenading with her husband at the assembly.

Her husband. Already it was easy to call James that.

As if he had told her enough privately, Captain St. Claire pushed to his feet. Down the table, voices quieted, gazes turned to him. He picked up his glass.

"Long have I known our magistrate," he declared, voice ringing. She could see him standing so on the forecastle of a ship, rallying his men. "Seldom have I seen him so happy. He has feted us well," he inclined his head to Eva, "*they* have feted us well, and you know how devoted he is to his village and his country that he will not serve us French champagne."

He lifted his glass of cider as laughter echoed. "May he be as devoted to his Eva and she to him. To Eva and James."

"To Eva and James," the others chorused before drinking deep.

With a satisfied smile, the captain sat.

Maudie popped to her feet, her own glass up. "And to those that brought them together."

"To friends," James hastily added.

"To friends," they all agreed, smiles flashing.

Eva leaned closer to him as Maudie sat. "What did you expect her to say—trolls and fairies?"

"Frankly," he murmured back, "I was more afraid she'd say smugglers and spies."

"Them too," Maudie said.

Eva started laughing.

"Now, that is a sound I hope to hear more often," James said.

Lost in his gaze, she didn't notice the servers coming until they had laid the wedding cake on the table before them. Honey dripping down its sides, plums poking out here and there, the rich spice cake begged to be cut. James set about carving slices.

The toasts and laughter continued for some time. Courses came and went. Friends and family moved around the table to speak to her and James, offer their best wishes, their love and support. She only caught glimpses of the earl, once speaking with Mr. Denby and another time to Mrs. Kirby. Between Captain St. Claire on Mrs. Howland's left and the guests who came to speak to her as well, James's mother had relaxed and was smiling happily.

Then, the wishes turned to farewells, as, singly or in groups, their guests took their leave. Maudie gave Eva a hug and eyed James.

"Keep fighting," she said.

He sobered and bowed to her. "Always, madam."

With a nod, she went to join her niece and nephew and Mr. Denby.

Abigail accompanied Mr. Carroll out the door. Mr. Priestly, James's secretary, walked with Mrs. North and her son. Mr. Greer attempted to leave several times before finally convincing his wife that she would not have an opportunity to converse with the earl. Lord Featherstone accompanied Mother Howland.

Captain St. Claire leaned closer to Eva and caught James's eye. "Do you wish me to escort your unwelcome guest out?"

Eva glanced down the table to where the earl was sitting. He appeared to be contemplating his plate, which was strangely full. Had the servers taken pains to keep filling it, or had he refused to accept even this part of their hospitality?

"Don't make trouble for yourself," James said to his

friend. "We'll all leave together. If you're ready, Eva?"

She gave him her hand, and he helped her up. They started for the door, Quillan St. Claire on her other side like the Queen's Guard.

The earl rose and moved to meet them. "An excellent repast. Thank you for inviting me."

What was this conciliatory tone? Eva wasn't sure how to respond, but James inclined his head.

"You should know we have already moved our things out of the magistrate's house."

"Very considerate of you," he said. "Mrs. Kirby was explaining it all to me."

Eva felt chilled. "I didn't realize you and Mrs. Kirby were on such good terms."

"Half the property in the village belongs to me, my dear," he said with a patronizing smile. "Of course I keep in touch with who's managing it."

"I manage it," James said, voice sharpening. "If you know anything about Mrs. Kirby, it is through my reports."

The earl waved a hand. "You argue semantics. Suffice it to say that you will not require that lease on Butterfly Manor. Ridiculous name for a house. I canceled the lease and ordered the staff to retrieve your belongings. You will all be moving in with me at the castle."

# CHAPTER SIXTEEN

JAMES'S FREE HAND FISTED AT his side. How many
times had the earl put him in this position of having to
do something he abhorred? Leaving his mother in London, preventing him from chartering the militia—those
were only the latest. Defying the earl had always come
with a penalty. He'd thought severing all ties would prevent the fellow from hurting him and Eva, yet here the earl
stood, asserting control. In another situation, it would have
been easy to refuse.

But James couldn't leave him alone in the castle. Who
knew what he might discover about Quill's activities? And
the earl might be in danger from those who had been using
the place. With only a few staff, could he protect himself if
their mysterious visitor started another fire? James might
detest the earl, but he could not put him in harm's way.

Neither did James dare look at Quill. That alone might
give the earl insight into his concerns. He knew to his sorrow how well the earl could use his emotions against him.

"I regret, my lord," he said, careful to keep his face
neutral, "that we shut up the castle. It is in no shape to
welcome you."

The earl smiled, like a wolf about to attack. "I anticipated
as much. That's why I sent your servants straight from the
church to see to the place. Lord Featherstone is helping

Mrs. Howland on her way there now."

Eva started. "That's why I didn't see Yeager about! How dare you! He isn't your servant. He's mine, and so is Patsy."

"Surely you would be more comfortable in the village, my lord," Quill put in smoothly. "I understand the magistrate's house is empty."

"And has already been consigned to Mrs. Kirby's care for leasing," the earl said.

He cut off their every escape. James gritted his teeth. "I will accompany you, then. We need not inconvenience Eva."

She stiffened beside him even as the earl inclined his head, smile smug.

"Surely we should not trespass on the earl's good graces, husband," she said, giving his arm a squeeze. "We can stay at the inn if need be until we can reinstate the lease to Butterfly Manor." She spared the earl a glance. "Mother Howland was so looking forward to returning to her childhood home."

"I am convinced she will do just as well at the castle," the earl said.

Meaning he intended to continue to use her as leverage.

"I know you had reservations about the castle's suitability as a home," James told Eva. "Perhaps you would be happier at the Swan. It's right in the village. Mother can stay with you."

Eva met his gaze, eyes narrowed as if she was trying to see deep inside him. If only he could tell her all the things in his mind, his heart. But never in front of the earl.

"That is very thoughtful of you, James," she said. "But I will go where you go, as your wife."

He should not feel so buoyed by her support. She put herself at risk by accompanying him. He had no doubt the earl would try to use her against him as well.

"What a fine, sensible woman you've married," the earl

said. "Eva, dear, you can accompany me while James bids farewell to his friend."

Something hard settled in his wife's eyes. "Why, I'd never leave my husband to such a task. Please go ahead of us. We may be some time. So many things to say to our valiant captain." She seized Quill with her free hand and dragged them both back to the nearly empty table.

The movement was just this side of rude. Some might even have considered it the cut direct.

James wanted to applaud her.

"You, madam," Quill said, as they stood at the foot of the table the servers were now clearing, "are a force to be reckoned with, and I can only lament that James married you first."

"And I can only lament that I don't understand any of this," she said. "James, why are you agreeing to live with him even for a moment? You know he's plotting something."

"Of course he is," James agreed. "But I need to know what he's plotting if I'm to fight it."

She didn't look convinced. "Then let me fight it with you."

"I'd prefer you didn't have to fight at all."

"So would I, but it's clear he's not willing to admit defeat. Captain St. Claire suggested we leave Grace-by-the-Sea to escape him."

James glanced at his friend, who held up his hands. "Don't look at me. I'm merely a minor player in this farce. But I stand by my assessment. Leaving might be your only option if you truly want to live away from the earl's influence."

"You don't understand, either of you," James insisted. "His fingers reach into every part of the empire. I can imagine nowhere we could go if we cannot make our stand here."

Again she squeezed his arm. "Then let us stand." She pasted on a smile, and he realized Mrs. Inchley was approaching.

The caterer inclined her head. "Was there anything else you needed, Mrs. Howland?" She had to be wondering why the three of them and the earl remained.

"We merely wanted to thank you," Eva assured her. "Everything was perfect."

She curtsied. "You are very welcome. And many happy returns to you both."

Eva nodded her thanks, and the caterer resumed her work. Eva looked to James. "How else can we delay the inevitable?"

James chuckled. "You'll only vex him."

"Oh, I'm counting on it."

Quill tipped his chin toward the kitchen behind the main hall. "Perhaps you should personally thank all the servers as well."

She smiled and strolled off, purple skirts swaying.

James stepped closer to Quill. "It seems Eva and I are stuck in the castle for the time being. I'll try to keep everyone away from the caves. Do I need to clean them out just to be safe? Is there anything incriminating to find?"

Quill pursed his lips. "Just Alex's fire circle. I would confirm that myself, but I won't be able to sail in until the tide turns, and that's after midnight tonight."

"Don't try it," James said. "You've already found another place to land, I take it?"

Quill nodded. James held up a hand before he could speak. "Don't tell me until we know the earl is out of our lives. I want to give him nothing to bargain for."

"And here you thought he'd give up his favorite plaything so easily," Quill said with a wry chuckle.

"I had hoped when he realized he'd lost his hold on me and Eva he would decamp," James admitted. "That may take longer than anticipated."

Quill patted his shoulder. "Hope springs eternal." He lowered his hand. "What about the caves, then?"

"I'll deal with them," James promised. And he would protect Eva and his mother as well.

Eva came out of the kitchen to see Captain St. Claire clapping her new husband on the shoulder as if they had settled on a plan, a plan to which she wasn't privy. Why was it so hard to trust James? So many in the village thought well of him—look at the turnout at their wedding. But any number of people, like Mrs. Greer, toadied up to the earl. Even Eva's astute father had been taken in by him.

Had she allowed James to do the same to her?

The need to believe him beat like a second heart in her breast. He'd gone along with her mad plan for a marriage of convenience. He'd made the arrangement that saved her fortune. He'd trusted her to find them a home.

Or had he intended to move them into the castle all along? She'd thought she'd saved her future from the earl by marrying James. Had she merely traded one scheming Howland for another?

She turned her back on them and went to talk to Mrs. Inchley about keeping the purple bunting from the columns. The longer she dallied, the sooner the earl might grow impatient and leave.

Her approach must have worked, for he and his carriage were gone when Eva and James finally exited the assembly rooms.

"At least we don't have to sit across from him as he gloats," Eva said.

"Oh, I have no doubt he's letting us know of his displeasure," James said. "He likely sent your carriage with the servants and baggage, and he's taken his own. We're expected to walk like the penitents we are."

"The penitents we *were*," Eva corrected him. "We don't dance to his tune anymore." At least, that's what she hoped.

James offered her his hand, and they strolled down High Street to where it met Castle Walk, then started up the path to the headland. He seemed as loath as she was to rejoin the earl, so she wasn't surprised when he stopped at the first turning with its little stone bench. Together they stood, gazing out over the sea. The day was advancing, the sunlight skipping across the waves, turning them to turquoise.

"Our lives will be different now, Eva," he said. "I promise." His arm moved around her waist, and she fit herself against him, warm, safe.

"I want to believe that," she said.

He turned his head to meet her gaze. "I would never lie to you."

Every line of that firm face attested to the truth of the statement. She ached to agree.

"Perhaps not intentionally," she allowed, dropping her gaze to the silver buttons on his waistcoat. "But it's becoming clear to me that you've spent your life dissembling to the earl. I begin to wonder if you know how to do anything else."

"I wonder too, sometimes."

The sadness in the quiet words cut through her. Oh, but the Earl of Howland had much to atone for. A shame he showed no signs of wishing to change.

She pressed a hand to James's chest and raised her gaze to his. "We have the right and ability to choose our own actions. I must believe that. I ask only that you believe we are partners in this venture, from beginning to end. You can share your feelings with me."

He sighed. "I will, Eva. Once we know he's out of our lives."

She frowned. "Why must we wait? Surely the more we are aligned in our thoughts, the stronger we will be against him."

"And the more easily he can tear at us," he said. "I have lived through it to my sorrow, Eva. I will not see him harm you because of me."

She lay a hand to his cheek. "Yet the distance you put between us is just as harmful. Perhaps I'm as impatient as he is. I told you love could grow between us. It won't unless you allow yourself to feel."

His eyes were dark, troubled. "I feel, Eva. Sometimes too much." As if to prove it, he bent his head and touched his lips to hers.

And everything in her rose to meet his kiss: her longings, her dreams, her hopes. The love that was growing inside her for this marvelous, maddening man. She wrapped her arms around his neck and held on.

A chittering pierced the cloud of emotion surrounding her. Eva pulled back and stared at him. "Did you hear that?"

"Do not," he said, "claim that was fairies."

She bent to look under the bench. The sun was at the proper angle to brighten the shadows below. A small, brown shape scampered into the bushes lining the cliff.

"A vole," she marveled, straightening. "I cannot tell you what a relief that is. Maudie's fairies remain unknown to anyone but her."

"Alas, I cannot say the same for the trolls," James said, offering her his hand. "I fear we are about to face one at the castle."

Eva clung to his hand, preventing him from continuing up the path. "Do not shut me out, James. We have a chance for a future together."

He squeezed her hand. "I feel it too, Eva. Give me time. I need to know you and Mother are safe."

And how could she argue with that? Always he thought of others: the villagers, his mother, her. She nodded, and they continued up the path to the castle.

"His lordship is sitting in the withdrawing room neat as you please," Yeager confirmed when they entered the great hall a short time later. "Don't let him fool you. He's been pacing a hole in the carpet. You have him that worried, Miss Eva."

"It's Mrs. Howland now," Eva reminded him. "Make sure you use it as often as possible in his hearing."

Yeager grinned. "That I will." His smile faded. "Are we staying, then? I wasn't sure whether to believe him when he gave Mr. Pym the order."

"For now," Eva said. "But don't unpack."

"Again," he muttered, but he nodded agreement.

James ran a hand up her arm, warmth trailing. "You needn't face him. I can make your excuses."

"We do this together," she insisted, latching onto his arm. "It is our wedding night. Surely he would not expect us to entertain him. We will bid him good evening and retire to fight another day."

"Aye, captain," he said with a smile.

The earl glanced up from studying the fire as they entered. His face seemed more lined than she remembered, but perhaps she was hoping to see any sort of weakness.

"Ah, back so soon?" he asked.

"Back and fatigued," James said. "It has been a busy day."

"Your mother said the same thing," he mused. "Am I to be left alone this evening, then?"

The question sounded melancholy, particularly for him.

"I fear so," Eva said with a bright smile. "We intend to retire."

"We will see you in the morning, my lord," James added as if to ward off any argument.

He merely smiled. "Sleep well."

"What, has he put snakes in the bed?" Eva whispered as they left him. "Or do even the castle ghosts obey him? Has he ordered them to haunt us?"

"There are no ghosts," James assured her as they started up the stairs. "But have Patsy check the bed carefully for any sign of snakes before you retire."

They reached the landing, and he kissed her hand before turning for the room he'd been using. She wanted more: his thoughts, his heart. With a sigh, Eva made for her own room.

But the space was dark, the hearth cold, and holland covers once more draped the furniture. She stepped back into the corridor and glanced across the landing.

James was retreating from his room as well. He met her gaze. "Where is everyone?"

She shook her head and raised her voice. "Patsy! Answer me."

A door opened at the end of the corridor, and Patsy poked her head out. "In here, miss, that is, madam."

From the very farthest end of the opposite corridor, Mr. Pym waved a hand and called, "Master James!"

James glanced from his servant to Eva, frowning.

Eva threw up her hands. "He's put us as far apart as he can! Is he determined to be annoying?"

James strode to her side. "Not annoying. He's dividing us to conquer."

"Why does he care?" she demanded. "I'm married. He can't get his hands on my money."

"He can't force you to marry Thorgood," James clarified. "He likely assumes I have control of your fortune. He'll attempt to maneuver one of us into a difficult position, then demand money to settle the matter."

"That's blackmail," Eva protested.

"And only one of his tricks," James told her. "His favorite is to find something you care about and either hold it over you or destroy it in punishment."

"My harp," she said.

James nodded. "I hope I saved it, Eva, but I won't know until I hear from Thorgood. The earl threatened to sell it when I questioned his judgment over you. I asked the viscount to purchase it anonymously."

"That was very good of you, James," she said, her heart warming. "So, what do you advise now? Do we accept this inconvenience? Turn the other cheek and keep an eye on him?"

His gaze narrowed as he thought. "No. Call Patsy." As Eva did as he bid, he turned and waved to Pym, who hurried down to meet them.

"Find us two interconnecting rooms," he told his man. "Set up only what you need for us to sleep there tonight. We'll make other arrangements in the morning."

Patsy slumped. "More packing and unpacking."

"Not much longer," Eva promised.

"He'll notice," Pym predicted.

"Let him notice," James said. "It will only tell him we are determined in our course. He couldn't stop the wedding, and we will not allow him to interfere in our marriage."

Eva blinked as realization hit. "Wait, James. That's exactly what he tried to do—rush here from London to stop the wedding. How did he know we were marrying and where? We were so careful. Who told him early enough that he could reach the church nearly in time?"

# CHAPTER SEVENTEEN

HE SHOULD HAVE THOUGHT OF that. "You're right," James told Eva. He turned to Pym. "Do you know anyone who would have alerted the earl?"

Pym's eyes rounded. "No, Master James. All of us on your staff have cause to dislike him. We're loyal." He looked pointedly at Patsy.

Eva's maid stiffened. "Well, we're all loyal to Miss Eva," she declared. "The earl treated us shabbily as well. We've no love for him."

"But perhaps a little fear," James reasoned.

"A healthy fear," Eva insisted. "It must be someone in the village. That horrid Mrs. Greer, perhaps."

James shook his head. "She would never presume to write to the earl directly. No one in the village would."

Pym cleared his throat. "You have Mr. Priestly write the earl on a regular basis, sir."

Priestly? He and his father had always been in the earl's pay, but James had thought he chafed under it as much as James did. Did the secretary have more love for the earl than they'd thought?

"I doubt Priestly would go behind my back that way," James said, "but I'll speak to him in the morning. Between the two of us, we should be able to determine who's passing word to the earl. In the meantime, see about those rooms, if you will."

"I know just the ones," Pym said. He motioned to Patsy, who suffered herself to follow. Eva and James brought up the rear.

They settled on a suite of rooms with a sitting room in the middle. James uncovered the settee so Eva could sit, while Pym and Patsy went about making the two beds and bringing in nightclothes.

"So, you've been dealing with the earl all your life," Eva said as James came to sit beside her. "Any advice on how best to behave in his presence? I obviously didn't manage it well, or I wouldn't have been exiled here."

He was suddenly very glad she'd ended up in Grace-by-the-Sea. "My father thought he had the way of it. Keep your head down, speak only of obedience, and hide."

She shuddered. "Wretched way to live."

"I agree. I spent my childhood watching him fawn and grovel and complaining bitterly to my mother when he thought no one would hear. I never understood his attitude."

"So you decided to fight instead," she said.

He wasn't sure why he was telling the tale, but something urged him to continue. "I did indeed. My father took me to London after I graduated university. I went intending to show the earl *this* Howland wasn't about to bow. But the earl was cordial, encouraging. He welcomed me as if I was his own son. I couldn't understand it. All I could think was that Father must have done something terrible to be treated so badly."

"I take it you learned otherwise," she said.

He nodded. "Father's health was already fading. The earl was grooming me to take his place. He wanted me to see what obedience might bring me. Thorgood was courting then, so I was even allowed to join him on his social rounds. We had known each other since we were lads. Many have remarked how much we resemble each other."

Eva cocked his head. "Perhaps in coloring and physical features, but Thorgood doesn't fight like you do."

"He doesn't fight in the same *way* I do," James countered. "His is a quieter revolt. He is the heir, you see. He can only do so much without jeopardizing the reputation of the House of Howland. I understand. We've always gotten along well. I suppose it wasn't surprising that we would both take a liking to the same lady."

Her brows went up. "Oh, I can imagine how that went."

"Not the way you suppose, at least at first," James admitted. "Thorgood was very gracious when she showed a preference for me. The earl was not. His attitude went from benevolent to bullying overnight. He ordered me to stand down. She wasn't meant for the son of a second son, you see."

Eva shook her head. "I hope she had something to say to that."

"She did." Remembering didn't hurt as much as it once had. "Her parents were of a similar mind. Better a husband who would one day be earl than a husband who might never amount to anything, especially when he was out of favor. Like me, she knew her duty."

"Duty." Eva sniffed. "It sounds as if she decided not to take a risk. Her heart cannot have been involved."

"So I tried to tell myself."

She cocked her head and studied him a moment, as if she saw more than he had let on. "So, I'm your comeuppance."

He reared back. "What?"

She straightened with a nod, as if satisfied by her assessment. "The earl wanted me for Viscount Thorgood as well. You wished to steal a march on him. I wouldn't blame you if it was true, but I'd like to know."

"It's not the same," James protested. "I asked Thorgood about his intentions toward you. He doesn't love you. You said you didn't love him."

"I don't," she agreed, "and I'm glad to hear I was right about his feelings as well. But you must admit, marrying me allowed you to stick your thumb in the earl's eye."

"You as well," he said.

She smiled. "Quite right. Well, aren't we a pair?" She schooled her face. "I'm sorry he treated you so poorly. That's not how family should act."

"Oh, he long ago disabused me of the notion we are family," James assured her. "I'm a tool, to be used and discarded at his will. Thanks to you, no more."

"No more, soon," she amended. "First we must convince him his power is broken. We'll deal with that tomorrow."

Just then Patsy came out of the lady's bedchamber and dropped a curtsey. "The bed is ready, Mrs. Howland."

Eva rose. "That's my cue to retire. Sleep well, James. Tomorrow we fight in the arena."

She was as brave as the gladiators she intimated. "Good night, Eva," he said, getting up as well. Once more his feelings gathered, demanded action. He bent and brushed his lips to hers.

And, for a moment, the world fell away, until there was only her.

He pulled back, legs a bit shaky. Her tremulous smile said she'd been as affected. He watched her walk unsteadily to her room. Only when the door closed did he wander into his, thinking.

Every inch of Eva was weary, but sleep refused to come. Patsy had helped her change for bed, dressing her in a fancy white lawn nightgown festooned with ribbons and lace.

"For your wedding night," she'd said when Eva had asked about the gown.

Some wedding night. Then again, she and James hadn't intended to pass the night together. But that kiss, and the one coming up from the village! How was she to forget them and pretend a marriage of convenience still satisfied?

She tossed to one side and then the other. Listened to the coals settle in the grate. This bedchamber was closer to the rear of the castle. Perhaps if she tried, she could hear the waves.

Instead, she heard the floor creak as someone crossed the sitting room. Eva sat up in bed. Surely the earl wasn't still awake and spying on them. No, he'd send a servant. But even they must have retired by now. Their mysterious visitor wouldn't attempt entry to the chamber story with so many people in residence. Then who could be about?

She slid from the bed, thrust her feet into her slippers, and hurried out of her room to the sitting room door. Cracking it open, she glanced left, right.

Just in time to see James disappearing down the stairs.

Why? Where was he going? He was still dressed in his wedding finery, so he hadn't even attempted to go to bed. Once more fears poked at her. Just when she thought she had the ledger balanced, he did something to add to the debit column. Could she truly trust him?

She must, or this marriage stood no chance. But even if she gave him her trust, she didn't have to sit idly by. She could help him in whatever he planned. She slipped out the door. At least the servants had left a few lamps burning in the night. Perhaps they too feared who might be prowling the corridors.

She reached the landing and peered cautiously down into the great hall. He had reached the bottom of the stairs and had turned for the kitchen. Was he hungry? She felt as if she wouldn't eat for days after that feast.

She crept down the stairs after him, careful to keep to the edges to avoid any loose treads. When she reached the main floor, she slid around the corner to look down the short corridor that led toward the kitchen. Though the castle was of recent origin, the designer had taken pains to make this part of the building resembled a fortress, with rough stone walls and narrow windows that now showed the inky black of night. She might well have been on her way to the dungeon.

She took a hesitant step forward, and a hand came down on her shoulder. She gasped and jerked out of the grip.

Moving away from the wall, James put his finger to his lips, then tipped his head to the left. She followed him to the kitchen.

No lamps burned here, but there was a slight glow from a fire that had been banked in the massive hearth, and a little moonlight trickled in through the windows at the back of the room. She made out a long worktable down the center, the gleam of pots hanging along one wall.

He glanced around as if to make sure they were alone, then turned to her. "What are you doing, Eva?"

Eva put her hands on her hips. "What are *you* doing, James? The truth, now."

His face offered her no clues as to his motives. "I'm simply making sure there's nothing here the earl can use against us."

She spread her hands. "In the kitchen?"

"In any part of the castle," he insisted.

Eva dropped her hands. "It won't wash."

He sighed. "Very well. I'm trying to make sure our mysterious visitor hasn't returned." He moved to the hearth, took down one of the spills, and stuck it into the banked coals. The little splinter of wood flared.

"Surely no one would sneak into the castle with the earl in residence," Eva protested. "You know something more, something you don't want to tell me."

He didn't answer as he straightened, and, in the silence,

she heard the tread of footsteps, coming closer.

He grabbed her hand and drew her over to the wall. A stout wooden door that might have been a pantry opened to reveal curving stairs leading down instead. He pulled her inside and shut the door. Then he stood still, face lit by the sputtering spill, as if listening. Eva listened too. The door was thick enough she could detect no movement through it.

He turned toward a lantern hanging from a hook on the wall and lit it with the spill before tossing down the wood and grinding it out with his heel. Pulling the lantern off the hook, he started down, and she followed him a couple of turnings, where there was no danger of being seen.

"Who was that?" Her whisper echoed off the stone walls. Eva clapped a hand over her mouth.

"I don't know," James murmured back. "It could have been Yeager or Pym, keeping an eye on things."

"Why would you care if one of them saw you?" Eva asked.

"Because I don't want anyone investigating what lies below." He nodded down the stairs. "These lead to the caves Mrs. Tully told you about. I intend to check them. You can wait here if you like. It will be cold and damp, and you aren't dressed for either."

She glanced down at her nightgown. "What, no white lawn? I assure you, sir, it is all the rage in London."

James shrugged out of his coat, juggling the lantern in the process. "If you're certain you want to come, take this, and follow me."

Hugging his coat close, she did.

James moved down the stairs, pausing every so often as if listening for noises above and below. Whoever had come into the kitchen hadn't opened the door, for she heard no sound of extra footsteps on the stone. From below came only a soft, rhythmic slush, like the waves on the shore.

"Why do you want to check the caves?" Eva asked, voice once more reverberating.

"I'll tell you when we reach the bottom," he said.

Why was he delaying? It wasn't as if anyone else could hear them.

Could they?

She swallowed and kept following. Ahead, an arched doorway looked out into blackness. James stepped down and lifted the lantern high.

Eva gazed around and up. And up. Everywhere she looked, light touched rock. Rock walls, damp and dark. Fallen rock on sandy soil, like teeth sticking up. Rock disappearing in front of her into darkness.

"It's huge," she said.

Her voice bounced around the space, the echoes crossing each other until it sounded as if the cave spoke back.

Eva grinned. "Ha, ha, ha," she called.

The cave giggled.

"Don't," James said as she opened her mouth again. "If there's anyone here, they already think we're mad."

She sobered, glancing around again. Was there someone else here? Would even breath echo? She held hers, listening. All she heard was that rhythmic noise, louder now. Where was it coming from?

"Is that the sound of the sea?" she asked, careful to keep her voice quieter now.

He nodded toward the darkness. "It comes in through an opening called the Dragon's Maw in that direction. We should be nearing low tide now."

Which meant the water would be coming in farther soon. She glanced around again. Were those rocks darker? Was that how high the water rose?

He swung the lantern one way and then another, sending light streaming across the space. Whatever he saw didn't seem to please him, for he frowned.

"What are we looking for?" Eva asked.

"Evidence of occupation," he said. He moved toward a circle of darker rock. As Eva followed him, he began kicking them apart, each movement as loud as a gunshot.

She stopped short of joining him, shuddering at the noise. "What are you doing? That looks like a fire circle. Doesn't that mean someone has been here?"

"If they have," he said, "I want nothing that might suggest as much to the earl."

She couldn't see the earl venturing down those stairs. But then again, perhaps he'd been the one to send someone into the castle to begin with. She tugged James's coat closer, looking out toward the waves. They were visible now that he'd moved deeper into the cave, foam tinged white and lapping at the stone.

And there, drawn up against the sea, was a boat.

Eva cocked her head, studying it. She hadn't sailed much, just a few times on the Thames with her father's friends, who owned a yacht. This was smaller, as if it had been designed to hold only a sailor or two.

She nodded toward it. "Isn't that more concerning?"

He followed her gaze and stiffened.

"Go back to the castle, Eva," he said. "Now."

# CHAPTER EIGHTEEN

JAMES LOOKED IN EVERY DIRECTION, feeling as if his gaze ricocheted off the rough stone walls like their words. No sign of any movement. No sound of other voices. He'd told Quill not to sail in, and the tide was wrong for this boat to have landed tonight in any event. Quill would have told James if he'd left a boat behind.

Who else had landed in his cave?

Despite his warning, Eva hadn't moved. She watched him now. "I'll leave if you insist. But first tell me why."

Perhaps he should. He'd wanted so badly to protect her, but was keeping secrets from her merely putting her in more danger? She had vowed they were partners. Marriage of convenience or not, the law tended to view a husband and wife as one. When they finally quit the castle, she might wonder at the nighttime rambles Quill had planned for him. Perhaps it was best she knew all.

"Someone's come through the castle," he said. "I don't know who or why, but they'll be returning for their boat. I don't want you here when that happens."

"And I don't particularly want to meet them on the stairs," she said. "Especially in white lawn." She craned her neck as if to peer out into the darkness. "Let's see if they left anything to identify themselves."

He could not feel so calm about the matter, but she was

right. The boat might tell them more about who had used it and when. Together, they ventured closer.

It was plain wood, with no ship's marks or owner's name that he could see. A single bench down the center and at each end would accommodate two to four men. The oars lay inside, awaiting their use. So did a long pole wrapped in canvas.

She wrinkled her nose. "Did this come through the Dragon's Maw?"

"It must have," James said. "That's the only way into the caves from the sea. That pole and canvas formed their mast and sail."

He crouched beside the wood, studied the sand beneath it. "The seawater's dried on it. It hasn't moved since the most recent highest tide."

"When was that?" she asked as he rose.

"Near midnight last night." He glanced around but still could spot no sign of any other disturbance. "It looks like they left the cave through the castle. Which means they'll have to return or abandon their boat. Very likely they didn't expect the earl, or us."

"Could it be someone from the village?" she asked. "Someone who knows about the caves."

"Possibly," he allowed, "but few own ships large enough to carry this one and offload it near the castle. Likely it took at least two men to bring it in."

"Wouldn't we have noticed two strangers?" she asked.

He motioned her up the rocks toward the stairs. "We were a bit preoccupied with the wedding."

"So was most of the village," she said. "Perfect timing. Still, it must be inconvenient to come in that way."

"And dangerous," James agreed. "The opening is called the Dragon's Maw in part because of the boulders that stick up near the entrance like teeth. Sail in that way, and a revenue cutter can never follow you."

"But it could be waiting until you come out," she argued.

"And so you abandon your boat for another day and exit through the castle, leaving a dram of rum for the cook."

"Or the earl." She turned to him, wide-eyed. "Or the magistrate. Oh, James, promise me you aren't in league with smugglers."

"Never," he assured her. "I'm merely explaining what's happened in the past."

"And that fire ring?" she challenged. "Who built that? I cannot conceive someone rowed in for a picnic in the dark."

"The fire ring was built by men working for Quillan St. Claire." There, he'd said it, and the air tasted cleaner.

"Captain St. Claire?" She frowned. "Then he's a smuggler?"

"Not of illicit goods," James clarified. "He's merely built up a fiction of the Lord of the Smugglers to hide his true activities. Quill has a number of contacts in France. He and his men sail over, gather information. Sometimes they bring back those in danger from the Corsican madman. What he learns, he sends immediately to the War Office in London. It was through Quill England first learned of the ships massing across the Channel."

"And he never brought back anything but information and those fleeing Napoleon's wrath?" Her voice was laced with skepticism.

"To my knowledge, no. I gave him a key to the castle and permission to use the caves. I do my best to keep others from intruding on his affairs. The rest I leave to Quill."

She arched her brows. "You must trust him a great deal."

"I would trust Quill with my life. But know this—he isn't involved with our mysterious visitor. There's someone else using the castle. And we can't afford for the earl to discover Quill or the visitor."

"You assume the earl isn't involved," Eva said. "Maudie

said he was connected with smugglers. The visitor she met claimed to know the earl's mind. Perhaps smugglers are leaving a dram, or more, for him."

James sighed. "It's a possibility, but if there truly are smugglers using the caves, why hasn't Quill run afoul of them before now? With that cipher, we could easily be looking at the work of French spies. I can only hope Mr. Carroll uncovers its secrets soon."

She tugged his coat closer, and he felt it too—a chill, a damp, creeping up his stockings and down from his face.

"With this boat here, we know they are near," Eva said. "We can lie in wait, send for the dragoons, the Navy."

"All good suggestions," James said, "except that we don't know when they'll return or even if they'll return. Neither the Navy nor the Army has men to spare, and I cannot bring anyone here without alerting the earl."

She raised her chin. "Even he would take the English side."

"Are you certain?"

She hesitated before answering, then shook her head. "No. The earl thinks only of himself. If it would profit him, he would allow the entire French army to camp on his lands." She giggled, the sound encircling them. "Can't you see it, James? Ordering Napoleon to pay his rent on time?"

He chuckled. "He would pay too. Even the little emperor must quake at the earl's command." He looked back at the boat. "I'll alert Quill and Lark. Both can keep watch for ships at sea, and Lark can be on the lookout for strangers in the area. In the meantime, the best we can do, for all our sakes, is to send the earl back to London before he discovers any of this."

Eva linked her arm with his. "Then let's show him how deliriously happy we are. That ought to sour his stomach."

He smiled. "Let's hope it's that easy. For now, we should

return to the castle and attempt to escape notice."

Eva agreed, and they started for the stairs. Her feet protested, and she paused to shake a rock from her slipper. The pink satin was torn and stained.

"It appears you weren't dressed for it after all," James said, handing her the lantern. Before she knew what he was about, he swept her up into his arms. She could see flecks of gold in the blue of his eyes, or perhaps it was the reflection from his thick lashes.

"Do not argue with me this time," he said, setting out for the stairs once more.

"I wouldn't dream of it," Eva said, warm in his embrace.

He frowned at her, as if he couldn't decide whether she was being impertinent. She refused to tell him she'd been dreaming of being in his arms again since he'd kissed her on the way to the castle.

"I can climb the stairs," she protested as he reached the smooth stone steps. "It's far too narrow to carry me."

"Very well," he allowed. He set her down, arms still around her, head cocked as if he studied her. Her heart began pounding as hard as if she'd run the distance from the French boat.

The French boat. Spies.

He must have seen the fear in her eyes, for his arms tightened. "We'll sort it out, Eva," he promised. "I won't let anything happen to you."

But something was happening to her. She could feel it. Since coming to Grace-by-the-Sea, she had taken risks—trusting him, working with him to thwart the earl, marrying him. Each step had been concerning, glorious. Was she willing to take the final plunge and make a true marriage with him?

Just the thought had her stepping out of his embrace.

"Thank you, James. For everything. We should go."

He regarded her a moment. Her chin was tipping up before she knew it. What, was she begging for his kiss?

He motioned her to lead him up the stairs. Blowing out a breath, Eva picked up the skirts of her nightgown with her free hand and started climbing.

The way back seemed harder. Like echoes, thoughts of the boat, Quillan St. Claire, Napoleon, the earl, and her feelings for James bounced around her. James said nothing, and she could only conclude he was also thinking hard. Still, the earl, their future, seemed so minor when England's safety might be at risk.

James put a hand on her shoulder as she reached the door at the top. Taking the lantern, he extinguished the light, plunging them into darkness. He brushed against her as he bent. In the gap at the bottom of the door, no light showed.

"Let me go first," he murmured as he straightened. "If there's anyone about, I'll lead them away."

There he went, protecting her again. It seemed he'd been protecting people all his life. Small wonder the villagers were so devoted to him.

She was beginning to feel more than devoted.

He eased open the door and slipped out, and she waited in the silence, alone. She didn't have time to wonder before he was back.

"No one around," he murmured. "Follow me."

The return trip was accomplished quickly and quietly. They saw and heard no one. Once inside the sitting room between their bedchambers, Eva lit a lamp and went to sit on one of the chairs by the fire.

"Give me your boots," she said.

"My boots?" he asked, glancing down at them. "Why?"

Eva pulled off her ruined slippers. "Because Pym will wonder how you managed to scuff and dirty them while you were sleeping." She rose and went to the window, heaving up on the sash.

"What are you doing?" he asked.

She tossed her slippers out and leaned over in time to see them fall into a bush in the moonlight. "Disposing of evidence."

"I will not throw out my best boots," he informed her.

"Your *best* boots," she pointed out. "Meaning you have another pair." She pulled back in and closed the sash.

He crossed his arms over his chest, shirtsleeves pale against his waistcoat. "There must be another way."

Eva waved a hand as she returned to the settee. "Feel free to use the washbasin in my bedchamber. Patsy should have left the pitcher full. I can throw out the water. Just don't get mud on anything."

"You have a remarkably devious mind," he commented as he came to sit near her and began removing his boots.

She would have taken umbrage, but he almost sounded admiring.

"I had to think that way to outwit the earl," she told him, leaning back against the satin-striped settee and closing her eyes a moment. "He was all kindness and compassion after Father died, but I'd seen him enough times to know he could be wily. So I wasn't surprised when he began dropping hints about me marrying Thorgood. Though I do think the viscount was surprised when I ended up in his bedchamber."

There was a thud, and she opened her eyes to find he'd dropped one of his boots on the carpet and was staring at her.

"His bedchamber?" he asked.

She shook her head, remembering. "We'd gone to the country house in Somerset, my first visit, and the earl led me up to what was supposed to be my bedchamber to change for dinner. He'd even told Patsy to go there, then sent for her on some excuse. I was partly undressed when Thorgood walked in. I think the earl expected me to seize my good fortune, claim ruin, and demand a wedding. I told Thorgood to find somewhere else to change. He was very good about it."

He chuckled as he bent to remove the other boot. "He wanted to marry even less than you did. He still mourns his first wife's passing."

She watched him as he tugged at the black leather. "Do you?"

He raised his head. "No. I long since realized my infatuation with Felicity was exactly that—a boy's first love. It saddens me she died so young, leaving behind a husband and daughter who adored her. But I don't mourn her the way Thorgood does."

She should not be so relieved to hear that, but at least if his heart had not gone to the grave with Lord Thorgood's wife, he was free to give it to another.

Namely, her.

# CHAPTER NINETEEN

JAMES WASN'T SURPRISED THAT EVA slept late the next morning. He'd also had a little trouble waking after a difficult night. Today they would have to settle many matters—the earl, Priestly's possible connection, the French spies.

And his growing feelings for Eva.

He could admit it only to himself. He was coming to care for her. Since Felicity's defection, he had never allowed himself to feel for another. It was safer, for him and for the lady. Yet Eva engaged every emotion: joy, hope, love. And fear. The bright future they had envisioned was so close. He knew how easily it could be taken from them.

Yet how could he hold her at arm's length? She was sunlight, burning through the fog around him. He wanted to open his heart to her. He wanted to feel love in all its messy, marvelous entanglements. She'd taken a tremendous risk on him. He wanted to prove to her that her faith was justified.

He'd agreed to a marriage of convenience. Would she think he'd tricked her if he suggested they make a real marriage instead?

Pym had poked up the fire and brought James tea and toast with jam when Eva ambled out of her bedchamber in her dressing gown and stockinged feet. He felt a little guilty that he'd managed to save his boots and not her slippers. Still, her wiggling toes looked rather endearing as she moved toward him.

Blinking against the sunlight streaming through the windows, she perched beside him, hairbrush in her grip.

"What now?" she asked.

He allowed his gaze to linger on the tousled mass of her hair. The urge to touch, to stroke, had only grown. He forced himself to focus on her question.

"Now I expect an inquisition from his lordship," he said.

Despite his intentions, she must have noticed his look, for she touched the billowing curls, cheeks pinking. "Sorry. I hadn't had a chance to tame it yet."

And he had no desire to see it tamed. He held out his hand. "May I?"

She sat back, slight frown on her brow. If she could not trust him with this simple task, what hope did he have?

As if she saw the questions behind his eyes, she slowly offered him the brush. "Careful. It fights back."

He accepted the brush with a solemn nod. She turned her back on him, as if to give him better access.

He ran the brush gently through the dark waves. They sprang from his touch, like a young colt, eager to prance. He caught her wincing and slowed his efforts. The thick curls were soft, yet strong, like Eva herself.

She shifted on the seat. "Perhaps I should finish the task."

Reluctantly, he returned the brush. "As you wish."

As she accepted the brush, Pym trotted into the room. "His lordship ordered a big breakfast and is waiting on you below."

"How very thoughtful of him," Eva said, swinging the brush back and forth by its handle. "Please inform his lordship we have other plans."

Pym set about his hopping from foot to foot. "I'd be delighted, Mrs. Howland, but perhaps he would take it better if you told him yourself."

"Oh, I can assure you he'll take it better from you," Eva said, eyes narrowing.

James put out his hand to still the brush. "I'll speak to him, Pym. That will be all."

His man-of-all-work offered a grateful smile before leaving.

"You don't have to rescue everyone," Eva said.

"And neither should Pym bear my punishment," James countered. "I share your desire to rid ourselves of the earl once and for all, but nettling him won't serve that purpose."

"It might make the process more enjoyable," Eva suggested.

When he eyed her, she laughed. "Oh, very well. I'll do my best to be polite. But we need a plan, James. Either we tell him about the boat and your suspicions of a French incursion, or we force him out of the castle so you can investigate further."

"Let's try the latter," James said. "He never liked rusticating here. Perhaps we can pluck that string."

Eva smiled. "I'm rather good at plucking strings."

Not, unfortunately, when it came to the earl. He was wrapped in a thick wool banyan when they came downstairs, as if the sunny day had grown chill. As he sat at the head of the table in the great hall, the hand that held his toast was trembling.

"I wasn't sure you were coming," he complained as Eva and James took seats at one side of the table. "Your mother insisted on a tray in her room."

"Well, it is our honeymoon," Eva said with a treacle-sweet smile to James.

"You needn't posture," the earl said, fork stabbing a plump sausage. "I know it's not a love match."

Eva fluttered her lashes at him. "Now, who would have

told you that?"

James watched him. He merely chewed a moment before answering.

"I have many friends in the village, dear. Ask James.

Eva's gaze darted to him, and he nearly slumped at the doubt that had crept in.

"I was not aware you corresponded with anyone but me," James said.

"You are not aware of many things," the earl replied. He nodded to the dish of coddled eggs. "Do fill your plate, Eva. I'm sure you must be hungry."

Eva speared a sausage instead.

"Was there a reason you decided to stay in Grace-by-the-Sea?" James asked, reluctantly filling his own plate. "The London Season won't end for another month."

"And Lady Howland must miss your company," Eva put in.

"I will return in good time," the earl said. "I haven't visited the spa in ages. I thought it time, what with the new physician. You will join me."

It wasn't a question. But tarry at the spa? Not when he had so many other matters to attend to. Yet who knew what the earl might get up to if James left him to his own devices.

Something pressed against his foot, a gentle touch. He glanced at Eva, surprised. Her gaze was on the earl.

"I'd be delighted to join you," she said. "Though you may find it thin of company. The other guests seem slow to accept Doctor Bennett."

"Your company will be all I need," the earl assured her.

James nearly choked on his eggs.

"Good," Eva said, spooning up some eggs herself. "Then James can attend to his other business in the village."

The minx! She'd manipulated the earl brilliantly. As if he noticed as well, the earl narrowed his eyes. "Business?"

"I must reinstate the lease," James said. "And there are some other matters that must be accomplished to leave everything for your new steward."

The earl sat back. "New steward? Are you resigning your position?"

Before the earl could sack him, certainly. "It seemed appropriate under the circumstances."

"Nonsense." The earl returned to his meal as if the decision had been made. "It would be impossible to replace you. You know too much about the various properties."

"So I understand," Eva said with a triumphant smile to James. "Now, off you go. So much to do."

James leaned over and pressed a kiss to her cheek. "Are you certain?" he murmured.

"I'll miss you too, dearest," she said. "But I'll make sure your cousin has an interesting time at the spa."

That was what he feared.

There. At least this time she could take comfort in the fact that she had rescued James. The worry on his face had nearly given away the game, but he reluctantly excused himself. She could only hope he would use the time to speak to Mr. Priestly and Mr. Denby about what they'd learned.

And perhaps a little time thinking about her.

She still could not believe he'd wanted to brush her hair. She liked her curls, but, from her first nurse to Patsy, every other lady in her life had complained about them. His reverent touch had stirred something deep inside her. Oh, to feel so admired, so loved.

"I must congratulate you," the earl said, bringing her back to the present. "I didn't think he could be so easily swayed."

"He's stronger than you know," Eva said. She dug into

her coddled eggs.

"So, apparently, are you," the earl said, watching her.

Eva refused to acknowledge the comment. She finished eating then rose. "If you'll excuse me, I should prepare to accompany you down the headland." She left before he could respond.

When she returned a short time later, serpentine redingote covering her pink sprigged-muslin gown, she found the carriage waiting. It seemed the earl walked nowhere, unlike most of the visitors to the spa. Was he intent on causing a stir?

"Lady Howland sends her greetings," he said as they set out. He had replaced the banyan with a tailored black coat and breeches. "She misses your company, as do Thorgood and my granddaughter."

"A shame you decided I had to leave, then," Eva said, turning her gaze to the trees.

"A decision I deeply regret," the earl assured her.

Because it had turned out to her benefit, but she couldn't bring herself to say that to him.

"I am always amazed how small the village is," the earl mused as they started down from the headland. "We could put every house in a tiny corner of London and still have room for more."

She'd once thought as much, but she could not agree with him now. "And yet *I* am continually amazed by the size of its people's hearts. They have certainly made me feel welcome."

"Position and wealth generally have that effect," he said. "At least, on the surface."

He was determined to be a raincloud on her summer day. She scowled at him. "I did not advertise my wealth, unlike some."

He smiled. "You didn't have to. Quality will out, my dear."

She was quite glad when the carriage stopped at the spa and she could put a little distance between them.

Doctor Bennett was speaking with Mrs. North and her son when Eva and the earl entered. The Norths were the only ones in residence. The breeze from the door ruffled the pages on the big book at sat at Jesslyn's desk, and water dribbled down into the fountain as if it were weeping.

The earl went to sit on one of the wicker chairs.

"Enjoy yourself," he ordered Eva, as if he expected her to perform for him.

Eva turned her back on him and went to join the Norths and Doctor Bennett.

"Where is everyone?" she asked after exchanging greetings.

"Everyone who is anyone is here," Mr. North drawled, swinging his quizzing glass.

"Oh, really, Dickie," his mother scolded. She turned to Eva. "I was just explaining to Doctor Bennett. The others seemed determined to buttress Miss Chance. I could not convince them to return. And now Dickie and I will be leaving on the afternoon stage."

"Great deal of bother," Dickie grumbled. He sounded like Patsy.

"I have not had the luxury of leaving the spa to go in search of Miss Chance," Doctor Bennett confirmed. "And my free time has been taken up in trying to settle into the village. But I am certain we can resolve this issue. Now, pray excuse me while I speak with our other guest."

Eva almost told him not to bother, but she glanced at the earl to find that he had leaned back in the chair and closed his eyes. Perhaps it was the blue of the walls, but his complexion looked almost grey.

"Of course," she said, and the doctor took himself off.

Dickie North offered Eva his arm. "Would you favor me with a promenade, Mrs. Howland?"

Rude to refuse, especially when his mother was beaming as if Eva was an old friend. Eva agreed, and they commenced strolling past the lonely wicker chairs staring out at the sea.

He prosed on about his horses and the weather, and she offered approbation or commiseration, as appropriate. But the conversation was sufficiently unengaging that she could allow her mind to wander. Perhaps that was why she noticed when others joined them.

The first was Mr. Harris. He went straight to Mrs. North and spoke at some length, and she could only conclude he was bringing her a message from Miss Chance and the other refugees from the spa. The second was Mrs. Greer, and she made her way to Eva's side, forcing Dickie to a halt in both his stride and his monologue.

"Mrs. Howland!" the spa president's wife gushed. "What a delight to find you here."

"Mrs. Greer," Eva acknowledged. "Do you know Mr. North? This is his last day with us."

Mrs. Greer didn't so much as glance his way. "Good journey, sir. Now, Mrs. Howland, you must tell me. How is the earl enjoying his sojourn? Is there anything we can do to make him welcome?"

Dickie lifted his chin as far as his complicated cravat would allow and stalked off. Mrs. Greer did not appear to notice. Her gaze was fastened on Eva's face, as if she waited for a word from a master.

Eva glanced to the earl. Doctor Bennett had evidently prescribed a dose of spa water, for the earl held a crystal glass in his hand. The way he frowned down into it, however, told her he had little intention of actually partaking of the waters.

"I believe he is sufficient," she told Mrs. Greer. "But thank you for asking."

She peered at Eva. "Perhaps I should ask him myself, just

to be certain."

James had said people tried to reach the earl through him. It would serve the old codger right if Eva introduced Mrs. Greer to him. Someone would end up getting the cut direct. She glanced the earl's way again.

Mr. Harris had moved to his side and was conversing earnestly, the earl nodding along. Then the Newcomer bowed and left.

Interesting. Never in her wildest dreams had she considered that the most popular fellow at the spa would be the earl.

She pasted on a smile. "I think that's a marvelous idea, Mrs. Greer. Allow me to make you known to him. I'm sure he'd like to hear all about life in Grace-by-the-Sea."

# CHAPTER TWENTY

JAMES MADE USE OF THE time Eva had given him. He alerted Quill as to what they had found in the caves, then did the same with Lark. He found the latter at the Mermaid Inn near the shore.

"Only a while longer," he told James when they sat at a table to the back of the public room. "When Jesslyn and I marry next week, I can move into Shell Cottage with her. We've already fitted out a study. Until then, you sit in my office along with anyone else who fancies a bite."

Laughter rang out from a group of fishermen near the long counter that bisected the space.

"It isn't ideal," James agreed. "But it will have to do." He set about explaining what he and Eva had discovered.

Lark blew out a breath. "I cannot like it, especially after that cipher Aunt Maudie found. Mr. Carroll mentioned he may be getting close to solving it."

"Good," James said. "That may tell us more about our unseen visitors."

"In the meantime," Lark said, "I'll send word to the Excise Office to see if we can step up patrols by the revenue cutters."

James thanked him and left.

His next stop was the flat above Mr. Carroll's Curiosities, where Priestly lived. It was only a simple sitting room, the bedchamber just beyond. James had given his secretary a holiday after the wedding, but he found Priestly in his rooms, tea things on a table by the window and pot steaming.

"May I offer you anything, sir?" he asked after welcoming James.

"No, thank you," James said. "I came with a question for you, Priestly. If you had a choice, would you prefer to work for the earl, or me?"

Priestly didn't hesitate. "You, assuredly, sir. The earl always put me in a bit of a pucker."

James cocked his head. "Enough so that you would fear to disobey him?"

Priestly blinked. "Yes, that is no. What are you asking?"

"Someone told the earl Eva and I planned to marry," James explained. "You were one of the few who knew both the wedding date and how to contact the earl."

He washed red. "I would never... That is, how could you..." He paused to tug down on his plain blue waistcoat. "If I have ever given less than satisfactory service, sir, I will tender my resignation immediately."

"I don't want you to quit, Priestly," James said. "I want the truth."

His face tightened. "That is the truth. I would never betray you to the earl. If you cannot believe that, then perhaps it's best if you find another secretary."

In the end, James managed to convince him that he believed his innocence. Yet as he left, he could not think of anyone else who might have had the knowledge and access to the earl. He left the village wondering which pair of eyes was watching his every move.

Eva and the earl had returned from the spa by the time James reached the castle. It was a long afternoon and evening. The earl was complaining and capricious, but he insisted on their company, and James could not decamp without leaving his mother at the fellow's mercy. As it was, she clung to Eva as if afraid of blowing away otherwise. He could only be relieved when his lordship called for an early night. Only then could he catch Eva up on what he'd learned.

She'd curled up on the settee in their sitting room, toes tucked under her wrapper, body leaning against his, and he could imagine an endless number of nights like this—sharing their days, their hopes and dreams.

"So, we have nothing more to go on," she summarized when James had finished.

Her clean apple scent teased his nose. "Unfortunately, no. But I thought I detected a new level of frustration in the earl tonight. He may be convinced to leave soon."

"From sheer boredom if nothing else." She yawned. "Forgive me, James, but I must sleep. I'll see you in the morning."

Cold air rushed over him as she pulled away and rose. It was nothing to the yearning inside him as she padded to her room.

"It isn't hopeless, sir," Pym said, coming through to bank the fire.

James straightened. "I never said it was. I have high confidence we'll best the earl yet."

Pym smiled as he bent over the hearth. "Not with the earl. With Miss Eva."

James glanced toward the door to her room. "You think so?"

Pym set down the poker. "I think she's quite taken with you. I'd certainly like to see you happy before I go."

James eyed him. Was that short frame more bowed than he remembered? "Why, Pym, are you planning to retire at last?"

He winked at James. "You never know. Now, may I help you with your boots? I couldn't find them last night, and I'm sure they could do with a good polish."

"I'm not ready for bed just yet," James said. "But I'll be sure to leave them outside my door."

After his man left, he waited until the house was quiet, then ventured down to the caves. The boat still sat at the high-water mark, as if taunting him. He thought it would be a long night as well.

Eva was up ahead of him the next day. She was already dressed in a pretty pink muslin gown, and her hair was piled up behind her. He came to wish her good morning.

She patted the seat beside her. "Will you sit? We must talk."

Something pressed down on his shoulders, and he sat more heavily than he had intended. "What about?"

She fiddled with her cuff, as if studying it for flaws. "We must, of course, deal with the earl, and with the matter of who has been using the castle. But another thought kept me awake last night. What is to become of us, James? Our marriage, our future?"

Could she have reached the same conclusion he had? His pulse quickened, and he twisted his neck to see up into her face. It was pale, as if she hurt. Disappointment tugged on him.

"What's wrong, Eva?" he asked. "Are you regretting our decision already?"

"No," she hurried to assure him. "Well, yes, but not for the reason you might think."

He straightened. "And what do you believe I think?"

She licked her lips, drawing his attention to the pink. "You might think I regret pledging myself to a Howland." She glanced up to meet his gaze, her own wide and bright.

"And I don't, James, because it's not any Howland. It's you. What I regret is agreeing to a marriage of convenience."

Something shot through him, like sunlight stabbing into the darkness. But before he could respond, someone rapped at the door, and Yeager hurried in.

"Forgive me, ma'am, sir. It's the earl. He's had some sort of attack. Pym's gone for the new doctor. His lordship is asking for your company, Mr. Howland."

James shook his head. "Of course he is. Did you believe for one minute he was telling the truth? He's merely trying to garner sympathy."

Yeager made a face. "I did wonder, sir, but he should have acted at Drury Lane, he's that convincing."

"He would be." James nodded to Eva. "I'll deal with this."

"Be careful," she said as he rose, "and let me know if you require reinforcement."

He smiled his thanks and followed Yeager from the room.

The earl had taken a large suite with its own sitting room on the same side of the castle as the room James had originally been using. James found his lordship's valet and a footman in attendance. Lying on the great box bed, his face pinched and grey, the earl looked surprisingly frail. Very likely he'd planned it that way.

"James, my boy," he said. "Thank you for coming. The rest of you may go."

Even said feebly, the statement was a command. The servants trickled from the room, Yeager with a commiserating look to James.

"Yesterday too much for you?" James asked, venturing closer.

The earl slowly turned his head to look at him, as if even that little movement was an effort. But the blue eyes were as piercing as always.

"Yes, if you must know," he said. "My physicians advised me against travel of any sort. The trip from London followed by the exertions of the wedding and the constant attention to my duty took their toll." He nodded toward the chair that had been drawn up near the bed. "Sit down. I won't crane my neck to converse with you."

Of course not. James took a seat.

The earl drew in a breath, chest shaking in the effort. "Now, before that ham-handed country physician arrives, I will have your promise, sir."

"What promise?" James asked, crossing one leg over the other. "I thought Eva and I made it clear we need no blessing from you. We owe you nothing in return."

"Some might disagree," he said. He aimed his gaze at the canopy as if evoking Heaven's help. "I am still her trustee."

"Only until we provide evidence of our marriage," James said. "Then Eva and I control her fortune."

"You mean *you* control it," he spat out, gaze spearing back to James and fire dancing in the blue. "That isn't lost on me, boy. You've played your hand masterfully. I've tried being conciliatory, but you'll clearly have none of it. Yet you forget—you're still a Howland."

"Howland is my surname," James acknowledged. "A fact that I regret some days. But you can no longer use it as a sword hanging over me."

"If not a sword, then a cudgel." He paused to cough, and red drops appeared on his fingers.

James stiffened. Everything else about his supposed sickness the earl might contrive, but blood?

As if ashamed of the matter, he quickly tucked his hand under the covers. "You have some affection for Thorgood, I believe."

James steeled himself. "The viscount and I have always been on good terms."

"And Lady Miranda, so much like her dear mother?"

He could feel the noose tightening. "Of course."

"Then surely you would not see them penniless."

"Hardly penniless," James pointed out. "You have the house in London, the country estate in Somerset, the castle."

"And little left to support them." His voice was heavy with sorrow. "The castle here is entailed, but we may have to sell the rest. Why do you think I ordered you not to start a militia? The leader is generally required to pay some of the cost. We no longer have that luxury. The crops have done poorly the last few years. My investments began to sour the moment that Irishman died."

He likely meant Eva's father. "I have seen little trace of penury here in Dorset."

"Which tells me I have undervalued your abilities," the earl assured him. "All I ask is that you use those abilities and your newfound wealth to benefit your family."

James leaned back in the chair. "You just admitted you invested poorly. Why would I pour Eva's money after bad?"

His gaze darkened. "Everything you have you owe to me—your position, your income, your very name. You will do as I say."

James rose. "That argument no longer sways me. I will leave you to recover."

"Wait!"

Turning for the door, James paused and looked back at the earl. He had propped himself up, and sweat stood out on his brow. Seeing he had James's attention, he collapsed back against the pillow.

"I'm dying," he said, tugging the covers closer. "The fools in London give me another month at most. That chit was my last hope of leaving my son and granddaughter solvent. You stole that from us."

"*That chit* is my wife," James said. "Her name is Eva, and she deserves far more than to be some pawn in your game. If you wish to lay blame for this mess you're in, I suggest you look in the mirror."

The door opened then, and the earl's valet hurried in with the doctor. "Doctor Bennett, my lord."

James intercepted the physician as he straightened from his bow. "My cousin tells me he is dying and has little time left. I would appreciate your thoughts on the matter."

Doctor Bennett searched his face as if looking for motive. "Of course, Magistrate. If you would give me a moment."

James withdrew to the other side of the room, but he wasn't about to leave. He knew how easily the earl might convince the doctor to further his lies. He watched as Doctor Bennett listened to the earl's heart and chest, checked his pulse, and peered into his eyes, nose, and mouth. Then he stepped back and considered the man on the bed.

"Let me be clear," he told the earl in a voice designed to carry. "My obligation is to my patient first. I expressed my concern for your health when you visited the spa yesterday, but you assured me your physicians had the matter in hand. What have they told you?"

"A scirrhus of my lungs," the earl admitted. "Tending toward the cancer. It's in its final stages. We've managed to keep it quiet, but I imagine that won't be possible now." He shot James a malevolent glance.

"Based on a limited examination, I must concur with their diagnosis," Doctor Bennet said. "Peruvian bark may give you some relief for a time. I'll prepare a mixture and send it up to the castle. Do you have laudanum?"

The earl nodded.

"Then there's nothing more I can do." He turned to James. "Does that satisfy you, Mr. Howland?"

James's throat felt tight. "Yes, thank you, Doctor Bennett. I'll see you out."

"Think on what I said," the earl called after them.

As if James would think of anything else.

Eva had breakfasted on tea and wonderful jelly rolls from Mr. Ellison's bakery, and still there was no sign of James. But something was going on. A steady stream of servants had traipsed up and down the stairs. And, when Eva had poked her head out the door, she'd sighted Mr. Pym and Doctor Bennett heading toward the opposite end of the corridor.

"What's happened?" she asked Patsy when her maid came to retrieve the breakfast dishes.

"It's the earl," Patsy whispered, as if she thought he was listening just outside the door. "His valet, Mr. Simmons, won't confirm it, but I think he's dying."

Much as Eva disliked the earl, she couldn't wish that on him. And she couldn't quite believe it, either.

A footman appeared in the doorway. She seemed to recall him from the earl's London house. "Pardon me, Mrs. Howland. There's a lady here to see you, a Mrs. Catchpole. She says it's about the staff."

Patsy drew herself up. "The missus has all the staff she needs, thank you very much."

"It depends on how big a house we take," Eva reminded her. "And Mother Howland is still seeking a cook so Mr. Pym doesn't have so many tasks." She turned to the footman. "Ask her to wait in the great hall. I'll be right down."

Patsy pouted, as if she was certain Eva intended to hire a new lady's maid, but she hurried to do her job and left.

James's mother was in the corridor when Eva exited her room. Gowned in a simple lavender dress with a white tucker, greying hair curled loosely and wrapped in a bandeau, she looked as if she'd lost her way.

"Is it true?" she asked, face puckered. "Is his lordship about to leave us?"

"If you mean as he returns to London, I certainly hope so," Eva told her. "But as to anything else, I know as little as you do."

She bit her lip, gaze dropping.

Eva touched her hand, bringing her gaze up again. "I was never clear—where did your lovely harp end up with all our packing and unpacking?"

She blinked. "Why, I think I saw it in the music room. I could play."

Eva smiled. "You certainly could. It would do us all good to hear it."

Still she hesitated. "If you're sure the earl wouldn't mind."

"If he minds, he can tell us," Eva said.

They continued down the stairs together, then separated as Mrs. Howland headed for the music room. Eva caught her glancing around as if to make sure no one else noticed.

At least marrying James had prevented Eva from developing that habit.

She pasted on a smile for the woman who was waiting for her. Young, buxom, with brown eyes sparkling with interest, she dropped a hasty curtsey.

"Mrs. Howland. Thank you for seeing me. I wouldn't have troubled you, but I recently discovered something of concern regarding the castle, and I thought I should bring it to your attention."

Was she about to relate something about the spies or Captain St. Claire? Eva took her arm and drew her closer to the fire, then held out her hands as if its warmth was the only thing that had attracted her.

"Forgive me, Mrs. Catchpole, but how are you connected with the castle?" Eva asked, keeping her voice low and steady.

"Oh, sorry!" She smiled. "Mr. Bent, the previous staffing agent, retired. The Spa Corporation appointed me to take his place." She laughed. "You should have seen me mum's face when I told her. Me, in charge of assigning staff to all the best people. Imagine!"

Eva smiled despite herself. "I'm sure they have the utmost faith in you to put you in the position. We don't need additional staff at the moment, though."

She hitched up her gown. "Oh, I thought as much. The earl usually brings his own, from what I've been told. No, I wanted to talk to you because we seem to have lost the key."

Eva blinked. "The key?"

"To the castle." She scrunched up her face. "Bit of a dust up there. It seems the magistrate gave Mr. Bent a key so he could send maids to clean from time to time. The last was Mrs. Bascom, who has left the area. And no one's seen the key since. I searched high and low, I can tell you."

"You think she took it with her?" Eva asked.

She shook her head, golden ringlets bobbing. "She was always a good worker, that one. We cleaned together at the Lodge from time to time. Very conscientious. Even brought a little can to oil hinges and such. But, given the trouble with her husband, I'm afeared that key ended up in the wrong hands."

Eva was missing something. "The trouble with her husband? Was he a servant as well?"

"Oh, no, Mrs. Howland." Like James's mother, she glanced in each direction before leaning closer, and the scent of roses washed over Eva. "He was a smuggler," she whispered, "part of the band the magistrate and the militia captured last month. What if he took the key with him?"

What if he'd done more? Could Mr. Bascom have been the one who had given the French access to the castle?

"Thank you for bringing this to my attention, Mrs. Catchpole," she said. "You can be sure I will discuss the matter with Mr. Howland and the earl."

She grimaced as she straightened. "Well, you needn't tell the earl unless you feel you must. He's not one to forgive, is he now? But if you must tell him, let him know that we had no reason to suspect Meg Bascom nor her husband. She never gave the least trouble. And none of us was aware of her husband's unsavory pastimes."

And still probably didn't know the extent of them. "You needn't worry. I won't mention the matter to the earl unless needs require. I'm not privy to his plans, and my husband and I haven't settled on our staffing needs, but we will contact you when we're certain. Please let me know if you should locate that key."

"Oh, I will," she promised. "And thank you." She curtsied. As she rose, her smile brightened.

"Now, there's a sight any lady might sigh over."

Eva turned to find James and Doctor Bennett coming down the stairs. They did rather make a pair—both handsome, both distinguished. But James seemed the more vibrant. She could feel his strength, his determination as they reached the great hall.

Mrs. Catchpole hurried for the kitchens, offering a sassy smile to both gentlemen as she passed. Eva went to meet them.

"Everything all right?" she asked, glancing from one to the other.

"The earl is resting comfortably for now," Doctor Bennett said. "I'll leave the magistrate to explain the details." He bowed to Eva. "It was very good to see you again, Mrs. Howland. I hope you'll both visit the spa when time allows."

"Sir," Eva said with a nod.

He saw himself to the door.

"What did he say?" Eva asked. "Did he find anything the least wrong with the earl?"

"More than I expected," James said, hand rubbing the back of his neck. "Come with me to our sitting room. You were right. We must talk."

# CHAPTER TWENTY-ONE

JAMES LED EVA BACK TO their sitting room and closed the door behind her. He then checked the bedchambers on either side to be sure none of the servants was about.

"Why the need for secrecy?" Eva asked, going to the settee. "What you know, the servants know. I realized that ages ago."

"The servants will shortly know that the earl is dying," James said, coming to join her, "but I'd rather they not know what I'm considering doing about it."

Her eyes widened. "He really is ill?"

James nodded. "A scirrhus of his lungs."

She shuddered at the mention of the deadly internal growth.

"Advanced, as I understand it," James added. "He claims he has no more than a month to live."

She clasped her hands in her lap, face falling. "Oh, James, I'm so sorry. I know he's done terrible things, but he is part of your family."

"He is, whether I like it or not," James agreed. "My concern now is for Thorgood and Miranda. The earl claims he's mismanaged the funds, and they are close to destitute."

"That can't be right," she said with a frown. "The earl was one of my father's wealthiest clients."

"I'm guessing he disregarded your father's advice after

he passed."

"Arrogant," she said with a sigh. "It probably galled him that anyone else might know more. So, how bad is it?"

"If he's telling the truth, economies will have to be taken," James explained. "The London house and the estate in Somerset may have to be sold."

"That's temporary," she pointed out. "You're liquidating assets rather than building a stable foundation."

He couldn't help his smile of pride. "Sounds like your father wasn't the only financial genius in the family."

Her cheeks pinked. "I may have learned a thing or two along the way, but my father never intended me to take over for him. I can point you to some other gentlemen he respected. They could help you determine what must be done."

"I wouldn't want to enlist their aid until I know the whole of the problem. But it does sound as if funds will be needed and soon. The earl accused me of stealing his only hope—having Thorgood marry you."

She snorted. "If that was the best he could do, he's in poor shape indeed."

"Still, I share his concern. I will not see Thorgood and Lady Miranda suffer for his negligence."

She cocked her head, sending curls tumbling down one cheek. "What can you do?"

He sighed. "I don't know. I could return to London with him, review the ledgers to see if I can find something he missed. But I don't like leaving you here, especially when we suspect the French of infiltrating the area."

"Speaking of which, the new employment agent was just here. She lost the key used by her staff to come clean the castle, and she suspects one of the maids, a Mrs. Bascom, might have given it to her husband, the smuggler."

"She might indeed," James said. "And that would explain why the light first appeared in the castle window as well.

Mrs. Bascom was signaling her husband at sea."

"But did he ultimately give her key to someone else?" she asked.

"Someone with ties to the French." Frustration pushed him out of his seat. "But we still don't know who or why they were leaving ciphers in the castle."

"And who brought that boat into the caves," Eva added.

"They must be near," James said, starting to pace. "I should rally the militia. This is one of the reasons they were formed."

She rose as well. "Only a few will know of the earl's predicament. Catch the spies first, then deal with the family crisis."

"Logical," he allowed. He stopped and ran a hand back through his hair. "But I cannot shake the feeling that the family crisis is more urgent than we know. Why else would the earl risk coming all this way as sick as he is?"

She nodded. "You need money, immediately."

"I suppose I do."

She waited, as if she expected him to announce some grand scheme to raise funds. Short of selling off assets, he had no such plan.

"There's another way," she said. "My fortune."

"No," James said. "That money is yours. I thought we agreed on that."

"So did I. We married to ensure our freedom from the earl. I find myself under another yoke, that of trust. I want to trust you, James, but I struggle."

He had hoped they had come farther. "I can see why it would be difficult to trust a Howland, but I had thought you'd made an exception for me."

"And so I have." She crossed to her bedchamber.

He frowned after her, not sure of her intentions. All he could think was that he'd failed—his village, his family, and the woman he was coming to love.

Eva returned with a sheaf of parchment.

"What's that?" he asked as she started for the hearth.

"Our agreement." She rolled the pages together and stuck them into the fire.

James jerked forward. "Eva!"

She turned to him, face resolute, as the heat caught the paper and sent flames licking upward. "No, James. It's done. I give you full control of my fortune. Use it to save Thorgood and Lady Miranda. They are my family now too."

"Eva." Could she hear the admiration in his voice? He stepped up to her, put his hands on her shoulders. "You didn't have to do that."

She nodded, curls trembling. "I did. I'm falling in love with you, James, and I don't want my fortune to come between us. I want you to know I trust you, with my fortune, with my heart, with my life."

He gathered her close, rested his head against hers. "Thank you, Eva. That gift is more precious than you know. I am honored by your trust, especially since I'm falling in love with you too."

"You are?" She leaned back, searching his face. It was the work of a moment to kiss her.

Once again, light and hope blossomed from her touch. She kissed him back, bright, pure, and he knew they would find a way forward.

At length she sighed, pulling back just enough to lean her head against his shoulder. "So, you'll do it? You'll use the money to help them?"

"No," he said, cradling her close. "You can use the money. What you burned was one copy, Eva. Julian Mayes has the other in London."

"Oh!" She leaned away again. "Well, we can burn it too."

James took her hands in his. "No, Eva. We keep the arrangement. I never want you to worry about whether I'm after your fortune. Once we determine how bad things are for Thorgood and Miranda, you can decide how to help them. And thank you."

Her lower lip trembled, and he had to kiss her again. They had a chance for a real marriage, and he would be forever grateful.

Eva could have stayed in James's embrace—protected, cherished—forever. But they still had far to go to unravel this mess.

She made herself step out of reach. "So, we are agreed how to deal with the financial crisis, if there is one. We should tell the earl."

He was watching her as if he'd very much like to resume their kisses. Her heart whispered the same longing. She turned to the fire and hoped he'd think the heat had brought the color to her cheeks.

"Telling him would probably keep him from ruminating," he allowed.

"And possibly from plotting more interference," Eva added. She glanced at him in time to see him smile. To think, such a look might be hers for always.

*For better, for worse...*

"I wouldn't wager on that," he said. "The earl gains too much pleasure from manipulating people. I trust you will never let me grow that toplofty."

Eva laughed. "But James, you're one of the most toplofty fellows I know. It's part of your charm."

He laughed as well.

Their plan decided, they went to see the earl. His valet met them at the door.

"He's sleeping," he reported in a whisper. "I don't expect him to wake until after tea."

"If he wakes before we return," James told him, "let him know that Eva and I are ready to do our part to help the family."

The valet looked a bit mystified, but he agreed to relay the message.

They next went to find Mother Howland. She was just draping her harp, her hands gentle, tender.

"James, Eva," she greeted them, straightening. "How are you? How is the earl?"

James led her back to the withdrawing room and over to the settee, then waited until she and Eva had sat side by side before answering. "Eva and I are fine, Mother. But our plans may have to change. The earl is dying. He may not have much time left."

She pressed her fingers to her lips a moment. "Will he return to London?" she asked as she lowered her hand.

"If I know him, he will insist on it," James said.

She nodded. "Then I will go with him. The countess will need me."

Eva put out a hand. "She was never particularly kind to you that I could see, Mother Howland. You don't owe her a duty."

"Certainly I do," she said. Her warm gaze brushed Eva as gently as her hands had draped the instrument they both loved. "The duty we all owe each other—care, respect, kindness. She will not know what to do with herself when the earl passes. I can help her, Thorgood, and dear Lady Miranda."

Eva patted her arm. "Know that you take my respect and admiration with you."

Her cheeks turned red. She looked to James. "If I must be there long, will you send my harp to me? I've missed it so."

"We'll make sure you have it," James promised.

"In the meantime," Eva said, "could you bear to keep an eye on the earl now? James and I have business in the village."

James looked at her askance, but his mother answered readily. "Of course. And I do hope you'll be able to take Butterfly Manor after all. I was always happy there. I know you would be too."

Eva hugged her. "I look forward to sharing that happiness with you."

Mrs. Howland beamed.

They returned to the great hall, where James stopped her with a hand on her arm. "What are you up to, Eva?"

There was no concern in the question, only curiosity, and, she thought, a willingness to assist, whatever she suggested.

She pressed his hand on her arm. "You've had to fight too long alone. You have help—me, Captain St. Claire, Mr. Denby, Jesslyn, Abigail, and Maudie, to name a few. Our mysterious visitor may be gathering allies, if that boat is any indication. We should do the same."

James lifted her hand to press a kiss against her knuckles. "I would follow you, madam, to the ends of the earth."

She could lose herself in that gaze. "You needn't go so far, sir. The village will do."

Having left the castle and its dying owner behind, Linus Bennett frowned at the sign over the door of the shop in the middle of the village. All the Colors of the Sea. He hadn't lived along the sea until now, but he hadn't thought there were all that many colors associated with it. And why name a shop that way? It provided no guidance as to what was inside, though he could see an eclectic collection of goods displayed in the window. Still, this was the location given by the lady who had responded to his advertisement in the local weekly newspaper about caring for Ethan.

He stepped inside to the chime of the shop bell. Miss Archer came through a curtained doorway. One look at him, and she jerked to a stop, smile of welcome fading.

"You," she said.

Linus bowed. "Miss Archer. Forgive me for troubling you. I must have gone to the wrong address."

He started to turn, but her voice made him hesitate. "Who were you seeking, sir?"

He held up the letter he had received. "That's just it. She doesn't provide a name, but she is apparently interested in caring for my son, and she seems to have some qualifications."

She frowned as she moved to join him. "That cannot be right. Let me see it."

He was almost afraid to hand her the paper with that militant look in her eye, but he held it out, and she scanned over the contents. Her head came up. "Wait here."

Mystified, he could only nod as she stalked back across the shop and disappeared through the curtain.

He glanced around. Interesting place. One table held tatted collars for lady's dresses, another leather goods of various sorts, and still another wrought-iron wall sconces. And the paintings…

He wandered closer despite himself. He'd been wrong. The sea held a myriad of colors and moods, and each had been painstakingly rendered in the pieces before him. Some showed power—waves high and curled, splashing as they crashed into the Dorset cliffs. Others held peace— sun beaming through parting clouds, water soft and misty. And one showed a light gleaming in the castle, offering hope in the darkness. It was as if the painter had reached inside his chest, touched his heart.

"Doctor Bennett?"

He pulled himself back from a great distance to raise his head and acknowledge the call. A slight woman with tightly curled white hair and great brown eyes regarded him steadily, Miss Archer, still frowning, right behind.

"I'm Mrs. Archer," the older woman explained when he met her gaze. "I wrote to you because I thought I might be able to help with your son. I raised two children of my own. I used to help at the church school Mr. Wingate, our vicar, holds during the winter. My days are rather lonely now. I thought your son and I could do each other good."

Miss Archer's face fell. "Oh, Mother, I didn't realize you were lonely."

Her mother smiled at her. "It's all right, dear. I know you have work to do with your paintings. I wouldn't have a home but for you. I just wanted to be useful."

*Her* paintings? Linus's gaze darted from the masterpieces to the ginger-haired lady who had gathered her mother close. What a remarkable woman.

But that didn't mean her mother had the temperament to care for Ethan. His son had always been the quiet sort, and his mother's death had only driven him deeper. Still, Mrs. Archer looked so hopeful as she disengaged from her daughter that he had to try.

"Perhaps you could come by tonight or after services on Sunday," Linus told the older woman. "That way you can determine if you and Ethan will suit."

She beamed at him. "Thank you, Doctor Bennett. I'd be delighted."

He inclined his head in thanks, then turned to leave, but he could feel her daughter's gaze on him all the way out of the shop.

It took a bit of effort for Eva and James to gather all the players later afternoon, and even then they could not collect everyone. Doctor Bennett had patients to tend at the spa, some Newcomers who had just arrived, and Mr. Carroll promised to join them shortly.

"A few more moments and I will have it," he told them,

waving the cipher above a counter covered in books and journals.

And so it was by nearly evening that they arrived at Shell Cottage. The front door had a fresh coat of paint since Eva had walked past with Mrs. Kirby, and flowers were blooming in boxes under the windows.

But James's brows went up when Mr. Crabapple answered their knock.

Immediately the scrawny fellow stepped back and straightened his cravat. "Magistrate, Mrs. Howland. We were expecting Mrs. Harding."

"I'm here, Warfield." The widow sashayed up the walk and accompanied Eva and James inside.

Everyone else was already there. Lord Featherstone, the Admiral, Miss Tapper and Mrs. Baugh, Mr. Harris, Jesslyn and her brother, Lark, Abigail Archer, Quillan St. Claire, and Mr. Priestly, James's secretary, were all crowded in the little withdrawing room, until it was hard to make out the plastered walls. Maudie came to link arms with Eva. She was back in her black gowns, but she'd threaded a purple ribbon through her grey curls.

"Have you made the acquaintance of the Lady of the Tower yet?" she asked eagerly.

"No, alas," Eva admitted with a smile.

The others were waiting expectantly.

"Thank you all for coming," James told them. "And thank you, Miss Chance, for making room for us."

"The trolls were busy," Maudie confided to Eva.

"You're welcome, Magistrate," Jesslyn said with a ready smile. "How might we help you and Eva?"

"Some of you are aware of a part of this story," James began, "but allow me to summarize for the rest." His look was cool and purposeful, and Eva's heart swelled with pride.

"In the last month," he continued, "a light has appeared

in the castle window at odd times. We now believe it was lit by Mrs. Bascom, wife of Henry Bascom."

"The smuggler!" Maudie crowed.

James inclined his head. "Exactly so, Mrs. Tully. She apparently had a key to the castle so she could come in and clean. That key has gone missing, and we fear it has reached the hands of our enemies."

"French spies," Maudie put in. "I knew it."

"What's this?" Mr. Harris demanded, while everyone but the Chances, Lark, and Captain St. Claire raised voices in alarm.

James held up his hands to quiet them all. "Once again, Mrs. Tully is correct. A note was found in the castle, written in code. It may well have been placed there by a French agent. In addition, Eva and I discovered a boat in the caves under the castle. As far as I can tell, it doesn't belong to anyone in the area."

Mrs. Harding drew her shawl closer. "Are they on our shores, then?"

Before James could answer, there was a frantic pounding on the door. This time, Jesslyn went to answer. She returned a moment later, with Mr. Carroll. His coat was unbuttoned, and his glasses were askew.

He held out a piece of paper toward James. "I did it! I solved the cipher!"

The others crowded closer, voices once more raised in surprise.

James took the paper from him, Eva close to his side.

"It was substitutionary," Mr. Carroll was explaining, eyes shining. "It took a bit to work it out, but once I determined the vowels, the rest was easy."

James looked down at the words on the parchment. "Location of landing confirmed. Report number, capability of defenses so can send advance guard. Stand ready to receive."

"Capability of defenses?" Jesslyn echoed. "Who's defenses? Against what?"

"The trolls," Maudie said.

"The French," Lark corrected her, voice as solemn as a church bell. "Magistrate, the invasion is coming through Grace-by-the-Sea."

# CHAPTER TWENTY-TWO

EVERYONE STARTED TALKING AT ONCE.
"This is terrible, horrible," Mr. Crabapple lamented, hands worrying before his coat.

"We must rally for the sake of England," Lord Featherstone told him.

"No, send for the dragoons," Miss Tapper argued.

"The Royal Navy," Mrs. Baugh insisted.

"You're all off," Maudie said. "We should call for the trolls."

"Whatever you do," Quill murmured, moving closer to James, "you must have Carroll share that code with the War Office."

James held up his free hand. "Easy. We don't even know what we're dealing with."

Mr. Carroll shook his head. "I think this makes it fairly clear, Magistrate. Who else would leave such a message but the French?"

They were all nodding, even Quill.

Miss Chance stepped forward. "What can we do, Magistrate? How can we stop them from invading?"

"You can do nothing." Mr. Harris stared at them as if they were all mad. "Don't you see? A village of this size cannot fight the French army. You're already defeated, and I refuse to go down with you."

He pushed past James and Eva and slammed out of the house.

Eva glanced around. "Do you all feel that way?"

Mr. Crabapple drew himself up. "Certainly not."

"He's a Newcomer," Lord Featherstone explained with a sigh. "Nothing to be done there."

"But the rest of us stand ready to support you," Miss Chance assured James.

"The village, most of those who came for the spa," Lark agreed. "I'm sure we can even count on Doctor Bennett."

"I wouldn't go that far," Miss Archer muttered.

Quill's mouth tilted up. "It seems you have your own army, Magistrate."

James glanced around. Everywhere he looked he saw determination. These were not Newcomers. They were the friends and family of Grace-by-the-Sea. Eva was right. He was not alone. As if to prove it, she squeezed his hand.

"So," she said, "what would you have us do, husband?"

James smiled. "The French loved their revolution. Let's give them another one."

Anyone watching the castle Sunday and Monday would not have noted anything unusual. There had been a flurry of activities for nearly three weeks now. What followed was merely more of the same.

James, Eva, and his mother attended church services and were seen talking with any number of villagers. Doctor Bennett came to check on his patient on Sunday afternoon. The magistrate drilled his troops as usual on Monday morning, with the usual disarray. Quillan St. Claire called on the newlyweds later that morning. So did Abigail Archer.

Both of the Howland coaches were brought up to the door of the castle on Monday afternoon, and several servants scurried back and forth with luggage and provisions for a trip. James escorted his mother and the earl to one of the coaches, the earl leaning heavily on James's arm.

"Safe journey back to London," James called as he shut the door.

With a cry to his horses, the coachman drove them off.

James then led Eva and her maid to the other carriage, whose top had been pulled up to shield the occupants, and the kiss he shared with his bride would have left no doubt that theirs would not be a marriage of convenience much longer.

"Return to me soon, my dear," James said.

"In all haste," Eva promised.

For some reason, their coachman dallied a bit before heading for the village. Only Patsy alighted before Butterfly Manor. The other servants filed out of the castle in a line that snaked down the headland, heading for the house that would soon become the home of Mr. and Mrs. Howland. At times, it even seemed as if a few people climbed the other way. Finally, as dusk began to gather, James himself locked the door and rode his horse down the drive.

And once more, Castle How sat alone.

But not empty.

"How long must we wait, do you think?" Abigail asked Eva where they sat in the servants' hall behind the kitchen. The only light came from a hooded lantern Jesslyn had brought with her, but, from their vantage point, they could see the door that led down to the caves.

Maudie wrapped her shawl tighter. "Ghosts don't walk until midnight."

"Even the Hound of the Headland?" Eva teased.

"He only rises on stormy nights," Jesslyn explained from her place at Maudie's side.

"And I suppose we have no young wastrels to draw him even then," Eva allowed.

Abigail shifted on the bench. "Young wastrels? I think he would prefer to prey on arrogant men. We certainly have enough of those. Forgive me, Eva, but I'm surprised the magistrate was willing to concede he needed help and allow us a role tonight."

"He's coming to learn the value of partnership," Eva said. "But all our efforts tonight may be for naught. We've made it clear the castle is empty and ripe for the picking, but we can't be sure these Frenchmen will return. They may abandon their boat. Its loss is a small price to pay to keep their identities hidden."

"Lark fears they will return to France in all haste," Jesslyn said, "to report what they've learned to the Emperor."

"All the more reason to stop them," Abigail said.

Eva nodded. Not that the four of them would be directly involved. James and the militia would have surrounded the castle by now. They'd arranged for the men to arrive in ones and twos and hide themselves among the trees to watch for the least sign of the enemy. Captain St. Claire and his men had sailed into the caves as the tide turned earlier in the day and were waiting below. And Lark had gone out to a revenue cutter that was watching the shore over the waves. If the French chose to approach the castle by sea or by land, they would be caught.

Eva was just glad that Doctor Bennett had been able to convince the earl to return to London for care. She wasn't sure how they would have laid the trap if he had remained in residence. It was no doubt a sign of his infirmity that he had agreed so readily.

"But I shall hold you to your promise of support for Thorgood and Miranda," he'd said, as if he would bargain even now.

"We will do what we must to keep them solvent," James had vowed. "I'll come to London soon to make the arrangements."

He had nodded. Either he trusted them to do the right thing, or he was once again plotting something. Only time would tell.

Abigail stiffened now. "Hst!" She lay a hand on Eva's arm.

Eva heard it too. The slight creak of a door opening, the clack of a heel against the polished wood floor of the great hall. She frowned at Jesslyn, who shrugged as if just as mystified.

"Stay here," Abigail whispered. She had arrived wearing a dark hooded cloak, which she draped around her now to become a shadow. She slipped through the kitchen and out into the unlit corridor. Eva, Jesslyn, and Maudie remained frozen on the benches, and Eva thought they were listening as hard as she was. She nearly fell off her seat when Abigail materialized back in the servants' hall.

"Someone's in the great hall," she whispered. "I just caught sight of a shadow near the hearth, by one of those tall statues."

They all glanced in that direction, as if they could see their mysterious visitor.

"What's he doing?" Abigail asked, face bunched.

"How'd he get past the magistrate and militia?" Jesslyn whispered back.

Maudie shook her head. "Why is he bothering? Only fairies use that hidey hole."

"Hidey hole?" Jesslyn asked.

"In the statue," Eva realized. "Quickly, now. We cannot allow him to escape. Abigail, go out the kitchen door and find James. The rest of us will keep this villain busy."

Abigail nodded and hurried for the door.

"What do you intend?" Jesslyn asked, rising.

"We'll defend the castle to our deaths," Maudie agreed, joining her.

"That's the idea," Eva said. "If this person has been watching the castle so carefully, hiding in our very midst, it's possible he's heard that Castle How is haunted. He may well have been counting on the legend to keep others away. Let's show him what the castle ghosts think of his scurrilous actions."

The moon had just risen, sending a silvery light across the grass and wildflowers that ringed Castle How. Hidden among the trees, James glanced at his men. They crouched around him, gazes steady, guns close at hand. Not one had balked at being ordered to serve, even when they'd heard they might be facing trained French soldiers.

Still, it could be a long wait. They had no way of knowing when their quarry might return or how many there would be. He could only hope they would all learn the answers to their many questions tonight.

"Magistrate, look!"

James turned toward the sound. Lawrence was staring back the way they had come. James saw it too, a glow where there should be none. A moment more, and he smelled smoke.

"Fire!" someone else cried.

James rose. "Lawrence, young Mr. Lawrence, Carroll, Greer—you're with me. Ellison, Hornswag, take the rest and see if you can put that out."

His men moved off into the darkness.

The rest shifted around him. The smoke was thicker now, the castle a hazy shape beyond the trees. James was debating sending the rest of them after the others when Greer pointed toward the castle.

"There!"

A cloaked figure slipped out the rear door and darted across the grass to disappear into the trees. His men raised their muskets.

James frowned. If this was their quarry, why was he moving away from the castle instead of toward it? If he had managed to make his way past them, wouldn't he be heading for the caves?

"Hold your—" he started.

A musket boomed.

With a cry, the shadow fell.

"Guns down!" James roared, surging to his feet. "Stay here and wait for my command."

Bending low, he raced for the fallen figure.

He recognized her the moment he reached her side. Abigail Archer lay on the grass, cloak spread around her, one hand pressed to her arm. Black in the moonlight, blood trickled past her fingers.

"You might teach them to recognize friend from foe," she said.

James crouched at her side. "How badly are you hurt?"

"I think it was a glancing blow, but it certainly stings." She winced as he helped her to sit. "More importantly, you need to know someone is in the castle and not heading for the caves. Eva and the others are trying to hold him until you can capture him."

No use for silence, not after that shot. "To me!" he shouted, and the rest of his men dashed out from among the trees. "Lawrence, Carroll," he said as they reached his side, "take Miss Archer to Doctor Bennett. Young Mr. Lawrence, fetch the others. Greer, follow me. Someone's in the castle. We aim to capture, not kill. Shoot without my direct order, and I will see you up on charges. Now, move!"

He and Greer rushed across the ground, stormed up the stairs, and burst through the door into the great hall. James held up his hand, and Greer tensed beside him, gaze wary.

The moonlight only reached so far. Darkness obscured the upper part of the stairs, the landing above. A dozen Frenchmen might have been sighting down their muskets even now.

Yet, out of the darkness came a wail, eerie and cold. Greer took a step closer to James.

Down the corridor from the kitchen moved a specter. Draped in white, it seemed to glide along the floor. The light of the lantern held in its grip gave it an unearthly glow.

Greer edged away from the menace.

The specter pointed a finger toward the great hall. "Beware!"

Was that warning for them or someone else? Before James could respond, a man leaped from the darkness to pelt for the door.

James intercepted him. "That's enough."

Greer lifted his gun and pointed it at the man, who slumped.

"Well done, Jesslyn!" Eva called, stepping into view from around the stairs.

"The Hound of the Headland would be proud," Mrs. Tully agreed, joining her.

The specter pulled the drapery off over its head with its free hand to reveal Miss Chance, who smiled at James. He saluted the three of them, then turned to the man before him.

"Well, Harris?" he demanded. "What do you have to say for yourself?"

# CHAPTER TWENTY-THREE

EVA MOVED CLOSER TO THE tableau, Jesslyn and Maudie at her heels. It simply didn't make sense that the man facing James should be Mr. Harris. He'd seemed so…so…harmless. Where were the rest of James's men? And what had happened to Abigail? Had James told her to wait outside for her own safety, not knowing what they might face inside?

"This is all a misunderstanding," Mr. Harris was chattering, hands up and eyes wide. "I am a friend of the Earl of Howland. He requested that I confirm the house had been locked properly. When I found the door unlocked, naturally I thought to look further. And then Miss Chance nearly scared the life out of me."

He lowered his hands to wag a finger in Jesslyn's direction. "Quite the prank, my dear. You nearly had me fooled."

"And you don't fool me for an instant," Eva proclaimed. "The earl has been ill. He never had a visitor except for Doctor Bennett for the last two days. When did he ask you to look after the castle?"

"Why, at the spa the day he visited with you," he said.

Eva looked to James, who was frowning. The earl had spoken to Harris that day, but she'd thought it only a casual greeting. Were they greater intimates, then?

"And how are you acquainted with my cousin?" James

asked, as if his thoughts ran along the same lines as Eva's.

Harris evidently thought he was no longer under suspicion, for he smiled. "I met him in London through mutual friends. A fine fellow. So generous."

"Is he talking about the same earl?" Maudie muttered to Eva.

Eva shook her head.

The thud of boots heralded the arrival of the rest of the militia. They crowded into the great hall, fanned out around James. Their gazes narrowed on Harris.

"Behold our intruder," James told them. "He claims the earl invited him here. I find myself in doubt. Turn out your pockets, sir."

"Surely there's no need," Harris started.

Mr. Ellison was having none of it. "Our magistrate asked you to turn out your pockets, my lad. Allow me to be of assistance." Handing his gun to another, he set about patting the fellow's body, strong hands moving fast. Harris winced.

Mr. Ellison delivered a pocket watch, a handkerchief, and a key that looked suspiciously like the one Eva had been given to the castle.

"Not much to show for himself," the baker said.

James fingered the key. "Except this. How did this come into your possession?"

"The earl gave it to me. How was I to lock the castle without it?" Harris aimed a scowl all around. "You have no call to detain me. I was only doing my duty."

"He's lying, and I can prove it," Eva said. She tugged on Maudie's arm. "Will you show me where the fairies hide their notes?"

Maudie nodded toward the militia. "You want this lot to know?"

Eva glanced around as well. The militia of Grace-by-the-Sea stood taller, as if they intended to earn her trust. They already had it.

"Yes," Eva said. "These are our neighbors, our friends. They deserve to know."

Maudie headed past them all to stop by the Grecian water bearer nearest the door. "There, under her arm. That's where I found the fairy writing."

Eva joined her to reach into the small hollow. She plucked out the paper inside.

"You found one too!" Maudie exclaimed.

Eva brought it back to James. "And why did you leave this, Mr. Harris?"

Harris twitched, as if he longed to grab the note and run, but his smile remained pleasant. "And what have you there? A love note?"

James opened the paper and angled it toward Jesslyn's lamp. The random letters and numbers seemed to jump off the page.

"A cipher," James said. "I'm sure Mr. Carroll can make short work of this."

Harris jerked away and ran.

Mr. Greer stopped him, and the other militiamen weren't far behind.

"Where are your compatriots?" James demanded as they brought him back to face him again. "If you give them up, it might go easier on you."

He sneered. "And if you let me go, it might go easier on you when Napoleon overruns your measly little village."

The militia bristled.

"So, you admit to working with the French," James said. "Do you claim the earl condones it?" His tone was stern, his face determined. Eva would not have wanted to face him in the docket.

Harris started laughing. "Condones it? The earl profits from it. Or didn't you know the House of Howland was in such dire straits?"

James didn't waver. Eva had never been so proud of him. "Whether we are in a difficult financial position or not has nothing to do with the loyalty an Englishman owes his country. What is your excuse, sir?"

"I know how to choose the winning side," Harris said. "You think the fires I lit were bad? Your little village will be swept through, picked clean, and left to bleach in the sun."

James stepped back from him, contempt written on every feature. "Ellison, Truant, take him to the village and lock him in the jail. Is the fire out?"

"Fire?" Eva asked, but his men were nodding.

James nodded as well. "Then the rest of you, light lamps and search the castle to make sure he's left no one and nothing else behind."

"They're coming for you!" Harris shouted as the men pulled him toward the door.

"We'll be ready," James vowed.

The other militiamen gathered lamps from the great hall, withdrawing room, and music room, then climbed the stairs to search the upper stories. James turned to Eva, Jesslyn, and Maudie.

"The Lady of the Tower, I take it," he said with a bow to Jesslyn.

"A poor likeness," Maudie admitted.

"But it certainly put the fear into our spy," Eva added. "Who knew damping holland covers could be so useful? I must remember to thank Yeager for storing them in the kitchen."

"And I should return them," Jesslyn said. "Do you require the lantern, Magistrate?"

"The moonlight is sufficient, but thank you," James said.

They moved off. As quiet settled over the great hall, Eva closed the distance between her and James.

"I'm surprised you didn't want to play the ghost," James

told her.

"Jesslyn is taller," she explained. "It made a better effect. Besides, I thought I stood a better chance of knocking him down if needed. So, you were right. The earl was involved in all this."

"So it appears," James said. "I didn't want to believe he would help the enemy, but we both know he was desperate. Harris and whoever sent him must have offered a pretty penny to convince my cousin to support their efforts."

"Perhaps they posed as smugglers," Eva said as doors banged and footsteps thudded overhead. "So long as they sent him something from France in token once in a while, he would have no reason to question them."

"But did the earl give him the key, or is that Bascom's key?"

Eva shook her head. "We'll have to ask the earl. What should we do now?"

He gazed down at the paper in his hand. "We must get this to Carroll."

Eva glanced around. "I thought he was a member of your troop, but I didn't see him. Didn't he answer the call?"

He lowered the paper, face falling. "He's escorting Abigail Archer into town. One of my men took her for the enemy and shot her in the arm. She's on her way to Doctor Bennett."

Eva gasped. "Oh, James, no!"

"I'm sorry, Eva. We'll go to her, as soon as I know the castle is hiding no more secrets. Can you manage things while I slip down and talk to Quill?"

"Of course." With a nod of thanks, he headed for the kitchen.

Jesslyn and Maudie passed him on their return. "But why cannot we summon the trolls?" Maudie was complaining.

"Because we don't know whose side they might be on,"

her niece rationalized.

Maudie humphed. "Well, they're good English trolls. Of course they'd be on our side."

"If Napoleon is indeed intent on taking his army through Grace-by-the-Sea, we'll have to rely on help where we can find it," Eva told them both. "But I still have hopes we can prevent that."

They waited in the great hall for the militia to finish its work. Eva checked the other statue, but the spot that would have held Maudie's hidey hole had been plastered over. Harris must have stumbled upon the one while searching the empty castle for safe places to pass messages.

James came back from the kitchen just before the last of his militiaman reported in.

"Nothing in that end of the house," James told them all, with a look to Eva. That must mean Captain St. Claire had seen no one either.

"Now," James continued, "before we return to the village, I will have an answer. Which of you shot Miss Archer?"

Jesslyn pressed her hands to her chest, and Maudie scowled at them all. The members of his troop looked at each other. For a moment, no one moved.

Then Mr. Greer stepped forward, face white against the red of his jacket. "I did. I didn't want to be slow to respond, so I left the gun half-cocked. It went off all too easily. I will never forgive myself if anything happens to Abigail."

Eva wasn't sure what James intended, but he glanced from Greer to the rest of his men. "We are all facing circumstances we never thought to face. We don't know how we'll react. But the more we practice, the more likely we will respond with the honor and skill expected. I'll ask Mr. Lawrence to draw up a schedule with more frequent drills."

"What about the French, sir?" someone asked.

"If they return to Grace-by-the-Sea," James said, "they

will discover what true Englishmen are worth. Now, company, fall in."

They hurried to line up and stand at attention.

"There's something about a man in a red coat," Maudie murmured dreamily.

"To the village, march!" James ordered.

They marched sharply out the door.

"We'll go as well," Jesslyn said. "Unless there's anything else we can do for you, Magistrate?"

"No, thank you," James said. "Your efforts are greatly appreciated." He bowed to her and Maudie.

Maudie patted his arm. "The fairies are very proud of you, I know."

He smiled his thanks as they left.

Eva glanced around at the dark house. "Then there may be Frenchmen in our midst, and we have no idea who they are."

James led her to the door and set about locking up. "They cannot hide forever, Eva." He shook his head as he twisted the latch. "I wonder, though, why I even bother to lock the door. Now, let's see how Abigail fares."

Abigail and her mother lived in rooms behind the gallery, as it turned out. Lights were glowing from the windows as James and Eva approached along High Street. At the back of the building, they knocked on the door.

An elderly woman with tightly curled white hair and a frail figure wrapped in a sea-green dressing gown greeted them. "Magistrate," she said, mouth turned down. "Have you come to tell us who shot my Abby?"

"It was an accident, Mrs. Archer," James assured her. "Would you allow my wife and me to come in? We'd like to explain the situation."

She stepped aside and let them in. The little flat consisted of a sitting room, small dining room, and two bedchambers. Mrs. Archer led them to the smaller of the two, where Abigail lay propped up in bed. Her face was white, her body stiff, and a bandage thickened the upper part of her right arm.

"Are you all right?" Eva begged, hurrying forward.

"Fine," she said. "No thanks to this oaf of a doctor."

Eva glanced to the side of the door, where Doctor Bennett was standing. He turned to snap shut his black medical bag. "I cannot be blamed, madam, if you choose to involve yourself in ramshackle affairs that end with you getting shot."

"And you also refuse to accept the blame for costing Miss Chance her position either," she returned.

"I most certainly do." He nodded to Eva and James. "Mr. and Mrs. Howland. I hope you can convince Miss Archer to stay abed and heal. She should not be painting with that arm."

"Oh, so now you want to rob me of my position too?" Abigail fumed.

He rounded on her. "No, madam. I am trying to save the life of one of the finest painters I have ever seen. I hope I may count on your support."

She blinked. "Certainly, sir. No need to shout."

He nodded. "I'll check on you in the morning before the spa opens. If you see Miss Chance before I do, please ask her to attend me at her earliest convenience. I have been trying to make her acquaintance to no avail. I have a position to discuss with her." With a nod all around, he departed.

"Well," Abigail said, and left it at that.

After letting Miss Archer know what had transpired at the castle, James led Eva back to the street. The moon had disappeared, but the eastern horizon was already lighting, streaks of pink and gold stretching across the sea.

"I must get this to Mr. Carroll," he said, laying a hand on her arm. "But there's no reason you can't go back to Butterfly Manor, attempt to sleep."

She regarded him. "Until I know what that note says, I doubt there's much sleep in my future."

He tucked her arm into his, more glad than he could say to have her beside him. "Then let's see what Mr. Carroll thinks."

They found the gentleman still in his uniform. "Are we marshaling?" he asked James, reaching for the musket that was propped beside the shop door.

James shook his head. "While you were getting Abigail to Doctor Bennett, we discovered that Mr. Harris from the spa was our French liaison. He attempted to leave this note in the castle."

He accepted the note, peering at it through his spectacles. "Never liked the fellow. He had no interest in books. Give me a moment."

He wandered back toward the counter, already muttering about Ps and Ss.

James followed with Eva.

"I have the code right here," the shopkeeper assured them, bringing out a sheaf of paper with notes all over it. "Let's see. Yes." He selected a pencil and began scrawling letters.

Mr. Carroll looked up. "Short, but to the point. It reads, *Do not land. Too many defenses. Seek another site.*" He blinked, then grinned at them both. "Then we're safe. The French know Grace-by-the-Sea can defend herself."

"Only if they receive that note," James said, holding out his hand. The shopkeeper lay the paper into it. "I will deposit this in the usual place and see if anyone takes the bait."

After thanking Carroll, they left.

"Then, is it done?" Eva asked as they headed for Butterfly Manor at last.

"For now," James said. "But the boat was still there when I talked with Quill. He and his men will be on the alert, as will the Excise Service and the Royal Navy, thanks to Lark. If the French return for this note, they will be found."

She seemed to accept that, walking along beside him as if they were out for a promenade. But, as they neared the house, she spoke and proved her thoughts had taken a different direction.

"Before we knew there were spies, we talked about our future," she said. "What do you intend, James?"

He stopped before the yard gate. "What do you wish, Eva?"

Her mouth quirked, and even in the misty light of dawn, he could see the twinkle in her eyes. "I asked you first."

"A marriage," he said. "A true marriage, husband and wife, together through good times and bad."

"One life, one mind, one heart," she agreed. "I want that too."

He bent and brushed his lips against hers, feeling the answering tremor in her. "Then, Eva Faraday Howland, will you be my wife and allow me to be your husband?"

"Yes, James. Nothing would make me happier."

She tipped her chin and kissed him. The sun rose, brightening the sky, bringing a new day, a new future.

Together.

*Two weeks later*

"You need more roses," Maudie said.

Eva glanced up from her work, trowel in hand. Their

home was certainly living up to its name this morning—butterflies danced from flower to flower, gold and brown and blue.

"But we already have an entire hedge," Eva said, pointing to the red and pink blossoms along the wrought-iron fence. "What about something that blooms more frequently?"

Maudie cocked her head, as if considering the matter. Then Eva realized she was listening. Tilting her head, she spied the carriage coming up Church Street. "He's back!"

She dropped the trowel and ran for the gate just as the carriage pulled up. James leaped down and caught her close.

"Oh, but I missed you," he murmured against her hair.

"And I missed you terribly," she said, pulling back to look up into his dear face.

"That's what happens between husbands and wives," Maudie said wisely. "Even if it's only been ten days."

"An eternity," Eva assured her.

Maudie nodded. "Then you'll want time alone. Call on me when you want to dance among the mushrooms again." She let herself out the gate.

James raised his brows. "Is that what you get up to while I'm gone—dancing in fairy circles?"

Eva wrinkled her nose. "Certainly not. The fairies are far too jealous of my good fortune. But Maudie and I did attend the assembly with Jesslyn and Lark." She sobered. "How did it go in London, James? Did you get answers to your questions?"

"Some." Arm around her waist, he led her back into the garden while Mr. Connors and Kip set about taking the carriage to the coaching house behind the manor. "I gave Mr. Carroll's decoder to the War Office. As usual, they weren't particularly excited about the matter."

"They don't want you to know you showed them up," Eva told him.

"Neither did Julian Mayes. He came to see me when he heard I was in town. He wanted to apologize. It seems he mentioned our agreement to his superior, Alexander Prentice, and Prentice immediately told the earl. That's how he was able to show up at our wedding."

Eva shook her head. "So at least that mystery is solved. I'm glad it wasn't Priestly who told on us. He's been very helpful while you were gone. Either he or Captain St. Claire have checked the castle every day. No one has come for the note."

James drew in a breath. "And I couldn't find the key that was in the earl's possession. So, someone still has access to the castle. We'll have to find another way to make sure the French know they aren't welcome in Grace-by-the-Sea. At least I am still magistrate and leader of the militia."

"And what about the finances?" Eva asked. "Were you able to salvage the estates?"

"Not quite." He paused to gaze out over the flowers as if taking comfort in the bright blooms. "Things were as bad as the earl intimated. He'd already sold everything we owned overseas. We'll lose most of the property in England as well."

"Oh, poor Thorgood," Eva said.

"We'll have to stop calling him that. The earl has passed. My cousin will shortly be confirmed as the sixth earl."

"Oh." Eva bit her lip a moment. "I should not be glad of his death, but I am relieved. James, we are truly free."

He nodded slowly, as if he couldn't quite believe it. "Thorgood intends to move himself, the countess, and Miranda to the castle to live. They will arrive next month, with my mother and your harp, Eva."

Eva beamed at him. "Then you'll finally have family in the area again."

James looked down into Eva's face. "I already have family. More than I ever believed possible."

Eva gazed up at him, love and pride and joy mingling. Her convenient husband had become more than she could have dreamed, and she would always be grateful she had come to Grace-by-the-Sea.

Home.

D EAR READER
      Thank you for choosing James and Eva's story. From the moment Eva walked onto the page, I knew she was just what James needed to become the hero he was meant to be. If you missed the first book in the series, about how Jesslyn Chance became betrothed to the dashing Larkin Denby, look for *The Matchmaker's Rogue*.

If you enjoyed this book, there are several things you could do now:

Sign up here *https://subscribe.reginascott.com* for a free email alert so you'll be the first to know when a new book is out or on sale. I offer exclusive free short stories and giveaways to my subscribers from time to time. Don't miss out.

Connect with me on Facebook or Pinterest.

Post a review on a bookseller site or Goodreads to help others find the book.

Discover my many other books on my website here *www.reginascott.com*.

Turn the page for a peek of the third book in the Grace-by-the-Sea series, *The Artist's Healer*. Spunky Abigail Archer is determined to see her friend, Jesslyn Denby, restored as hostess of the spa at Grace-by-the-Sea, even if that means ousting the new physician. Doctor Linus Bennett isn't about to lose his post to some crusader, but the pretty painter awakens feelings he'd thought long buried. As the French edge ever closer to the little village, could Abigail be just the prescription for healing Linus's wounded heart? Blessings!

*Regina Scott*

SNEAK PEEK:
*The Artist's Healer,*
BOOK 3 IN THE GRACE-BY-THE-SEA SERIES

by
Regina Scott

# CHAPTER ONE

*Grace-by-the-Sea, Dorset, England, July 1804*

S HE WASN'T MADE TO LIE abed all day.
Abigail Archer stared at the ceiling in her bedchamber. It wasn't a grand ceiling like those in Castle How on the headland above her shop or Lord Peverell's Lodge on the opposite headland across Grace Cove. The cream-colored plaster bore no coffering, no elaborate beams, no mosaic pattern or allegorical painting of mythical beings.

She could paint one. Perhaps Poseidon rising from the depths, waves crashing around him. But no, she didn't need the reminder of the autocratic fellows in her life.

The biggest autocrat at the moment wouldn't allow her to paint in any regard.

She carefully shrugged her right shoulder. Immediately, pain shot down her arm, causing her fingers to tighten. No, no painting. Not yet. But she would not be deterred.

Her mother bustled into the room. On the best of days, theirs was an uneasy truce. Now the carefully coiffed white curls around her mother's face, her neat printed cotton gown partially covered by a frilly white apron, and her purposefulness only served to remind Abigail of all she could not be at the moment.

"Let me fix your hair," her mother said, going to the

walnut bureau on the opposite wall to fetch the tortoise-shell brush. "And help you change into something prettier. Miss Pierce, the elder, sent over a lovely bed jacket—green quilted satin. Can you imagine?"

"That was very kind of her," Abigail said as her mother came around the bed, brush in hand. "But I can't move my arm enough to don it, and I doubt this bandage would fit inside even if I could."

Her mother frowned at the swath of thick cotton wrapped around Abigail's upper arm. "That is a problem."

It certainly was.

And it wasn't something she'd ever prepared for. Bullet wounds were unheard of in the village of Grace-by-the-Sea. She ought to know; she'd lived here for all her six and twenty years. She'd made cherished friends like Jesslyn Chance and now Eva Howland. She'd learned to read and write, learned to sail, learned to paint. She'd grown her own enterprise, provided for herself and her widowed mother. Now all that was threatened because she had been in the wrong place at the wrong time.

Her mother had nearly collapsed when two of Abigail's fellow shopkeepers, Mr. Carroll across the street and Mr. Lawrence, the jeweler, had half carried her down from the headland two nights ago.

"But what happened?" she kept repeating as Abigail curled up on her bed, holding her arm and the men had gone for the local physician. "Why are you bleeding?"

"Mr. Howland and the militia surrounded the castle," Abigail had managed, pausing to clench her teeth against the pain. "He suspects the French have been using it to send messages."

"Messages?" Even in Abigail's fog of shock, she could see her mother's face scrunching up. "But the French are still massing across the Channel. They haven't invaded."

Yet.

"There may be some in the area," Abigail said.

"How?" her mother protested. "Why?"

She would not lose patience. She tried so hard. Abigail drew in a breath, mustered the last of her energy to explain. "Jesslyn and I were inside the castle with Eva and Mrs. Tully, keeping an eye on things, when one of the Frenchmen arrived. I slipped out to alert the magistrate, and a militiaman fired his musket, thinking me the enemy. Now, if you don't mind, I think I shall faint."

She'd woken in her nightgown, with her mother fussing over her. The bullet had carved a deep trough through her upper arm, and that doctor had insisted she must rest to heal. And after all that, they had caught only one of the French agents thought to be haunting their village.

"It's fine, Mother," she said now. "I don't need to dress up. It isn't as if I have anywhere to go."

Her mother bit her lip a moment, then set about running the brush through Abigail's hair. Ginger-colored tendrils whipped past her eyes as if fleeing the vigorous strokes. She knew how they felt.

"Well, it never hurts to look your best," her mother said, avoiding her gaze. "You never know who might call."

A knock at the door of their flat attested to the fact.

"Oh! I wasn't ready," her mother fumed. She pulled a handful of hairpins from the pocket of her apron and dropped them and the brush in Abigail's lap. "Here. Do what you can. I'll delay him a few moments." She hurried out.

Abigail shook her head. She couldn't raise her right arm, and she could hardly dress her hair one-handed. She set the brush on the table beside the bed, then scooped up the pins and let them slide down next to it. Then she cocked her head and listened.

Through the door her mother had closed behind her came voices, three of them. She couldn't make out words, only pitches and tones. One of the higher, excited ones belonged to her mother, but the other? A lady visitor, perhaps, though why she would sound so reluctant was beyond Abigail. And that deeper one...

She stiffened a moment before the door opened and Doctor Linus Bennett walked in, black leather medical bag in one hand. Not that she would admit it to anyone who asked, but the ladies at the spa must be in alt at the very sight of him. Warm brown hair waved back from a brow that spoke of intelligence. Those grey eyes appeared to look upon the world with wisdom and compassion. The firm line of those pink lips promised no complaint. His color and physique attested to good health.

"Miss Archer," he said. "How are we today?"

"I have no idea how you are," Abigail told him. "But I'm ready to get out of this bed."

His brows rose ever so slightly, but he gave no other response to her testy tone. He came around the bed to her side and set his bag on the table, sending a few pins to the hardwood floor with a tinkle.

"No pain?" he asked, beginning to unwind her bandage.

"Not enough to account for." Though his gaze was on his work, Abigail felt her cheeks heating. Where was her mother? Always before she had remained in the room while Doctor Bennett examined her. It was bad enough that he must visit her in her bedchamber, with her in her nightgown, the sleeve cut away to make room for the bandage. In a moment, the bare skin of her arm would be in view.

He'd seen it two nights ago, of course, when he'd first attended her, and the other morning as well. But this time, alone with him, seemed too intimate.

Then the wound came into view, an ugly slash against her fair skin, red, raw, the gap closed with white stitches as good as her mother's embroidery. Abigail swallowed.

"The sutures are holding together nicely," he said, studying the wound. "No sign of inflammation." His gaze met hers, and breathing became difficult. He frowned and laid a hand on her forehead, the touch cool, commanding.

"No sign of a fever, though your color is higher than I'd like. How much laudanum have you used?"

"None," Abigail said, pressing her back against the wood of the walnut headboard to remove herself from his distracting touch. "I'm fine."

As if he didn't believe her, he went to locate the bottle on the bureau, held it up, and peered at the darker liquid sloshing about inside.

"Do not bother prescribing more," she warned him. "I won't take it. It makes me nauseous."

He set down the bottle and came back to her. "Have you been eating?"

"Broth and toast, as you apparently dictated," Abigail told him. "I could do with something more substantive."

"Gruel, then," he said, taking a fresh bandage from his bag.

Abigail stared at him. "Gruel? What of mutton, sir? At least plaice."

"Tomorrow, if you have no more nausea," he said, beginning to cover the wound anew.

"I only have nausea if I take the needless medicine you ordered. I cannot stay in this bed. I have a business to tend to, and I must help Jesslyn Chance prepare for her wedding."

His head was bowed enough she could only see the crown. The strands of brown looked far softer than his demands.

"I am assured Miss Chance can manage," he said. "Everyone has gone out of their way to praise her skills and organization. And as for your business, the visitors to the spa will simply have to shop elsewhere for the next fortnight."

Abigail jerked away, and the bandage slipped out of his grip. "A fortnight! You cannot expect me to lie here so long. I demand you let me up, immediately."

Linus Bennett had to clench his teeth a moment before responding. He'd dealt with difficult patients in the past, from Edinburgh, where he'd attended school, to Mayfair, where he'd had his last practice. But even his nine-year-old son, Ethan, when he had been injured and abed for weeks had been more receptive to his suggestions than Miss Archer, who seemed determined to thwart his care of her.

"You cannot get up immediately without risking a fever," he said, catching hold of the bandage to tie it off. "You could also break the sutures and reopen the wound. The bullet grazed your bicep, madam. Unless it heals properly, you will never lift your lower arm without pain. I imagine that would be rather inconvenient for a painter."

He leaned back to find her green eyes narrowed and her melon-colored lips working as if she was piling up words to hurl at him. Her color had only gone higher, and this time he was fairly sure of the cause.

She was furious.

"It would be more than inconvenient, and you know it," she finally said. "But my paintings aren't the only things in the shop. Nearly every woman in the area helps support her family through the crafts I sell on commission. If I make no money, neither do they."

The workings of this village continued to amaze him. He'd visited the famous spas at Harrogate and Scarborough and knew of inland Bath and Lyme Regis along the coast. None had such a generous arrangement. At Grace-by-the-Sea, families lived from the income of the shops, the goods and services sold to the spa where he had been appointed physician and the visitors it brought in. And the Spa Corporation that paid his salary divided profits among the village families quarterly.

"Perhaps one of your ladies could watch the shop for you," he suggested, snapping shut his bag.

She started to cross her arms over her chest and seemed to think better of it. "Perhaps they could, if I was allowed visitors to discuss the matter."

"You may have as many visitors as you like," he said. "So long as you do not disturb that arm. And if you have any sign of a fever or swelling, you are to send for me immediately."

Her face settled into tight lines. Her cheekbones were high and firm, the maxilla and mandible of her jaw well defined. Sculptors must long for such a face to model.

"I do not appreciate being ordered about, sir," she informed him.

Neither had Catriona.

He shoved the thought aside. Miss Archer was nothing like his late wife. Catriona had been blond and buxom, with a focus on her own pleasures. Miss Archer had a slender physique and hair the color of the bruised ginger he used in his preparations. It fell about her shoulders now in thick waves that seemed to beckon him closer.

All while the light in her green eyes warned him to keep his distance.

"Ordering my patients about is my duty," he said, picking up his bag. "So is helping them understand the ramifications of ignoring my counsel. Wounds that are not allowed to heal can turn gangrenous. I prefer not to perform amputations, but I understand there's a surgeon in Upper Grace who is delighted to pull out his saw."

The color that had concerned him fled, and she dropped her gaze to the quilt covering her lap.

He felt a twinge of guilt. He hadn't intended to frighten her, but she had to know what could happen if she didn't take care. Catriona had refused to listen to him. He would not lose another.

"No need to trouble him," Miss Archer murmured as if far more contrite. "I'll do what I must to heal."

Linus drew in a breath. "Good. Any other questions for me?"

Her gaze rose once more. Oh, but he'd been wrong. Not contrite. Merely gathering more ammunition.

"Have you reinstated Jesslyn Chance and Maudlyn Tully to their positions at the spa yet?" she asked.

He should have known she would bring that up. Miss Chance and her aunt had managed the spa between the time the previous physician—Miss Chance's father—had passed and Linus had arrived a week ago. The Spa Corporation president and his wife did not see the need for their services now that Linus had taken charge, but he began to think them indispensable. For one thing, many of the ongoing spa guests refused to set foot in the Grand Pump Room without them. For another, he was having trouble just getting the fountain that dispensed the mineral waters to operate correctly.

"I regret that I have been too busy to make Miss Chance's acquaintance," he said. "But I have asked everyone who mentioned the matter to have her visit me at the spa."

She shook her head. "When you intend to apologize, sir, you go to the person you have wronged. You do not demand that they go out of their way to find you." She narrowed her eyes. "You do intend to apologize, don't you?"

"I intend to correct the misperception that I insisted on their dismissal," Linus explained. "And begin discussions on how to reinstate some of their services."

Her chin edged higher. "Some?"

He met her gaze, hoping that his own held half that determination. She could not know how important this position was to him and to Ethan.

"I am the medical practitioner at the spa, Miss Archer," he told her. "There isn't need for another."

She continued watching him a moment, then nodded slowly. "Very well. I'll endeavor to have Jesslyn here when you call tomorrow morning. But I warn you, sir. I have started a crusade against your despotism, and I will not cease until I have satisfaction."

Learn more at
*www.reginascott.com/artistshealer.html*

# OTHER BOOKS BY REGINA SCOTT

**Grace-by-the-Sea Series**
*The Matchmaker's Rogue*
*The Heiress's Convenient Husband*
*The Artist's Healer*

**Fortune's Brides Series**
*Never Doubt a Duke*
*Never Borrow a Baronet*
*Never Envy an Earl*
*Never Vie for a Viscount*
*Never Kneel to a Knight*
*Never Marry a Marquess*

**Uncommon Courtships Series**
*The Unflappable Miss Fairchild*
*The Incomparable Miss Compton*
*The Irredeemable Miss Renfield*
*The Unwilling Miss Watkin*
*An Uncommon Christmas*

**Lady Emily Capers**
*Secrets and Sensibilities*
*Art and Artifice*
*Ballrooms and Blackmail*
*Eloquence and Espionage*
*Love and Larceny*

**Marvelous Munroes Series**
*My True Love Gave to Me*

*Catch of the Season*
*The Marquis' Kiss*
*Sweeter Than Candy*

## Spy Matchmaker Series
*The Husband Mission*
*The June Bride Conspiracy*
*The Heiress Objective*

*Perfection*

And other books for Revell, Love Inspired Historical, and Timeless Regency collections.

# ABOUT THE AUTHOR

REGINA SCOTT STARTED WRITING NOVELS in the third grade. Thankfully for literature as we know it, she didn't sell her first novel until she learned a bit more about writing. Since her first book was published, her stories have traveled the globe, with translations in many languages, including Dutch, German, Italian, and Portuguese. She now has more than forty-five published works of warm, witty romance.

She loves everything about England, so it was only a matter of time before she started her own village. Where more perfect than the gorgeous Dorset Coast? She can imagine herself sailing along the chalk cliffs, racing her horse across the Downs, dancing at the assembly, and even drinking the spa waters. She drank the waters in Bath, after all!

Regina Scott and her husband of 30 years reside in the Puget Sound area of Washington State on the way to Mt. Rainier. She has dressed as a Regency dandy, learned to fence, driven four-in-hand, and sailed on a tall ship, all in the name of research, of course. Learn more about her at her website here *www.reginascott.com*.

CPSIA information can be obtained
at www.ICGtesting.com
Printed in the USA
LVHW081005090820
662642LV00026B/1061

9 798636 296492